Mary Lide was born
Hugh's College, Oxfc
has lived in the USA (
at Ann Arbor), Franc
divides her time betw
previous novels inclu
and *Ann of Cambray*.

By the same author

MARY LIDE

The Legacy

Grafton
An Imprint of HarperCollins*Publishers*

Grafton
An Imprint of HarperCollins*Publishers*
77–85 Fulham Palace Road,
Hammersmith, London W6 8JB

Published by Grafton 1992
9 8 7 6 5 4 3 2 1

First published in Great Britain by
GraftonBooks 1991

ISBN 0 586 20896 8

Set in Palatino

Printed in Great Britain by
HarperCollinsManufacturing Glasgow

FOREWORD

From the start let me explain that this is not my story. I was drawn into it against my will as an outside observer. A barrister, it was my legal training that prompted me to keep a record of what I saw. It was only later that I became an active participant. The truth is, I knew little about Cornwall, had not a drop of Cornish blood in my veins, and had never even visited the county before the summer of 1898. That I should eventually settle there seemed as remote a possibility as learning to fly, to say nothing of becoming involved with the people there.

On the other hand, I will admit that it was my interest in old ways that took me to the West Country in the first place. In those days, when words like 'evolution' and 'science' were becoming fashionable, my one hobby (outside the law, that is) was anthropology, and Cornwall was reputedly a fertile field for students of the past. In the course of that first summer I remember feeling transposed in time, as if I had reverted back three hundred years to a medieval age, where land was still the only source of wealth, and those who were not landlords worked upon it as peasants. I was intrigued by local indifference to change, to ignorance of those laws and the social revolution that marked the end of Victoria's reign. Stagnation and poverty were self-evident, from the wretched little inns where I stayed to the fishing villages with their decrepit houses and non-existent sanitation. The mining towns were decaying, almost all the miners had disappeared. Yet, as a man trained to deal with discrepancies of evidence, I remember observing too that although on the surface the local populace seemed subdued, their subservience was only skin deep. Under the veneer of indifference there lurked an energy. I felt that when the time was right it would erupt in a burst of primitive rage.

Such contrast fascinated me. I saw Celtic power behind every pretended servility. I sensed it in the dialect based on the old Cornish tongue, I looked for it in every Cornish custom. When a few years later, my doctors ordered me to retire from active practice, Cornwall was the first place I thought of. Suddenly those little villages with their broken streets and their slate stone jetties appeared in all their postcard attraction. The cottages teetering upon the cliffs, the round-cheeked fisher-girls who lived in them, the vast expanse of sea, began to haunt me with unexplored possibilities; in short, if I were not a man whose life was built upon a sense of logic I would have said that I had been waiting for an excuse to return. And that very foreboding of unrest had become a lure to tempt me back.

Of course, I know there is a great difference between visiting an area on holiday and choosing it as a permanent place of residence. Yet I had relinquished my legal practice, had packed up books and furniture, had arranged to sell my London house, before it dawned on me what a risk I took. After forty-five years of living in one place I should have had more sense than to uproot myself so completely. Yet in the spring of 1912 I never thought of those difficulties, never considered that once in Cornwall I would not even have a home to call my own; or whether any suitable homes existed; or, supposing I could establish myself, what in God's name I would do with my time in a backwater of civilization. These were matters that I passed over, like a man in a dream.

Although warned by friends and neighbours I stubbornly went ahead with my plans. Being without wife or family, I told myself I owed explanation to no one, and to those inquisitive acquaintances who dared ask how I planned to spend my days, I replied, truthfully, that I preferred my own company to most other men's, was never bored in my own presence, and would find as much enjoyment in reading and writing about my new abode as I had done previously in my work on the Queen's Bench. Forcing myself to proceed slowly, travelling west by degrees, encumbered with all my baggage as if I were travelling to Africa, I crossed that river which divides the peninsula from the rest of England, as if shaking off my past like dust from my feet.

My decision, as I have suggested, was an impulsive one, out of character with my habitual caution. I hid from myself that growing expectation, also uncharacteristic, that sense of anticipation quite at odds with my previous life. Nor, to this day, can I explain why I settled in Tregaran, a seaside village so dissimilar from my native Cambridgeshire that it might have been built on the moon. A hundred times I have tried to convince myself that practical necessity influenced my decision; that finding there a gentleman's residence which suited me, I was persuaded to buy the house; that I felt no special affinity for the place, no special sense of belonging; more, that when I and my belongings were installed, I intended to insulate myself behind its granite walls as thoroughly as in my former city life. I still have not acknowledged that underlying excitement, that recognition of what was to be, that sense of truly coming home.

There have been times since when I have sought some other reason for my quixotic choice. Sometimes I have felt it was revolt against that isolation I had so long deliberately fostered, an unexpected protest against so many years of loneliness. Or I have put it down to my unaccustomed idleness – 'the devil finds mischief' sort of thing. Or, more simply, blamed the land itself, this strange, half-violent, half-somnolent county impossible to ignore, impossible to understand, with its knobs of hills poking up out of the moors like fistfuls of bones. But most of all the sea's pervasive presence had its effect on me, that presence which no walls, however thick, could quite block out. What had I cared about the sea in my inland childhood home? What meaning had it had for me in my long city life? Now, sometimes slate grey, sometimes blue-green, its change of colour reflected its change of mood and frequently captured my own. Even if I could have shut out the sight of the sea, there were times when its sound was heard all night, when its salt taste hung in the air, when its smell invaded the house, as if fronds of weed had been cast up on the front steps to rot.

My manservant, Hodges, who had elected to come to Cornwall with me, felt the same way, although he had a practical explanation. 'It's the people's manner, Mr Cradock, sir,' he broke out one day, soon after our arrival. He was laying out my dress clothes, for he saw no excuse for letting city manners slip because I was buried in the country. His own cockney voice suddenly sounded very marked, and his sallow cheeks had reddened with vexation.

'Polite as pie to yer face, pulling of their forelocks and the like, or bobbing of curtsies as if they was in the seventeenth century. Underneath, all screwed up tight, like one of their shellfish. How's a man to know what they think or what's beneath them smiles? And can't understand a dashed word they say even if yer did, if yer'll pardon me the expression.'

There was no need for him to apologize. I knew what he meant. It was like coming to a foreign land, and discovering you had been there already; it was like looking around you in a familiar place and finding everything mirror-changed.

All this is fanciful. Better to stick to the facts and lay blame, where blame is due, upon my curiosity. Say it was a lawyer's need to discover truth. Yet I swear that that spring day of 1912, soon after my arrival, I ventured out of the house with no other thought in mind than passing a few hours pleasantly. If future events make me a liar, then judge me as you wish. I have no other means of defence. And, in the end, no cause to regret my decision.

CHAPTER ONE

That May day the whole of Tregaran was in fête. For over a
month handwritten posters had advertised the event, and
each time a local man came to the house he mentioned
it, as if to ensure I should take note. Even I had sensed a
bustle in the air, as if everyone were revving up like one
of those new-fangled motor-cars I had just bought. I had
read a little about Tregaran Feast. It had been mentioned
briefly in Frazer's book, *The Golden Bough*, published a
few years earlier on the subject of ancient rites. I felt it
would have been foolish – cutting off my nose to spite
my face, as the Cornish say – to have ignored so famous
an example, and so, bundled up well in case of cold, I
walked down my garden and let myself out of the gate.

From where I stood, the village spread beneath me like
toy building blocks, the slate roofs shining in the sun.
Boats bobbed at anchor along the quay; the sea shim-
mered into a pale distance; all was perfectly delineated,
clean and fresh, without any taint of those human foibles
that were to sully it. If I had known what I know now I
should have stayed safe where I was, peering down from
my Gulliver's height, keeping my distance.

The festivities themselves had begun at dawn. Some
were obviously of antique origin (such as the cutting
of hawthorn branches, or may-flowers, by a chosen
'Queen of the Feast', followed by dances through the

streets performed by masked figures, crowned with horns). These pagan practices had been superseded by more Christian ones, to wit, a 'Methodist Tea', put on by the Methodist Chapel and paid for by the local squire, a tea consisting of big saffron buns, studded with raisins, and washed down with mugs of indeterminate muddy liquid.

The chapel itself, an ugly red-brick building, stood four-square at the centre of Tregaran, and now, in the late afternoon, local ladies were still bustling about its hall, with trays of plates and kettles of tepid water. The third ritual was about to begin, and it was this that most interested me. It was called 'Calling of the Pilchard Home'. The pilchard was a kind of fish that once had been Tregaran's main source of revenue. Even now, in summer, its shoals were awaited anxiously (although the numbers had much decreased from the days when millions had been caught at a time). Naturally I was curious about these rituals, how they were linked, why pilchard fishing was celebrated months too soon. I hoped, you see, to write an article on the May Feast and had actually declined an invitation from the local squire who had asked me to participate. I had no wish to be encumbered with obligations to a bunch of country nobodies, was still content to go my own way, with my own thoughts for company. But the mild sweet air, the scents and colours of the spring put me off my guard. I was half enchanted before I had gone a dozen steps. In short, I repeat, the only excuse for my behaviour was myself: the man who went down 'simply to observe' was different from the man who returned.

I should explain that the natural hollow where the village lay had been shaped by a small rivulet. This stream had its beginnings among the moorland rocks, further north, but here, below my house, cut its way

11

down through the cliff, carving out a typical Cornish half-moon bay with a harbour stretched across its mouth. All along its banks hawthorn trees grew in profusion, their pink-and-white flowers outlined against the sky, and when I came to the first cottages, I saw branches of the same tree wound across the doors and window-panes. I knew the fisherfolk must have gone out early that morning in the May Queen's company, for normally hawthorn was thought to bring bad luck, and I paused to make a note how superstition itself was rooted in antiquity.

The cottages themselves were so layered against the cliff that their fronts projected over the edge. In stormy weather spray from the waves below coated the windows white like frost. In some places the path was so steep that the doors of the houses were in the roofs, and the scoured white steps were littered with nets and lobster pots. Today there was no one there, and when I reached the quay it was deserted too, except for a few old men dozing on a wooden bench. But the doors of the fish cannery, too, were decorated with branches of may (although the cannery itself was closed, the girls who worked there presumably let off early to join in the celebrations), and the riggings of the boats were strung with garlands of the same flowers.

The central square was already crowded. At first I felt conspicuous in my city clothes. Local people stood in knots, nudging each other when I appeared, making way so I could take a seat on a large wooden contraption that filled one side of the square. It was sturdily built, draped with an awning like some reviewing stand, and lined with chairs, all at present unoccupied. I understood, without actually being told so, that this stand was reserved for the dignitaries, 'gentry' was the word villagers used, but since I made no attempt to approach it, after a while I was left alone although every move I made was carefully watched, to say nothing of every word I said. I withdrew into a corner where, taking out my pen, I began to make notes which I use now to refresh my memory.

In honour of the occasion the villagers were dressed in what I presumed was their best: the men in rough black serge suits, starched white shirts without collars, thick black boots; the women in dresses or skirts of bright colours, over which they had tied their big work aprons. The younger girls wore small straw hats perched jauntily upon their black hair. Mayflowers were woven around the brims, and posies were tucked at their waists. Their feet, encased in sturdy lace-up boots, tapped time as if to some dance music they heard in their heads. Their cheerfulness today was certainly genuine. Once they became used to me they talked freely among themselves, revealing a naïvety that I found touching after the sophisticated world of London. Although, like Hodges, I could only understand one word in ten, when a small man appeared (carrying a tray, from which a most appetizing smell arose), their cries of, ''Tis the pasty man, he'm come', and their hand-clapping made their pleasure seem complete. Soon everyone was jostling forward, thrusting threepenny bits into his hands, and biting into the crescent-shaped pastry with no inhibitions about spilling crumbs. Even babies in arms sucked on these Cornish 'delicacies' (although the size of the pasties was anything but 'delicate'), and, equally unconcerned, their mothers wiped their faces clean with the corners of their sleeves. Young men came to sit upon the low walls in front of the chapel, beer mugs in hand. They kicked the bricks with their thick heels and made jokes that only the girls seemed to appreciate, for they giggled beneath their hats and nudged each other in the ribs. Soon everyone was eating, laughing, drinking, completely at ease, and for a moment I felt a warmth of companionship that previously I had only read about. Then, as suddenly, without warning, the atmosphere changed, grew still, watchful. All chatter stopped, and all heads turned expectantly.

For the last half-hour or so thin threads of music had been drifting towards the square, lingering at the back of consciousness. Now, for the first time, a brass band could be clearly heard. The villagers seemed inordinately proud of it. They nodded to each other, as if to say "'Tis ourn,' and some of the children jumped in front to make a guard of honour.

The music started with a flourish, a rousing thumping of drums and a blast of trumpets that sent the seagulls screaming. Down the narrow street a group of bandsmen inched along, their faces flushed with effort, gloriously out of step for all they were playing a soldiers' tune more suitable for a military tattoo. Behind them came a second group, belonging to another village (for it seemed that every hamlet of any worth had a band of its own, which was 'lent out' on special occasions). This second group were blowing lustily, a different tune discordantly at variance with the first. And behind again, mincing over the cobbled street, a motley collection of ladies and gentlemen followed, looking as incongruously out of place as a bunch of orchids in a Cornish meadow.

The ladies were chatting animatedly among themselves, their broad-brimmed hats nodding like peonies, making a to-do about the uneven stones, and climbing up into the stand with little screams of fright, as women do, when trying to pretend they do not know they are the centre of attention. Their husbands arranged the children in front before clambering up themselves. Once in place, they tipped their chairs back against the timber supports, laughing too loudly, with a great deal of familiar back-slapping. And there they sat, hands in pockets, slightly embarrassed, pretending to look bored. They might have been settling down to watch a play put on by schoolchildren, and for a moment their self-conscious superiority struck a false note.

Behind them came the main part of the procession. At first it seemed as if a gardener's wheelbarrow had taken a wrong turn and been caught up by mistake. Two men were dragging along a small cart, using ropes which were entwined with hawthorn; a third, a great lusty chap with a mop of dark curls, walked behind to steady it, and on either side girls, acting as attendants, scattered sprigs of may under its wheels. The cart was a strange triangular shape, so covered with flowers that it scarcely seemed to have substance, while the flowers themselves appeared to have lost their colour as if it had been leached out of them. The whole was decorated with an arch of hawthorn, under which sat the May Queen, like a saint carried in a religious ceremony.

She was dressed all in white, and veiled like a bride, so that her face was hidden. Her figure was slight, certainly young, perhaps not more than a child's, for the arms which extended under her robes were so delicate the blue veins showed upon the skin. Although the cart lurched along, she held herself in place, her body arched forward like the masthead of a ship, head thrown back against the wind. Something about her stillness, despite the uneven movement of that rustic cart, her intensity, was astonishing in one so young, almost as if she understood the role that she was enacting, almost as if she understood the purpose of the ritual, and I felt a wave of excitement.

Over her veil she wore a rough may wreath; bunches of may were heaped in her lap; if this had been two thousand years ago she would have been the perfect Virgin Maid, the chosen victim, Queen of Birth and Sowing, on her way to the yearly sacrifice to ensure a good harvesting. And all around the square a sigh went up, as if the watchers recognized what she stood for, and both adored and grieved.

A spell seemed to have fallen over us; even the girls and youths were staring open-mouthed. I remember thinking, 'My God, wherever did they find her?' when a shout broke the silence.

A rough, black-haired man came shouldering his way through the bandsmen so that they faltered and lost the beat. He was perhaps in his late thirties, tall and powerful in his workman's clothes. He would have been startlingly handsome had not there been a bitter twist to his mouth and a wild glint in his eye, and his thick boots stamped the flowers with angry belligerence. Instinctively people stepped back to get out of his way but he ignored them as if they were of no more consequence than those scattered flowers under his feet.

'Get 'ee down,' he said in a broad Cornish voice. 'I said I'd not 'ave 'ee made a spectacle of, and I won't. Enough's enough.'

He was speaking to the veiled figure, and for a moment a shiver ran through the crowd. The men drawing the cart dodged to one side so quickly that the flower-decked ropes snapped.

''Twill bring bad luck,' a woman hissed and again there was a sigh, like a gust of air. But the man paid little heed to her words, stepped up to the girl and with one quick jerk threw back her veil.

Even without the covering, it was hard to decide how old she was, child or woman, a girl on the verge of womanhood. Nor was it easy to say what she looked like. Only afterwards did I remember the dark hair, gathered in a knot at the nape of a slender neck, and strange sea-coloured eyes, luminous as if a light shone through them. Only afterwards did I recall the

16

fine clear profile, so carved it could have graced an ancient statue.

She looked at the man with a strange expression, part understanding, part pitying. 'You be making of the spectacle,' she said, addressing him earnestly in a low and musical tone. 'There be no harm. See, Tom be here, a-keeping watch of me. Why don't 'ee walk along with us? The boys be waiting on the cliff to give the cry. They say a great big pilchard shoal be moving up the coast within sighting soon. You'd be some pleased at that; you'd not want the fishing to fail.'

Her words had a practical wisdom that belied her youth, and were meant to calm him down. They made the relationship between the man and the girl hard to understand. Seeing them both together it was obvious they were related in some way, but my first impression – that he must be an irate father come to bring an erring daughter home – was obviously false. And the anger itself seemed out of place, too intense for the offence. It jarred the nerves like an untuned instrument, revealing a pent-up rage that, like the procession itself, grew from the past, a true Celtic rage smouldering in the dark. And sensing it, the people in the square tensed with apprehension.

'Get away with 'ee, Zack, leave sister be.' The second speaker clarified the situation, although had he not spoken one look at him would have stamped him of the same breed. It was the young man who had been steadying the back of the cart. Now he leapt forward to confront his older brother, and once more a sigh ran through the crowd, of fear perhaps, or anticipation. For it was clear that this 'Tom' was not afraid of the older man, and for a moment stood eyeing him, sizing him up like a dog spoiling for a fight.

Then the younger, Tom, backed down, making an effort to smooth things over as his sister had done. His expression softened; his good-natured face broke into a smile that was warm and somehow touchingly gentle.

''Twould be some shame to end it here,' he began, appealing to the older man, trying to soothe him, to make him change his mind. ''Tis all a game, no harm in ut. And Alice be some good at ut.' A naïve argument this last, as if it were reason enough by itself. 'Besides, these be hard times, we'm in need of luck. Ask them.'

He pointed towards the crowd, who, following his lead, began to nod in agreement. 'There's a truth,' one shouted, while another, in the rear, cried, 'And wasn't Zack Tregarn once the best mummer dancer ever us did see? Heard 'un danced all night and fished all day, no call to be dog-in-the-manger now 'tis others' turn.'

This caused a burst of hearty laughter, the sort people use to mollify their own kind, and perhaps it would have succeeded had not a third speaker broken in. This voice was cultivated, low enough to be mistaken as a private aside, yet having a kind of strident undertone that made it audible to everyone.

'Whoever expects a Tregarn to do as he's told?' it asked. 'Whenever has there been something that the Tregarns don't spoil?' And then more quietly, with unexpected venom, 'If he wants to act the tyrant, let him find a wife.'

The speaker was a woman, or rather a lady. She was sitting in the centre of the stand, in the place of honour, surrounded by her husband and sons. There was a fleeting glimpse of a pale oval face, framed by coarse black hair, before she turned aside to whisper to her friends. She had not looked at Zack Tregarn; rather she had fixed her stare on some point over his head as if he did not exist, but the smile that for an instant had curled her red lips was aimed at him, and the laugh which now followed her whispers was meant to sting.

Zack Tregarn glared around him like a baited bear. He seemed to swell to twice his size and edged back against the cart as if searching for a footing. Then he lashed out, like an animal on a chain.

'Damn 'ee all to hell,' he cried. 'Damn 'ee all, as if we were put on earth to keep 'ee amused.' And to the lady in the stand, 'We bain't 'ere to pleasure 'ee, Missus Tregaran.'

I remember thinking stupidly, Tregaran, that's the name of the village, and the squire's, whose invitation is in my pocket: I remember thinking, equally stupidly, there's no love lost between his wife and the Tregarns, when several things happened at once. Zack Tregarn reached once more into the cart to drag his sister out; his brother Tom leapt to the other side to push him off; like a cannonball, someone hurled himself upon both.

It was one of the lady's sons, a good-looking boy, with a shock of black hair and large dark eyes. Although almost matching the Tregarn brothers in height he was reed-thin against their girth. Yet he wrapped his legs about Zack's and clung around his neck, pummelling him and Tom indiscriminately.

'Leave Alice be,' he was shouting incoherently. 'Brute, idiot.' Each word was another blow to Zack, each well-enunciated insult another goad. And for a moment Zack stood there, stunned.

Then, as if shaking off a fly, he shrugged the boy off.

'Run back to mammy, Johnny Tregaran,' he sneered, jerking his thumb towards the stand. 'She'm welcome to 'ee, if she choose. But keep yer nose out of Tregarn affairs.'

With what can only be called a flick of his wrist, he manhandled the boy down into a pile of lobster pots. With equal ease he thrust his own brother aside and

19

began to tear at the hawthorn arch so that its blossoms fell in showers about his sister's feet.

Some of the gentlemen had jumped up when John Tregaran had appeared. Now with a crashing of seats they scrambled down from the stand, intending to help the boy. While their ladies screamed, in earnest now, they thrust their way imperiously to the front of the crowd. The villagers gave way and then surged after them, as if in protest too, although what they were protesting about was never clear: the violence of one of their own, or the interference of these outsiders, their 'betters'? Behind them, the village youths, who all this while had been sitting in silence on the wall, suddenly came to life. Befuddled by beer, presuming some insult to themselves, they now began to push inwards from the outside, like a rugby scrum, at the same time letting out a strange rallying cry in an unfamiliar tongue.

This cry was taken up across the street where the local pubs were filled with mummers, waiting to begin the dance. A fresh wave of men streamed out, some of them already dressed in their green-and-white costumes, some carrying the horns which they were to wear on their heads, all sufficiently drunk to be raring for a fight, no matter what the cause or why. In a shocking instant the square was filled with gesticulating, shouting men, shoving back and forth, knocking the bandsmen off their feet and tearing the streamers down upon their heads. Above them, like a statue carved in ice, their Queen sat frozen, amid the wreckage of her flowers.

The ladies screamed again, throwing up their hands in horror. The village women, more sensible, tugged at their men's coattails, or swatted them upon their backs. 'Get away with 'ee, girt great fools,' they shouted to their Jims and Joes. Ignoring them, masters and underlings flailed at each other indiscriminately, until no one knew who was which, a grand free-for-all, perhaps not altogether as violent as it seemed – until a man staggered out with his forehead streaming blood from a flying piece of glass. Then a howl went up, and the fight took an ugly turn.

Zack Tregarn and his brother were in the centre, back to back, their broad shoulders hunched against the mob, which was raining blows upon them, gentry and villagers alike. They were easily discernible because of their height and their display of fraternal loyalty – puzzlingly illogical on the face of it: after all, it was their dispute which had caused the trouble in the first place. I remember thinking, again rather stupidly as it should have been clear from the start, there is some quarrel here, some family hatred that the villagers recognize. And then one last thing, before the bricks and stones began to fly in earnest, as if someone had made me see things in perspective, 'Whatever it is, those young people aren't part of it.'

For the boy had picked himself stubbornly out of the mud. Avoiding both villagers and gentlemen, dodging in between the groups of men locked now in real conflict, he forced his way towards the cart and climbed up in it himself. The cause of the trouble, Alice Tregarn, whose brothers were the object of everyone's dislike, was now clinging to the rails, her face pale with fright, as the cart swayed and tipped under the thrust of men. When she saw John Tregaran a ghost of a smile flickered across her lips, and her eyes lit up. He held out his arms. She lowered herself towards him trustingly. Then he was speaking earnestly into her ear, as if trying to drown out the noise, and she was listening just as earnestly, as if making sense of what he said. They might have been alone, just the two of them, and the thought came to me, almost extinguished before it was completed, 'If they are meant to be enemies they do not know the meaning of the word.'

The girl's gown was torn where her brother had ripped

21

it; her headpiece had slipped awry. The boy's tie had slid out of its collar and his coat was split. None of that mattered. His mud-streaked face had taken on a look that made him seem older than his years, and he gripped her so tight I could almost see the marks upon her skin. Her expression too had changed, become, not older, but more defined, as if what he was saying was the most important thing in her life. And the smile they gave each other at the end was full of mutual understanding.

Then the boy jumped down and disappeared among the crowds. The girl started forward, adjusting her dress and veil as if resuming her role, a thin white figure above the struggling mass. Again I felt that strange sense of calm, that stillness, which transcended this fleeting moment and carried us into a greater universe. I felt, somehow, that the more she appeared above this present world, having no part in it, the more she became of its essence. She appeared like the goddess to whom she was supposed to be offered as sacrifice, she became the symbol she was supposed to represent. And afterwards I remembered saying to myself, 'My God, when this is over, whatever will become of her?'

She held up her hand in the ancient gesture of benediction. 'Hush now,' she said, 'listen.'

Her voice went thrilling above the din, spilling out into the golden air where the setting sun had touched the roofs. The wind caught it and tossed it to the sea, the sea tossed it back again until the square rang with the sound, drowning all other noise into silence. And then, loud as a trumpet call, came another cry from the cliff above the harbour mouth.

I knew instinctively, without being told, that it was the voice of the young John answering, as they must have arranged, 'Hevva! Hevva!' the cry of the fishermen, 'A shoal! A shoal!'

Pyu us ena? Pyu us ena?
Pyu a wor?

Who is there, who is there?
Who understands?

Like an echo from the waiting girl, standing in the
wreckage of her finery, came the traditional response,
in a tongue older by centuries than our English one.

An moror! An moror!
Magag owr – ruth avel an howl
Maga owr – ruth avel an tan.

The sea rover, red gold as sun and fire.

It was a strange cry, sending a shiver down the spine.
So perhaps, in similar fashion, had the Celts cried out
when they first spied the invading Roman ships; so had
the crowds turned then, as one man, to face the sea; so
had their queen urged them on from her Celtic chariot.

Hearing that cry, the villagers forgot the quarrel. Every
man began to run, tearing off his jacket and best shirt and
throwing them to his wife, as he made a rush towards
the quay. Some clambered into their boats, cast off the
mooring lines and began to row with feverish haste out
to sea. Others, pulling off their Sunday boots and rolling
up their good trousers round their hairy legs, waded out
from the beach through the waves, dragging large nets
behind them. Little boys and older men panted up the
cliff to keep watch as they soon would keep watch day
and night for several weeks. Their shouts came down to
swell their excitement. 'Pilchards off Dolam Point, a girt
shoal of 'em.'

The women who were left picking up the clothes and
comforting the injured repeated the news cheerfully

among themselves. Driving their children before them they hurried to the beach, knotting up their skirts between their legs. ''Tain't never that it comes so soon,' they cried. 'But atter today, why, 'tis both meet and miracle.' And rolling up their sleeves they too made ready to anchor the nets when they were full.

So that was what was meant by 'Calling of the Pilchard Home', the fisherman's invocation to the sea. By now the fleet of boats had reached the cliff and was beginning to spread out like a fan, moving crab-like around the headland to form a barrier to drive the shoal towards the shore. And now a shout went up, the loudest cry of all, as the men began to point and gesture at a dull golden streak that rippled against the blue of the sea.

It grew and widened, a molten wave, a sea of fish, dashing in against the nets, thrashing the water white like a pot put on to boil. Waist-deep, the men pulled on the ropes and laughed, throwing up fish into the air so the waiting gulls could catch them on the rebound. And in their midst the Tregarn brothers worked side by side, hauling on the nets with all their might, the saltwater working on their bruises and weals, the cold water turning the cuts purple, all enmity forgotten in this mutual frenzy of capture. On the beach their sister wrapped the anchoring lines around her waist like the other girls, her hair caught back and her white dress tied up to her knees.

The square was almost empty, littered with the wreckage of the fight. A few survivors nursed their wounds; some hangers-on who had never joined in, some curious onlookers, among whom I counted myself, were left at one end like flotsam on the shore. Garlands trailed, wreaths hung crooked, the stand was knocked askew. Gradually the gentry there put themselves to rights. The ladies began to clamber down, still shaken from a spectacle they had not expected. They picked their way carefully, as if walking over coals, while the gentlemen, somewhat the worse for wear, closed ranks behind them to escort them home.

'By God, I'll have the bloody thing banned next year,' I heard one say, a stout red-faced older man, Squire Tregaran as I supposed.

He passed me with a glare. Still hemmed in place with the other loiterers, I averted my eyes, not wanting to be counted among the riff-raff.

'Blasted hotheads, I'll see 'em all in jail before I let 'em run riot in my village again.'

Squire Tregaran was blustering, as men do after an event which they feel they should have controlled and failed to do. His wife leaned on his arm, not saying anything, her face hidden demurely under the wide brim of her hat. Behind her trailed her sons, the older looking smug, the younger, John, grim-faced beneath the mud, and yet, head held high, with a kind of pride that was not only for himself. I suddenly thought, he's glad he gave the shout to distract the crowd, and then, thank God he timed it right. But I remember thinking too, with a strange foreboding, when he gets home there'll be the devil to pay. And I found myself looking at him with a feeling almost akin to sympathy.

He and his parents were about to leave the square when someone took it upon himself to have the last word. From my days in court I have learned that there is always some joker who has to make the last joke, some 'big-mouth' who wants to be thought more clever than he is.

'What hotheads?' a voice behind me jeered. 'There were only two. One from either side. The first, a Tregarn, old enough to father the second, a Tregaran, if he had wanted to.'

That was the last straw. Squire Tregaran wheeled round

25

to attack. 'Who said that?' he shouted, his face purpling, his blue eyes bulging ominously. He waved his stick. 'I'll thrash that lie out of you.'

He advanced towards us, thrusting with his stick, ready to take on the lot of us. The others, all those who could, threw pride aside and took to their heels. Only I stood on my dignity, notebook in hand. And that is how I first became acquainted with the Tregarans, when the squire's stick descended on my head.

What happened afterwards is anti-climax. A middle-aged gentleman with a weak heart had no business in a village brawl, let alone to become its chief casualty. My poor Hodges had a bad time of it when I was carried back indoors. For a week or so I lay in a darkened room and he tiptoed about, while doctors were summoned, looking grave. But as I recovered, as flowers and apologies came daily from Tregaran House, as messages in the squire's name arrived, written in a feminine hand, full of regret and condolences, I told myself I had learned my lesson. The sound of the sea fretted my dreams, the soft spring air sent the sap rising; when I closed my eyes I saw a pair of blue-green ones. And whatever the lesson was, I forgot it soon enough.

CHAPTER TWO

During this period of convalescence I learned a secret about my house, if secret is the right word for something that should have been obvious. I have mentioned before the all-pervading presence of the sea and, to prevent its effect indoors, I had had special curtains hung in the halls and bedroom to shut it out. What I had not realized was the way the bay, like a gigantic amplifier, magnified sounds so that at certain times they came clear as a bell, I suppose tricks of wind or tide. Now, lying on my bed, I began to recognize the splash of oars, the rattle of sails, the reeling in and out of nets or lobster pots, and the voices of the men responsible for all this activity. To Hodges' scandalized concern, as soon as I could bear the light again I insisted on having the casement windows opened wide so that I could eavesdrop. And when I was recovered enough to resume my normal life I took to walking on the cliffs where I could listen even more closely. I told myself I was like a scientist studying a primitive tribe, using speech to unlock their secrets. I lied to myself. I wanted to learn their thoughts, to worm my way into their lives.

The cliff path I used was frequented by the villagers at special times for special reasons. Early in the morning, at daybreak, came the miners on their way to the small mines whose workings riddled the cliffs and made them treacherous. Next came the local women bound for Truro on market day with fresh-caught fish, or home-made jams, or vegetables from their little gardens. Sometimes there were children hunting for mushrooms under the hedge, sometimes young girls off to work in the 'gentry houses'. I learned to avoid all of them, chose my times of coming and going carefully, keeping out of sight – or so I thought, not knowing then that little can be hidden in a village where what is not known is invented.

I used to let myself out of the garden gate, follow a narrow path between deep hedges, winding through a succession of fields until they dipped within a footfall of an abyss, below which a series of bays indented the coast like a string of pearls. A great thatch of gorse and thorn grew along the edge, bent by the wind into a kind of tunnel, provided with gaps on the seaward side for peering through. Equipped with a telescope I spent many happy hours there, watching and listening. And as spring lengthened into summer, and weeks of fine weather turned that tunnel into a natural greenhouse, sheltering all kinds of rare plants, flowers, grasses, ferns, I felt myself a naturalist, observing plants and animals, and men, with equal scientific detachment. Pride caused my downfall. Because I felt myself immune, I came to think myself an expert; because I imagined I watched and judged unseen, I thought myself unseen. And I believed I understood everything.

I soon knew which boat edged out slowly, rowed by older men; which came swiftly, propelled by young strong arms. Pleasure craft I ignored, fewer of these, rocking past without a care in the world, filled with idle holidaymakers. It was the fishing fleet that interested me, the working boats which went about their daily business methodically. And among them, the Tregarn boat naturally caught my attention.

It was a long and strangely elegant craft, riding low in the water. I came to admire the grace with which its narrow wooden prow cut through the waves, and the precision with which its owners manoeuvred it in and out of the rocks, turning it smartly aside just when collision seemed inevitable. Its dark green paint blended with the greenish water in a way that was somehow aesthetically satisfying, and its deck was a model of neatness, the piles of lobster pots, the coils of nets, each arranged with a minimum of clutter. Its coming and going were timed with mathematical precision, early in the morning, rain or shine. I could have set my watch by it. A distinctive sound heralded its arrival, a swish and slide, as if its hull were slicing through the ocean. Usually Tom worked it alone, but when Zack accompanied him I noticed a tension in their rowing style, as if they were competing in a race. They sat one behind the other, straining on the oars, forcing themselves along by strength alone, the blades turning and twisting like precision screws. I took perverse pleasure in timing my excursions with their passing, so many steps out, so many steps back, as if on land I could keep pace with their progress at sea, as if at least in this, I was their equal.

Unlike the other fishermen the Tregarn brothers seldom spoke. When I parted the branches to look down at them, a hundred feet below, their silence seemed like a weight, anchoring them in place as they drifted from one cove to the next checking their lobster pots. Their movements had a pattern as spare and clean as a ritual dance; their nets came reeling out of the sea like webs; their boat floated like a shadowed layer above the ocean bed.

All this should be proof of how much I myself had changed, mellowed, perhaps, softened. My former life had not allowed much time for poetic description. Nor did I think of myself as spying. And if I had, I would have claimed I meant no harm. Amateurs don't. It pleased my fancy, that is all, watching there in secret, and when one day I heard a different voice coming from the boat, it seemed entirely right to listen.

Tom's voice was immediately recognizable, the low musical timbre of it, as if he found something of humour in everything. He was accompanied by a stranger, or at least at first I thought so. When the boat came into view a passenger was leaning over the gunwales, unthreading a twisted line of twine, while the slack curled in loops around his feet. The boy's head with its black hair was bent, he wore old clothes, he could have been one of twenty of the village lads, until he suddenly looked up and smiled, with John Tregaran's smile.

'There,' he said, 'I've got it clear. Now shall I thread the hooks back on?'

Without waiting for Tom's answering nod, he plunged his hands into a bucket where the bait was kept, and squatting down in the boat began to prepare the lines. Tom did not hover over him with exaggerated solicitude as the fishermen usually did when escorting 'foreigners' for pleasure, but in an offhand way kept an eye on him, meanwhile continuing with his own work, poling for lobster pots, emptying them on the deck and then sorting the catch rapidly. When both jobs were finished to his satisfaction he gave John a second oar, and sitting on his side on one bench, rowed with him round the headland.

Their style of rowing was more leisured, companionable, as if they felt in harmony rather than in competition, and they chatted in the intimate way friends have when they are speaking privately. From the start it was clear Tom dominated the partnership, telling the boy what to do, instructing him, although it was also clear that John was no novice. Probably it was natural for Tom to take charge,

30

he being older, and the skipper of the boat; certainly his attitude was not the usual one of a fisherman towards a member of the 'gentry' class, and it was puzzling. On the other hand, John Tregaran seemed perfectly happy, like a boy in the company of someone he admired. Whatever he had done or said at the village feast seemed to have been forgotten; there were no signs of the lad who had attacked so impulsively, and although in the following days he was often out with Tom (never Zack, only Tom), he never deviated from his role of submissive pupil. And once I remembered that now the school holidays must have begun, it made sense to accept this as a summer occupation, albeit perhaps a long-standing one dating back several years.

Yet the relationship was puzzling in other ways. The first time I had seen them in the square they had appeared as enemies, and after what had passed it might have seemed that friendship between them would be impossible. If anything, what John had done seemed to be regarded as a favour rather than an attack, for I once heard Tom thanking him. That left only one other reason and after a while I became suspicious. A good-looking youth, clearly a member of the 'ruling class', a handsome young fisherman, what could they possibly have in common except some mutual physical attraction?

Since the well-publicized case of the writer Oscar Wilde (in which I had played a minor role for the prosecution), homosexuality had lost its taboo, although the laws against it were if anything more savage. That it was epidemic among upper-class schoolboys I knew from firsthand experience; why not among fishermen? But although I watched carefully, I never saw a sign of it. And I must say truthfully that there was an innocence to them, a carefree trust, that made suspicion seem vulgar. (This is the last time I try to excuse myself for spying. It was only afterwards that I could accept my actions for what they were; that I could admit to envy; that I could understand that I resented and feared their comradeship simply because I was excluded from it. But that understanding came much later. Now it took several weeks of careful watching to find out what it was that bound them, for bond there certainly was.)

It was not at all what I expected. That day the sky was dull and lowering, threatening rain, and I had almost decided to stay indoors. The green of the boat was barely discernible against the grey of the sea, itself as cold and hard as granite. The two figures were still clearly visible, although a mist threatened to envelop them, and wisps of vapour trailed after them like a halo. John Tregaran suddenly straightened his back, and squared his shoulders, as if making up his mind.

Even at a distance his dark eyes dominated his face, almost as dark complexioned as a native of the southern Mediterranean. The sun had accentuated the angles of his high cheekbones and angular nose, giving an unexpected fierceness to his looks, as if he were some Spanish grandee. He would become a handsome man, I thought, if a sensitivity about his mouth did not turn into weakness. I had the strange feeling that I was about to witness a transformation, as if from under that shroud of mist a new person would be revealed; as if until now some unexplained reason had made him hide himself, a reason which no longer had importance and could be overlooked.

'I can't and shan't go off without saying goodbye,' he said. 'That's final. It'd not be right. Nor fitting. As well you know.'

His voice was different too; he spoke now with the sort of decision that before had been lacking. He did not face Tom, stared towards shore with an intent look as if searching for someone. His gaze seemed to pick me out behind the covering of gorse and for the first time I felt a pang of guilt as I ducked down out of sight. But even so it did not occur to me to leave.

Tom leaned on the oars, keeping the boat still against the current. His good-natured face was drawn into a frown, full of concentration. ''Tis not for me to say 'ee nay or yea,' he said at last. 'I bain't Zack. I don't think right or wrong as black and white as he does, with naught in between. To my mind 'tis all grey, same as today.'

He gestured with his hand, taking in the sky and sea. 'I passed the word on, as 'ee asked,' he continued. 'That's fair enough. But mind, now, I've no notion what the response'll be. That's not up to me neither. Though I know what 'ee hopes. And mayhap I hopes 'ee gets it.'

He gestured again. 'Now rewind them lines in quick, or we'll be tied up on the rocks like a Monday washing.'

It was the longest speech I'd heard him make, and whatever it referred to, sincerity showed in every word. I watched John take it in, digest and finally accept it. But the set of his shoulders showed it had not altered his opinion. 'Very well,' he said crisply, his accent suddenly less 'countrified', more educated, if that's how to describe it. 'Then say there's no cause to hide. We can't be punished twice for the same fault. Say there's still a choice, either here, tomorrow at this time, or there, at your house, in the evening. I think you'll agree that, of the two, here will be much more pleasant.'

He turned his back, settled down to his work. I watched the pair of them for a long while after that, adjusting the telescope to keep them in sight. They didn't speak again, took turns throwing out the lines, dragging up the pots and re-baiting them, then rowed quietly along, hands close on the oars, their bodies bending in rhythm. If some parting were imminent, Tom knew the cause. But

33

what the message was about, and who it was meant for, only became clear the following morning.

I was standing in my usual place when a sudden noise startled me, not a noise at sea but a rustling through the underbrush as if some large animal were making its way down the cliff. I have mentioned the tangles of bushes at the top forming the tunnel. In places these extended over the sides, overgrowing the rocks so that even the steepness was hidden. This mesh of gorse and thorn was criss-crossed with narrow tracks, along which sometimes small boys scrambled looking for gulls' eggs. Now a second fall of stones, a great outburst of birds' squawking, marked someone's presence; there was a ripping sound, a cut-off cry, and a momentary glimpse of a dark head half buried in the bracken. Before I could swivel the telescope round, the head disappeared and an answering shout came from below. The Tregarn boat had just nosed in to the bay and John was standing up, gesturing towards the cliff.

Tom sat still, arms wrapped about the oars, trimming the boat, apparently unperturbed by the continuing slide and rattle from above. And in a moment or two the object of all this commotion slid on to the beach in a last shower of turf and rubble.

Alice Tregarn picked herself up, shaking the dust from her long cotton skirt. Its flounces hung in ribbons, and its pale pink was stained green and brown. Without shoes, her hair unbraided, she looked now more like a gypsy than a statue, but the smile she gave was the same that had dazzled John Tregaran in the middle of the fight at the May Day feast.

She ran down towards the water's edge, her bare toes gripping and curling round the seaweed left uncovered by the tide. When she had clambered up to the furthest rock, she sat down, letting the water swirl round her skirts, and dipping her hands and feet into its eddies. The wind blew her hair out in wisps, the light made her eyes shine, she was the most alive thing I had ever seen. Even the mockery in her voice had a lilt to it. 'Well now,' she laughed, a laugh just like her brother's, 'you said to meet at the usual time and place. Here I be, but 'ee forgot the tide. Can't come no further out than this.'

The mischievous flash in her eyes added, 'What next is up to you,' as she sat peeling off limpets and throwing them towards the boat, as if that was all she had come for.

Tom continued to lean impassively on the oars, keeping well offshore. The shallow water ahead revealed new rocks cresting below the surface and he would not or could not come closer. John was still standing up in the prow, vexation and amusement in his expression. He opened his mouth in protest, then, without a word of warning, dived off, sending a wave surging over the side, almost over-tipping the boat. He swam underwater for a while, surfacing close to the rock where Alice sat, sending another wave washing over it so that she too was swamped. 'How's this?' he spluttered. She didn't move, sat there smiling to herself until he hauled himself up beside her, his hair plastered to his skull, his clothes streaming.

'For two pins I'd push you in.' His remark was not exactly gallant, and he grinned as if the thought was tempting. 'Except 'twould be no sport, you swim like a fish.'

'And when I get home someone'll notice.' She had not stopped throwing shells into the sea but something in those few words put him on his guard. He squatted silently, wrapping his arms about his chest for the wind was cold. Out in the bay, Tom trimmed the boat, and gave a gesture that could have meant anything before settling down to his fishing chores. For a while the two on the rock remained side by side, throwing shells and pebbles into the sea until Tom had vanished round the headland, and the only sound was the lapping of the water and the crying of the gulls still circling the cliff.

Then John said, 'It never bothered you before. Don't tell me you've gone all lady-like and particular. Is that why you've let the summer waste away without once joining us? And now I'm leaving . . .'

He let the sentence trail off. 'God damn,' he broke out, 'surely Zack's not that mean. He knows how we've gone fishing all our lives, how close we've always been, the three of us.' Again he let his voice trail off.

She went on peeling shells, still not looking at him. 'You know Zack,' she said at last. 'Comes a thought into his head, and there it sits, like a thundercloud. But it's not only him. What about you Tregarans?'

She broke off then said, suddenly, passionately, 'They hate my family, you know; they hate me too. 'Twas different, perhaps, when we was younger, they could pretend it didn't matter, something we'd outgrow like chickenpox. But after the May Day feast, they can't forget. Hasn't your father already said he'll cancel it? Hasn't he forbidden it next year because of us? And isn't your having to leave partly a'cause of it?'

He didn't deny the charges. 'Just the last few days,' he was pleading, 'for old times' sake. You've managed it somehow today, then try again tomorrow. Just like we always used, you and me and Tom. You can think up some excuse. It isn't the same without you.' He started to add, 'It's what makes . . .' then shivered into silence, as if a coldness had caught him.

'It'd mean a lot to me,' he began again, 'some memory to take with me.' He still didn't explain where he was going but she must have known, for she shivered as if in sympathy. The end of that unfinished sentence hung in the air between them, 'It's what makes things bearable.'

She put out her arm and touched his. 'I know,' she said. ''Tis the same for us. Tom do miss 'ee something fierce.' The end of her sentence, too, hung unsaid. 'And so do I.'

She smiled at him, began to unsnarl her hair, braiding it into one long plait. 'Zack'll find out,' she said. 'He always does. He's on the watch these days anyhow, threatening me for everything. If I catch you, he says, I'll take my belt to you, as if I was some kind of horse. Checking on me, where I go, what I do, as if he expects something wrong. Times me to the village shop and back, and if I'm late, 'tis "Who've 'ee been talking to, what've 'ee been up to, then?" as if I were a criminal. If it weren't for Tom he'd drive me mad.'

She sighed. 'Tom do say it's a'cause of our Mam. Zack can't bear to think her gone, Tom says, that even after all these years her death's a hurt. He were the oldest son, see; he can remember all the little ones that died afore I was born, and it's made him afraid. It makes him responsible like for me.'

She sighed again. 'I don't remember my Mam,' she said, 'but I've seen her photograph. Tom says she loved to laugh, our house was full of fun when she was alive. Myself, I think she gave her laughter to Tom and me, and left Zack naught. I think Zack's afraid I'll die too, just like the others did. I think he's feared for me because I'm like she was.'

She sighed for the third time. 'But I'll come,' she said slowly. 'There, I promise. Zack or not, I'll think up some excuse. Every day until 'ee goes.'

She threw up her head as if scenting the wind. 'I never wanted not to,' she said simply. 'And we'm in luck. 'Twill turn fine this week; can't 'ee feel the it? Smells like sloes simmering on the hob.'

She sniffed appreciatively, then jumped up and stretched out her arms as if to gather in that sun, a gesture that was suddenly familiar. For a moment she stood there on tiptoe, outlined against the sea, the wind blowing her skirts, like the figurehead on a ship. Then, briskly practical, 'So now that's settled, do 'ee get on home afore 'ee catches your death of cold. I'll wait for Tom.'

She gave him a little nudge. 'Go on,' she said. 'No need to wait.' And when he still hesitated, 'I promise. Cross my heart and hope to die, and may the Giant of Long Leet take 'ee. Can't say any more than that, ain't that enough?'

Before he had time to reply she jumped up and began to run along the beach, her wet dress flapping round her legs, her thick braid flopping down her back. He watched her until she rounded the headland, then straightened up and turned towards the cliff himself, presumably searching for the same path she had used. I heard him scratching for footholds among the roots, and before the gulls began their screams of protest hurried off myself, not willing to make my presence known. And as I went, I heard another noise, equally in haste, the beat of hooves, as if a horse were galloping up the field. From the tunnel's end I caught a glimpse of a great grey beast disappearing over the crest of the hill, as if its rider had whipped it up, so that only the thrum of its passing lingered. The identity of horse and horseman remained a mystery, a farmer perhaps surveying his livestock, a rider about his own business, but in the days to come I was to remember them.

The next week passed in a blur of sun such as sometimes occurs in the west of England. It burns like a red ball out of the morning mist, drying up the dew until the grass turns brown. The leaves of bushes whiten with

38

dust; the bracken stalks curl, the smell of gorse is like hot jam. It is a time when nothing stirs, a time for lazing on the beach, for sitting without thought while the warmth burns through to bone. Each morning, at the appointed time, the Tregarn boat slid towards the cove, laden with its baited lobster pots. Each morning I counted the three figures on board, working without haste to retrieve and replace pots and lines, six hands pulling and releasing in unison. And when the work was done, Tom tied the catch into a net, sent the anchor rattling to the ocean floor and let the boat drift on its chain towards the point of rocks where Alice had sat to gather shells.

The men untied their boots and knotted them round their necks, while Alice bundled her skirt into her petticoats. All three leapt overboard at the same time, and began to swim, John with a great splashing of fancy over-arm, Tom solid as a whale breasting along with a canvas bag on his head to keep it dry, Alice skimming just beneath the surface. They waded out on the beach, dried themselves off with wisps of grass, threw themselves down on the sand and began to eat, with hearty young appetites.

The food was Cornish, obviously prepared by Alice in the early dawn, country food that city people despise: pasties, easily recognized and without which no meal in Cornwall is complete; smoked pilchards wrapped in leaves; apples, cooked in thick pie-crusts, sugar-glazed; clotted cream spooned out from a pressed glass jar, the whole washed down with cider cooled at the water's edge. Having dined prodigiously, Tom walked restlessly about, no lying idle in the sun for him. A working man, unused to holidays, he let his clothes steam on him, kept moving constantly looking for things to do: digging for clams, hunting crabs in the small rock pools, beach-combing among the wrack of weed that piled along the high-tide mark, sometimes even climbing partway up the cliff towards the caves made by the openings of the mine shafts. But he never went inside, just stood and shouted as if the weight of all that rock frightened him.

Alice had no inhibitions. She lay back facing the sun, the skirts of her faded blue dress spread round her to dry in white salt streaks. The sleeves were rolled up above the elbows; her skin was golden against the golden sand, her dark hair touched with gold like a raven's wing. Only the clasping and unclasping of her fingers showed that she was awake, as she played with some pebbles, feeling them like worry beads.

John lay beside her, equally awake, although he kept his eyes closed. The veins on his neck stood out; his eyelids flickered; from time to time he shifted on the hot sand as if making himself comfortable. Time was running out for him, the 'chaperon' was conveniently absent, now he had to speak. But when he did begin it was to continue a quarrel.

In actual fact Alice spoke first, her voice low although the treacherous wind funnelled the words up into the air for all the world to hear. 'Don't scold,' she said, biting her lip. ''Tisn't that I don't care to write. But how's a letter to come to the house without anyone noticing? And how could I answer? 'Tis gone beyond the drop-hole in the hedge when we was young. Besides,' she looked away, ''ee'd laugh. I'm not schooled for letter-writing, fancy like.'

'As if that matters,' he said almost angrily. 'It's what is thought and felt, not how it's said. Come to that, I'm no dab hand myself. But I'll not be back for more than eighteen months. That's long, if you count the days. As I shall. And I'm afraid we'll forget. Afraid, that is, if you don't write.'

He said 'write', but the word he meant was 'wait'.

40

After a moment he added, 'Then we'll use Tom. He won't mind if we send news through him. Zack can't object to that.'

There was a steely note now to his voice that made her sit up straighter and begin to brush the grit from her clothes, as if brushing away its sound. She fixed her large brooding eyes on him, for the first time letting their full force be felt.

'That's not fair,' she said, with her brother's earnest honesty. 'Don't blame Zack for everything. And to my mind, time don't count when a thing is meant. But there's too much resting on us both for plunging on, all blind-like. I don't see a way clear ahead, and that's a fact. I wish . . . I wish I did.' And for a moment she let her hand with its powder of sand brush against his back, no more than a hint, a promise of a caress.

It must have been what he was waiting for. He seized her fingers between his own, turning them, as if trying to learn their imprint. 'There's no one in the world but you,' he muttered. 'Never has been back to the start of remembering. But now we're grown I . . .' He hesitated, as if nervous about rushing in, as if afraid of alarming her. 'When I saw you as Queen,' he cried, 'I knew you'd changed. I felt, I don't know, that you'd gone somewhere far away, and I was left behind, as if you'd never come back.'

'Where would I go?' She tried a laugh. 'Whatever makes 'ee to imagine such a thing, when 'tis 'ee that's going and I that stays? And everyone knows May Day would've been spoiled if 'ee hadn't interfered.'

Again that little half-gesture of affection. 'Always has been the three of us,' she said, 'always will be, Tom and 'ee and me, the Three Musketeers. Remember when 'ee fell and broke your arm reaching for that bird nest, and how 'ee made Tom take me home before coming back for

41

'ee? And when we beached the boat how 'ee and he swam it off through the storm? And when we got waylaid in the mist how 'ee both argued which way 'twas? And when . . . but there's no end of remembering, 'tis all printed in your thoughts and his, and mine.'

'Perhaps.' The bleak note was back. 'But it's not Tom I'm interested in.'

'Once 'ee was,' she said. 'He meant the world to 'ee.' There was a reproach which he acknowledged with a nod of his head. They sat in silence for a while, thinking perhaps about that past when they had all three been close, those simple summers of long ago. At last, 'I know,' she answered him simply, ''tis me 'ee want. And that's what I'm a-feared of most.'

On an impulse she put her hand up to his cheek, and let him kiss the palm. It must have been the first time she had done such a thing, for as suddenly she turned ruby red and snatched her hand away as if it burned.

Then, slowly and carefully, as if she were repeating a lesson learned by heart, 'Who else is there but 'ee? Who else is there to remember? I'll count the days too. But 'tis not the waiting that bothers me. 'Tis all that past, before we was born, all those two hundred years of hate that we've inherited. I can't start it up again. And that's what Zack is really frightened of, that's what I'm frightened of meself. Zack says it overshadows us, like this cliff. I don't know we'm strong enough to lift it up.'

'We've got to try.' It was his turn to be passionate. 'Whatever happened in the past is past. It's not our fault. Zack's got to recognize that. And so must you.'

She had turned aside to brush down her clothes. The wind blew back their folds, moulding the damp cotton to her breasts. The sun shone against the form inside; slight as a reed she leaned into the wind with that calm, familiar stillness that seemed natural to her. Beside her, his body thin where hers was curved, John held her fast around the waist so he could look at her. A smile began to curl along his mouth; he put a finger out to touch hers. 'So let's not fight,' he whispered. 'Let's not waste what time is left. Tom's not here, we're all alone. And I want to make love to you.

'I'd not hurt you,' he went on. 'I'd mean no harm. I just want to lie beside you here, holding you tight. Just kiss you without stopping for an hour, a week, just wrap you up to keep you safe. Why, Zack should be pleased; I'd keep you safer than ever he could.'

He was making his actions fit his words, winding her round in her own clothes so that her arms were bent back and her body fitted into his. And for a moment it seemed he would win for she let him cover her mouth with his and swayed against him as if her will was gone. Then with a struggle that was almost violent, she broke away, her breath coming in great panting sobs. ''Tain't right,' she said, 'I know what comes of kissing close like that. I'm not that innocent. Keep your distance, Master John.'

Her use of that 'Master' made him grow white, as before her face had grown red. 'Don't call me that.' He was angry. 'Don't use that word. There's enough difficulty without dragging that up. Whenever has what I am or you are come between us?'

'You'm a Tregaran,' she said. 'I'm old enough never to forget that. But you'm right. We shouldn't quarrel. For one thing Tom might hear. And for another . . .'

She hesitated. 'And for another, I don't want to neither. I care too much for 'ee.'

With a gaiety that was forced she suddenly smiled at him. 'The tide's a-turning,' she said, ''ee've forgot it again. We'll be trapped. Race 'ee to the rocks and back.'

With a toss of her head she was gone, the sand spurting in dry puffs beneath her feet and her blue skirts fluttering.

The boy watched her for a moment without moving. That mixture of resentment and confusion he had shown before flickered across his face. What is she playing at? it seemed to say; is she pretending, to lead me on? Or is she simply being herself and is it I who have changed? He ground his fist against the sand. Is Zack right to mistrust you? that's what that gesture said. Is your innocence real; are you a child or a flirt? I can't tell And if I could, what difference would it make, you've caught me fast, so fast I can't ever escape.

After a while, his own emotions under control, he reached down for his shirt and followed her more slowly. He found her round the point of rocks, kneeling beside Tom admiring his finds, and while the brother and sister spread out the shells and flints of stone for him to choose, he watched them with a strange expression. It was as if, standing above them, he felt himself a giant, about to smash a fragile thing to bits, as if their childlike laughter taunted him, as if it shut him out.

Then, as the first tidal currents began to spread along the beach, 'Be quick,' he said curtly, 'you're the ones who don't want to be late.' He led the way into the water, wading out until it came up to his hips, then diving in, leaving them to go back for the remnants of their picnic. On board he loosened the anchor rope, unshipped the oars, waited scowling while Tom clambered in and reached to haul her after him.

Tom seemed impervious to his mood. He went on smiling, turning everything into a joke. Perhaps he did not notice, but there was an effort to his chatter, as if he were trying to balance things, like trimming a boat. Behind them, Alice trod water, hanging on to the anchor chain, a mermaiden, in her element. Her smile was the one I'd seen before, both ageless and young, godlike and human, and it sent a shiver down my back.

44

It took me a while to recover after that, too many ideas crowding all at once, too many nuances needing assimilation. I had to make an effort to walk away, as if I were leaving part of myself behind. And when I did, for the second time I heard a horse's hooves thrumming in the distance.

The next day I watched in vain. As Alice had predicted, the weather continued fine; other boats passed and repassed; the Tregarn boat never made its appearance, although I waited until long past noon. I was hungry, tired and vexed when at last the obvious conclusion dawned on me. And as I approached the open field a third time the sound of a horse made me draw back. But this time the sound did not go away.

The horse was standing in the middle of the path, snorting uneasily, its grey flanks curdled cream with heat, the flies buzzing round its long cream tail. Its rider was impeccably dressed, seated sideways as if glued into the saddle. Her black-skirted habit was arranged to show the neatest foot, her hat was set at a rakish tilt; in her gloved hand she held an ivory-tipped crop which she tapped against her side, as lady-like a turnout as one could wish. Only her face gave her away, that look of suppressed anguish that I had seen before.

The reason why Mrs Tregaran did not move was the man who was standing in front of her. One hand was on the bridle holding her horse in check; the other was laid across its nose so that it snuffled against his arm. Zack Tregarn hadn't changed, either. Despite the heat he wore the same rough miner's clothes, waistcoat and jacket, heavy workman's boots. His voice was thick with rage. To her splutter of protest, 'Your land, your land,' he was repeating with a snarl, 'That's rich. 'Tweren't ever yourn; you married it. And my right to it's better by fifty-fold than that precious husband you'm so fond of.' (He sneered the

45

word.) 'As for telling me to get off what's mine, leastways I comed here openly. And I speak my mind openly too, no sneaking about, meddling with other people's lives.

'Don't matter what 'ee say,' he went on, ''ee can't pretend to me. Don't use my girl to stir up muck. Keep your boy off, or I'll tip him over the cliff.'

Evelyn Tregaran suddenly looked away, a faint flush colouring her white skin. 'That's cruel,' she said, suddenly very quiet. 'That's not worthy of you.'

He stood there letting the horse fidget with its bit and swish its tail. 'Whenever did cruelty bother 'ee?' The question was bleak. 'I can't say I ever noticed before. Leastways not where I was concerned.'

She had paled again, her skin like ivory against her dark hair. 'There's lots to be said about that,' she burst out, almost sounding like her son. 'If I'm the way you think, you know it wasn't always so. And you know who's to blame.'

When he didn't reply, hardening her voice, giving it that malicious whisper, 'If you dispute whose land this is, at least grant me the right to ride my own horse. Let go.'

'Not 'til 'ee agree.' He stood there, blocking her, solid, large, impenetrable.

'Liar,' she suddenly screamed at him, as if her nerves had snapped. 'I've no reason to stir up the past. The thought of my son with your sister makes my blood cold. What would he get out of it? All the gain's on her side. Keep her and that brother of yours away from him.'

'Alice's just a silly chit of a child.' He spoke as if she hadn't interrupted him. 'Your son's old enough to understand. Why don't 'ee tell him the truth too? Tell him nothing's ever gone smooth between our two families, nothing ever will, and the sooner he accepts that the better for him. And it'll not change in our lifetime.'

His voice was calmer now, suddenly more ominous than his previous shout. It made her flush again. Angrily she raised her crop so he was forced to step back and let go the reins.

'Anger won't help,' he said in the same tense way. ''Tis too late for anger. Just remember what I say, or 'twill be the worse for 'ee.'

He turned on his heel and strode away. But as he passed the place where I lurked, 'If it's trespassers you'm after,' he jerked with his thumb, contemptuously, 'here be a real one. Threaten him.'

Mortified, I stuffed the telescope into my coat pocket and clambered out into the open. Zack Tregarn was already disappearing down the path towards the village; for the second time I was left to face the consequences.

Evelyn Tregaran recovered her composure first. Showing admirable presence of mind she leaned over the horse to steady it, gentling it for a moment or two to catch her breath. Then she turned towards me, forcing her mouth into a smile although her dark eyes were hard. To my muttered excuses, 'Well now, Mr Cradock,' she said, 'no need for that. It's we owe you apologies. Twice you've caught us off guard. But that's Cornish life for you, as ingrown as a toenail. Don't judge us too harshly because of it.'

She was still breathing heavily, but the smile she gave me now was genuine, and she unfastened her hat as if to let the wind fan her hair. 'He's an odd man,' she said, pointing with her crop. 'Mad as a hatter. Visions of past grandeur, that sort of thing, like lots of old families. He's convinced he owns our land; says it once was his, before the Tregarans stole it. And then there's that brother of his, always hanging about with his silly grin, trying to push his sister forward, make a lady out of her, poor thing. She's wild enough without having her head turned. Lately I've passed by here once or twice, tempted by the fine weather, as I expect you've been.' She paused then, her voice faintly, ever so faintly, pointed. 'I've seen the two of them with my son. My fault perhaps,' she went on artfully, trying to gauge how much I'd heard, trying to guess what to reveal and what to hide, trying to pretend a truth. 'In the old days we used to let our children run with the villagers, although I never held with too much familiarity. All right for a while, I suppose, then former friendships can become a liability. I'm afraid the Tregarns are taking advantage of poor John's interest; possibly he's not been as discreet as he ought. He was fond of them once and he's, what was the phrase, a "silly chit" himself, not over-sensible.' She smiled again. 'You know how careless young boys are,' she said. 'Or so my husband says.'

She broke off, 'But there, I'm boring you and keeping you standing. We're just glad to have you up and about. Now you're better you must come to dine.'

Impulsively she leaned towards me with the same flattering interest. 'Come tonight,' she offered, 'do. Just a few neighbours. We're not quite such peasants as you think. And I'd like you and John to meet before he goes, so you won't be left with the wrong impression.'

She laughed down at me. 'Wouldn't blame you,' she said. 'We must seem like medieval lords. Take pity on our countrified ways, Mr Cradock. We've heard about you, you know. Come and amuse us with all the city news.'

She tapped the horse so that it sidled past and headed towards the open field. 'Sevenish,' she called over her shoulder, 'black tie, nothing special. And show us you've forgiven us.'

The horse broke into a canter, a gallop, breasting the hill; she turned it to race along the ridge, deliberately I thought, so that her silhouette was shown off against the sky. Her hair, freed from the confines of her hat, streamed behind her; her straight back and clear profile gave her the look of a a Valkyrie. My first thought was, how well she rides. My second, she knows how to make the best of it; the third, what accomplished lies she tells.

As I dressed for dinner that night, like the old trial lawyer I was, I counted the lies. Or rather, the half-truths, which one learns to sift out for a jury's benefit, like chaff from wheat. That 'odd man' with 'visions of past grandeur', her 'lady of the manor' pose – on the surface, these things were not completely inaccurate, only her distortion of them was. And the careful little asides, the 'tempted by fine weather', the 'letting our children run with the villagers', all calculated to seem innocent, all calculated to put me off the scent. Likewise the clever rephrasing of Zack Tregarn's own words, to test how long I had been listening and how much I had overheard. An astute woman, I thought. But no one had taught her the first lesson of defence, never to explain too much. Nor the second, to ignore the obvious. Whatever reason she had to lie – embarrass-ment at being caught herself, irritation at being put in the wrong, or even genuine concern for her son (which last I doubted), one thing was painfully certain. She might pay lip service to 'class' and 'position'; she and Zack Tregarn might burn with mutual hate. Once, in the past, they had met as equals, and as more than friends.

CHAPTER THREE

Apart from accepting her invitation as a peace offering I had several reasons for attending Evelyn Tregaran's dinner, excluding idle interest, I mean. For one thing she fascinated me. She seemed to embody the dark side of that Celtic force whose opposite I had sensed in Alice Tregarn. Like her enemy, Zack, she exuded fire, sparking hammer against anvil. Then the way she'd tossed the invitation off, like a challenge, like an afterthought, piqued me. I wasn't used to such offhandedness. Most of all I wanted to see her with her sons, to unravel their family secrets, to spy on them as I had the Tregarns.

Yet even as I waited for my car to be brought round, even as I endured Hodges' complacent look ('We may be buried here alive,' it said, 'thank God, someone still keeps standards up.') I was also trying to guess what she wanted me for. That was the thing which most intrigued me, what use she meant to make of me. For she used people, that was clear, although she did so with finesse, and behind her charm there was a sense of purpose as if, on seeing me, an idea had leapt into her head. I admit to finding that thought intriguing. It wasn't often I was made use of, a lawyer isn't easily outfoxed. And as a last resort two can play the same game.

When I joined the other guests in Tregaran House they regarded me with the same cautious restraint as I did them. 'What's that chap here for?' their expression said, and they looked at me with undisguised curiosity, as if trying to guess why their hostess had invited me. As she was not yet in the room we had time to size each other up while our host made the rounds introducing me somewhat sheepishly and, when that was done, turning his back on the rest of us. I felt a sort of sympathy for him. It's not often a man is obliged to entertain someone he has almost brained and I suspected, despite his wife's sweet talk, he wished me to the devil. In fact he seldom spoke to anyone, devoting his remarks, what there were of them, to his steward (as I learned Cornish bailiffs were called). This stocky little man, Jim Polwren, was there presumably at the Colonel's request for he too kept to himself, looking uncomfortable in his best clothes. Again I felt a fellow sympathy. As for Colonel Michael Tregaran, he seemed to me a sad man. Beneath his bluster he was shy, almost morose. I thought, all this – beautiful house, beautiful wife, handsome sons – inside he's taut like a cord, wound up with self-disgust. It made me like him. It was a feeling I'd had cause to know, recognizing it in myself.

There were only three other guests, excluding Polwren and myself. At one end of the room the vicar, Mathew Trevenn, took up a whole sofa, seeming much as Hodges had described. ('A blatherer,' Hodges had said, 'too fond of his own voice except when Mrs Tregaran's about. Then butter won't melt in his mouth, meek as dish-water.') Seated opposite him was another local pair, a Sir Archibald Penquire and his lady wife of whom it was said no two more staunch Conservatives ever breathed, and who regarded me with alarm, as if by being there I threatened them. In fact, my first impression of this group was that we were sitting in some waiting room. Not because of the room itself (which was part of the old medieval hall, surprisingly untouched; I suspected the Colonel's hand in that) but the expectant atmosphere. There was a stream of disjointed talk, punctuated by long, suspicious silences with which people gathered in a public place try to preserve their anonymity. And when at last Evelyn Tregaran appeared in a rush of apology, one almost heard an audible sigh of relief, as her friends sat up and rearranged themselves as if preparing to make a move.

I realized this swirl of energy was typical of Evelyn, but again it caught me unprepared, as heady as the perfume she wore. Nor was I the only one affected. I saw the other male guests exchange glances and lean forward simultaneously as if jealous of each other and vying for attention. All except her husband, that is. He ignored her, still standing apart with Jim Polwren. And she ignored him. I had never seen such disregard as if he and she had nothing to do with each other, were less than strangers, not there at all. And I couldn't help thinking, if that's all marriage is, better to remain a bachelor.

By now dusk was just beginning to fall, that long sad twilight hour which gives English summers their melancholy, and through the windows wafted the scent of jasmine and stocks. The windows themselves opened out on to the park, a stretch of dark velvet grass bordered by trees which, on the eastern side, merged into a dense and ancient wood. The land sloped downward into a hollow, cupping the sea in a pale silver bowl. I shall never forget how that silver seemed to mirror the sky, and how the starlight reflected back its pallid gleam. This has been since time began, it seemed to say, all else is transitory.

By contrast Evelyn Tregaran's presence was the more vivid. Her, 'My dears, my dears, what can you think, I've been delayed by disasters unimaginable,' was calculated to banish melancholy as she began an absurd tale of a pair of missing shoes. She moved swiftly round the room, greeting everyone in turn, spending a moment or two with each. She had a habit of touching people as she spoke, and although I myself have a horror of familiarity I felt resentful that she left me till last. I was the outsider, presumably the honoured guest; I suppose it was natural that I sensed a slight. But when at last she welcomed me the clasp of her long thin fingers over mine was strangely soothing, as if she wanted to put my mind at rest.

She was dressed in black, shot with silver thread, a sophisticated choice that accentuated her pallor and added to her mystery. I had the impression of rustling silk, of pearls, and when she moved, a glitter, like the sea outside. But she still made no attempt to make me part of the group, as if saving me for herself, and although again flattering, this made other conversation difficult.

Her two sons had come into the room when she did, walking stiffly like some military escort. I remember they stood a step or two behind, side by side like two pages in their sombre evening clothes, a medieval effect that was enhanced by the lighted tapers they carried. I can think of no better way to explain her influence over them than by saying that this dramatic entrance did not seem to embarrass them. Or rather, not the older boy; John had lapsed into his subdued self and needed constant prompting to salute his mother's friends, as if he were a younger child. She kept her enthusiasm for the older son who was obviously the favourite, and again I felt a twinge of sympathy for the younger one.

She must have sensed it. Her abrupt, 'Come on, my dears, you must be starved,' was calculated to break the mood and set us all in motion. She led the way into the dining room, mincing quickly along with tiny steps; her sons followed, standing on guard as she took her place; the rest of us complied without speaking, as if tugged on strings, the Colonel sitting at the table's head in grumpy silence.

Talk returned to the Tregaran sons, and saw us through the main course of a meal which was surprisingly good. (As were the wines – Colonel Tregaran prided himself on his cellars, and on the deer which provided the venison.) To be precise, it was the older boy, Nigel, on whom attention continued to centre; like his father, John was ignored.

Nigel sat opposite me. His fair good looks, in contrast to his family's dark ones, his open face, his easy charming manners, reminded me of a young subaltern at Mess, a shrewd analogy as he had just come home on leave after joining his father's regiment. There were congratulations, a rambling discourse from Lady Penquire concerning her own father's army days, a few gruff recollections from Sir Archibald. For the most part Nigel took this interest modestly; only once or twice I caught him eyeing himself in one of the many mirrors on the wall as if enjoying being lionized. His light hair, his grey eyes, would have attracted anyone, but the look he gave himself, suggesting he found himself attractive, was somehow too complacent for his years, indicating a self-absorption that did not match the outward charm. It made me like him less than he thought he merited, while his smile, unconsciously deepening into a smirk when his mother spoke, suggested that he both revelled in her pride and yet felt he should disclaim it.

As soon became apparent, however, in praising him his mother had a secondary purpose. 'Nigel was captain of his House as well as cricket captain,' she was saying, with over-obvious emphasis. She smiled fondly at her older son who had the grace not to smile back. 'He'll be playing on your side, Aggie, in the annual local match. You know cricket's his favourite sport, after riding. He's brought his horse with him, the one that won the point-to-point.' She sighed. 'John'll have a hard time,' she said, 'to repeat that.'

It was the first direct reference I'd heard to John, and it struck a sour note. When Sir Archibald, trying his hand at humour, added heavily, 'Like your father, eh, Nigel, my boy, huntin', shootin' and fishin' and all that sort of thing,' she shook her head as if in warning. Sir Archibald meant trout fishing, of course, but his listeners took it in another sense.

'Not fishing, Sir Archie,' Nigel broke in. It was the first time he had spoken and his voice had his mother's intonation. He grimaced. 'Fishing's more in John's line. Can't think what he sees in it,' he went on, 'all that work, all that sea, all that rocking up and down. I prefer dry land myself.'

He might have meant this as a joke, it was hard to tell, but as a joke it was misplaced. His mother took it up at once. 'Nasty flappy things, fish.' She wrinkled her nose. 'And how they smell. The village reeks of them.'

Nigel laughed, leaned forward to pick up a peach. 'Saw Tom Tregarn the other day.' He slid the name in easily. 'Or rather smelled him a mile off. I was in the village and up he comes, bold as brass, as if we'd been bosom pals for years.' Again the grimace. 'He had a cannery girl with him and she smelled worse. Don't know how they stood each other. I suppose they're used to it, at least they can't tell "t'other from 'twich".'

There was an unexpected sarcasm in his voice. It gave him away. And perhaps he realized it. 'But there,' he added too quickly, 'she was pretty so I suppose Tom didn't mind. He always was an easy chap.'

The attempt to mollify caused an awkward pause. Evelyn used it as if she had been waiting for the chance.

'You've all heard, of course, that John leaves tomorrow,' she said confidingly. 'We're sending him to Nigel's school. We thought a little military discipline wouldn't hurt, would knock some nonsense out of him.'

She spoke as if her younger son were not there and since John himself did not reply, again there was an awkward pause. Then Nigel leaned back and bit into the fruit while the rest of us broke into chit-chat about the relative merits of different schools. Since I had not known before what John's leaving entailed I listened carefully. It seemed that instead of going to university as planned, he was to be prepared for Sandhurst and a military career, a surprising change. I wondered that he accepted it. Yet from his place mid-way down the table John continued to let this talk wash over him as if he had no part in it. Only for a moment did I see him grit his teeth as if to keep his anger down. Then he bent his head again, his face closed and secretive. In a strange way he reminded me of his father. But whereas his father's anger was all outward, for show, John kept his feelings hidden, banked down outside.

I suppose the awkwardness might still have passed and the evening ended as it had begun, in idle talk, except that Evelyn continued to provoke him. Either John's expression irritated her or his control did. Her voice became increasingly brittle, her manner loud, just as she had sounded in the square. She began to needle John, trying to break through his guard, gradually homing in for the kill. 'John doesn't like cricket, do you, John? He doesn't have Nigel's throwing arm. John doesn't like hunting, his heart's too soft.' Finally, as he lifted his half-filled glass, 'John, enough wine, we don't want you drunk.' This last with a throaty laugh that was meant to wound.

I don't know about the other guests but I found this performance disturbing. I wanted to tell her to be quiet. Yet the intensity of my own feelings surprised and silenced me. Once I too had been an unloved son with an older brother who was idolized. I still remembered the sarcasm; I still remembered vividly its paralysing effect.

It must have had the same effect on Colonel Tregaran. All this while he had sat at the head of the table, drinking his wine, talking, if he did, in low tones with his steward about estate affairs. Now, at each of his wife's sallies, he seized the bottle from the butler's hands and poured himself another glass, his red face growing redder as if he would explode. Finally he set the bottle down with a crash. 'For God's sake,' he cried, 'leave the boy alone. What harm does fishing do? Used to do it myself. Took a seventy-pound shark one day, right out there in Tregaran Bay, played him for an hour. Talk of fighting fish, never had better sport.'

It was a clumsy attempt to draw attention away to himself, but his younger son shot him a look that was far from grateful. 'That's not the sort of fishing I like,' John said, his voice hoarse with holding anger in check. 'I prefer the everyday kind with people I know, poking around rocks with nets and traps.'

He threw this out like a challenge. Good for him, I thought, remembering how it was when I was a boy. (And remembering, too, how pity hurts, how it's always the unloving parent that one wants to please.) It was at this point that the vicar, as peacemaker, must have felt obliged to put in his oar and rocked the boat. 'Always thought you'd take up science,' he said to John. 'You were good at zoology and botany and such when you were a child. Surprised to hear you've changed your mind.'

John Tregaran pushed his chair back so that it scraped across the floor. 'I didn't,' he said flatly. 'It was changed for me.' He glared about him, taking us all on. 'Paupers don't have much choice,' he said. 'Remember, I'm the second son.'

He didn't look at Nigel, but the dislike was there. 'You're right about one thing though,' he went on. 'I'd make a better botanist than soldier. As for these fishermen you poke fun at' (he stammered the word), 'I tell you that for honest men, loyal men, you'll never better Tom Tregarn. I owe him a debt that I can't repay. The Tregarns were here before we were. We're the jumped-up nobodies. Some day I mean to make it up to them, when I come back from this bloody place I'm banished to.'

He threw the words down like a challenge. There was a strange bitterness to them, the first I'd heard him permit himself. And speaking of the future was the closest he could bring himself to mentioning Alice. But her name hung there unspoken.

When he was gone, leaving us in stunned silence, 'You see,' his mother cried, 'that's what I have to contend with.' Her voice was still shrill; even in his absence she couldn't let go. 'This very afternoon one of those so-called "friends" tried to stop me riding across the cliffs. Not that John'd care. He's thrown in his lot with them. But God knows what would have happened today if Mr Cradock here hadn't come to the rescue.'

She turned to me, as if she had been holding me in reserve, as if this was the purpose I was to be used for. And when, caught by surprise, I muttered something noncommittal, 'The Tregarns are a universal nuisance,' she cried reproachfully. 'They're misfits, thinking themselves better than they are, claiming land as if they were in the Wild West, mining for gold instead of tin.'

She laughed without mirth, showing all her splendid teeth. 'Today I wished we were,' she said. 'I'd have used a gun if I'd had one.'

Once more her husband stirred. 'Leave them to me,'

he muttered, but she continued as if he had not spoken; as if, one victim gone, she had fastened on him next. Turning to the rest of her guests, leaning towards us so that we seemed enveloped in her confidence, 'They're tricksters, the Tregarns,' she said. 'Poachers, thieves, scum. I'm not going to let them drag my son into the gutter with them.'

She closed her painted lips firmly, sat back. There was another awkward pause. Then the other men rallied round gallantly. 'Poach on my land,' Sir Archibald blared, 'I'd shoot to kill,' while Vicar Trevenn, putting on his learned look, babbled of church land records that went back to the Domesday Book. But no one elaborated on her last remark about her son, that was clearly too close to the truth.

Her husband and I remained silent, he, I think, because he knew she was trying to goad him, and I, because no man likes to know it is not he himself who is wanted, only his professional advice.

For she had seized upon Sir Archibald's words. 'I'm glad you take that stance, Archie,' she cried. 'Every year they rob Tregaran woods. That famous herd of deer is their main target. God knows how they eat it all! They probably sell it back to us at Truro market's price. But if they claim the land as theirs, doesn't that complicate things? What about that tin mine they work from time to time? I want those woods fenced off and the cliff path closed. I want proof of ownership. And a good lawyer to make proof stick.'

Now she did address me directly, staking her claim on me, adding me to her list of followers. 'You're the expert on such things, Mr Cradock,' she flattered me. 'Give me an opinion. How can land ownership be proved, without an expensive lawsuit, I mean? How can we better them at their own game? They've still a little holding they say is theirs, a pigsty of a house, that mine. Couldn't we fight them with their own weapon and make a counter-claim to those?'

She poured out her questions in a steady flood as if she were the barrister preparing a brief. I didn't know where to look. Or what to say. One word from me and she'd have me caught, her pet lawyer in her court. But saying nothing was equally wrong, would put me on the defensive, would make me seem to sympathize with the other side.

I was saved by Sir Archibald. He cleared his throat and gave her a nervous glance. 'I say, that's a bit thick,' he began until, at his wife's nudge, he lapsed into a mumble. The vicar gave up speaking of his record books, tugged at his watchchain and examined it as if to remind himself of the time. Colonel Tregaran shoved his chair back and got up as abruptly as his son had done.

'Tregarn this, Tregarn that,' he shouted. 'I'm sick and tired of them. I'll smoke the whole lot out before I'm done.'

He nodded to Polwren, the two stalked out, and there was an imperceptible sigh of relief as if a climax had been reached. Ignoring the rest of us, as if a switch had been turned off, Evelyn Tregaran watched her husband's departure with a little smile that was full of triumph. 'That breaks through your guard,' the smile said. Then, turning back, she addressed me in her most dulcet voice.

'I hear you're a sort of scientist yourself, Mr Cradock,' she said. 'Your hobby perhaps, now you seem to have given up law. They say you haunt our cliffs, watching our flora and fauna.'

She gave a smile, full of malicious intent. 'Full of strange things, those cliffs,' she said. 'Always something going on. Tempting, isn't it, using nature's works to play Peeping Tom.'

And that was how I learned of Evelyn's power. And how she kept her cohorts in line.

And that was how the evening ended, at least in Tregaran House. Discomfited I drove away, my second encounter with Cornish 'society' proving almost as disastrous as the first. The last remarks rankled as she had meant them to. I almost found myself blushing. They were a warning that nothing remained secret long; they were a threat that if I did not help her I would be exposed.

But it was something more than that. For Evelyn Tregaran there were only two choices in her life, Tregarans or Tregarns. She automatically expected me to pick her side, and that was that, even if it meant unthinking allegiance to a cause I couldn't begin to understand. For her there was no middle ground, no room for non-combatants. But my sympathies that evening had been all for father and son, and she had sensed it. It hadn't pleased her.

What she didn't know was that the tension between husband and wife, between mother and child, between brother and brother, had reminded me of my own family. All I wanted to do was go home and slam the door and shut everything out, just as I had always done. But preventing such a cowardly withdrawal was the interest I felt in the young couple. Would their affection for each other last? Would separation be too much for them, could they withstand such hatred? I thought, if that's all the secret is, old hostilities choking an old house, the finding out is not worth the trouble, is like seeing a reflection of one's own self.

It was therefore in a thoroughly depressed mood that I was driven slowly home through those leafy lanes, the car itself an anachronism, a modern intrusion in that strange backward world. By one of those coincidences that fate delights in, when I got back the rest of the secret was revealed. And faced with another choice, I was truly caught.

I do not pretend this was preplanned, or that the 'enemy' made a deliberate counter-attack, although it might have seemed so. Nor did I mean to make a choice. Again choice was forced on me. But even if that had not been so, I would still have found it difficult to resist the appeal of this second encounter, so in contrast was it with the first.

By country standards the hour was late and I was about to point this out to Doreen, the maid, who announced the visitor when she bobbed her little Cornish curtsey. 'He'm been waiting some time, sur,' she said in her soft Cornish voice. 'I told 'ee you was gone, but 'ee said 'ee'd bide.' She curtsied again, wrapping her fingers in her apron. ''Ee's some persistent like,' she said, with an infectious giggle which would have made Hodges' hair stand on end. 'Not fer taking no fer answer.'

I watched her plump cheeks flush. Probably not, I thought dryly, as she turned to show him in. I had gone into the study and was sitting in front of the unlit fire. The curtains were not drawn and the same silver light came pouring into the room, giving it the same touch of mystery as at Tregaran House. The walls and furniture were transformed, their heavy familiar dullness lightened, even the books seemed to gleam. I felt myself caught up in it, as if in a dream. I was not even surprised when one of the Tregarns appeared; I might have been expecting him.

It was Tom. He had obviously taken pains to wash and dress in a manner appropriate for business, but unlike his adversary, Evelyn Tregaran, he got down to it without pretence.

'I've a favour to ask 'ee,' he said. 'Or rather not a favour, since I'm more than ready to pay whatever 'ee says is right.' He fumbled in his back pocket and drew out a bag which jingled satisfactorily as he set it down on the table.

His face was tense with concentration. 'They say in the village you'm a great lawyer chap,' he went on. 'That's what I want. Not one of them local fellows who'd rob their own mothers blind, and gossip it about atterwards. I want it written fair and square so there'll be no mistake, and then kept quiet.'

He looked at me, his eyes sharp with anxiety. 'I want to make a will,' he said. 'And I've picked 'ee for the job.'

I suppose I must have looked startled. 'All fair and square,' he repeated. 'Everything aboveboard. My share of the boat that Paw left to me and Zack. My share of the house and land.'

And when I still remained silent, 'There's nothing wrong in that,' he went on, ''cept Zack don't know. I've not told 'un and I don't want 'un told. And she's not to know neither, Alice I mean, that she's the one I've left it to.'

'Is that wise?' The lawyer instinct was too strong to let that pass. 'You're young and so is she. You may get married.' I thought of the maid's pink cheeks and almost smiled. Then, more soberly, 'Or Alice might. Then you'd have written off an inheritance that should go to your own family.'

Tom stood twiddling his cap. Although I'd twice motioned to him to take a seat he seemed more comfortable on his feet, legs braced as if on the deck of his boat. He never took his gaze from me. 'I'll tell 'ee what I think,' he said. ''Tis Zack I'm most feared of. He's that stubborn. If anything were to happen I'd not trust 'un to treat Alice right.' He hesitated. 'Not that he'd do her harm,' he burst out, 'leastways not harm as he'd see it. But if she defied 'un then he'd not stand that.

''Twould break his heart, what's left of it,' he added. 'He feels like a father to her. But he'll not have her mixed up with those Tregarans, not for all the tea in China.'

He leaned forward confidingly. I thought, here's a simple man, too trusting, too naïve for the modern world, yet I could not bring myself to despise him for his confidence. 'When our Mam died,' he said, 'and then our Paw, we promised to look after Alice. And we have. But she's not ours to order. So I want to make sure she's safe whatever happens in the future. I owe them that much.'

He paused again. Then he said abruptly, 'I know 'ee've been watching us. Zack told us so. And I've seen the top of your spyglass in the sun.'

His use of that word 'spy' again made me feel uncomfortable, as if nothing could be hidden in this secretive part of the world. 'Well,' he said, 'a man don't like being watched and I know 'ee'm in with the Tregarans. Leastways 'ee were tonight. But then, I told myself, he wasn't so that day in the square. And a knock on the head don't make for friends. And they do say you'm the best legal man we've had in years. Why, you'm famous. And that counts, your reputation like. So I took a chance, see what 'ee says, I told myself. No harm in asking.'

Strangely enough, or perhaps not so strange, his appraisal pleased me. I'd been judged before, and found wanting, but never quite so honestly. There was a pause while I reflected. 'But I want it fast,' he said, 'tonight. So that 'twill all be done and readied. So if she needs it 'tis there.'

I thought, it's not a will he wants, it's a list. A formal list of all the Tregarn possessions, so that he will know what's his to give to Alice whenever he chooses. Or has to choose. And then, that's something I could give to Evelyn Tregaran to use, if she ever asks for help again. But I swear that thought only crossed my mind as an ironic reflection.

Perhaps he thought I doubted he had anything worth giving, for he suddenly pulled out a crumpled sheet of paper and thrust it towards me. 'I wrote it down,' he said with a note of pride. 'I wants 'ee to take it and make it proper. I wants it all to go to Alice for her share. As for marrying,' he grinned disarmingly, 'I'll take my chance with that in me own time.'

The list was surprisingly long, all written in a childlike hand, round and laborious. I glanced at it, noting not only the boat and fishing gear, but the house – that 'pigsty' Evelyn Tregaran had called it – the tin and copper mines, most of them labelled 'closed', as well as various other properties of which he claimed half – a lot for 'poor peasant scum'.

Perhaps he guessed what I was thinking. ''Tain't much,' he said confidingly. 'We've come down in the world a bit since the old days when we was great. Zack insists we owned half the county, that some God-danged lawyer chap stoled it off us by a trick, begging your pardon. If he had his way we'd be in court fighting over every yard. No, I've left that work to 'un. This is just what I'm sure of.'

He moved closer, taking the paper back and turning it over to draw a quick map on the back, naming places with those complicated Cornish words that ripple off the tongue like honey. As he spoke, the little coves that I had seen came vividly to mind, basking in the hot sun, the tall cliffs looming over them, the empty sea receding into the misty blue.

'As for the boat,' he was saying, ''tis half Zack's too. But he don't work it like I do. Don't like fishing much, does Zack, mining's his real love. Down in the dark looking for tin.' He sighed. 'Not much tin left,' he said, 'tho' them cliffs be burrowed with mines like a rabbit warren. Been digging tin here since time began; no wonder 'tis all played out.'

He rolled up the paper and stood fingering it just as he

had done his cap. 'As fer boats,' he said, 'once they say we were captains fer a queen. Sailed round the world with Francis Drake in our own ship.' He grinned. 'Reckon it weren't much bigger than our present one but saying we were captains makes it sound more grand. And while we were away something happened. The Tregarans, see, had set themselves up a few years before, out of nothing. Some small chaps they were, no lordship about them, twisting land off their betters. Now they took another chance and married a Tregarn heiress so as to get the house. That house you visited tonight,' he said quietly, 'it once were ours. Go down into the cellars where the Colonel keeps his wine, you'll find the stones that my ancestors put there with their name scratched on 'em. Go into the woods where he keeps his precious deer, there be oaks that were old when we hunted there. Alice be good enough for his son, and he knows it. 'Tis only his wife that thinks different. She didn't think so once when she took up with my brother Zack.'

He stared at me, dark eyes unwavering. 'That's the truth,' he said. 'She came after him. Don't say he didn't respond, but she started it. And then, when she saw what Zack were like, weren't she afraid! 'Ee don't play with fire without getting burned.

'She tried to put 'un aside, see, and he wouldn't go. Stubborn. And he loved her. As she did him. 'Cept she loved Tregaran House more. And he can't forgive or forget that. And she can't forgive him for hanging on.

'I tell 'ee this,' he said. ''Tis common knowledge in part but it happened long ago and gossip do change things. But it's best 'ee know. Don't want to put 'ee in awkwardness like, with her and the Tregarans, if you do this fer me. So you just decide.'

He smiled his sweet smile, putting all his cards on the table without guile. I was helpless in front of him. I repeat,

I didn't mean to choose. I was a neutral outsider just practising my profession, and he was a fisherman, with a sense of family pride that made him take the world's responsibility on his back, like a Cornish Atlas.

But I knew as I sat and pored over his scribbles that I had already picked my side.

CHAPTER FOUR

Tom got his 'will', made to his liking, John went away, Nigel returned to his regiment to charm his colonel and pay court to the colonel's daughters. And Alice waited. I don't suppose Nigel felt any remorse; I presume John and Alice might have suffered, but they had youth and time on their side. I went abroad. I told myself that I was bored. The truth was I wanted to distance myself. I felt betrayal lurking. I know what Evelyn expected of loyalty; I know now what she wanted her friends for, and what she could do to an enemy. And I knew myself incapable of pleasing her.

One can't run away for ever. When I came back, more than a year later, I might never have gone.

It was spring when I returned; the hedges were over-brimming with flowers that trailed great swathes across the roads. The sea again lay blue and calm, a giant pond without a ripple to its smooth surface. Village life seemed unchanged, the fishing boats rocked out in the pre-dawn light and back at noon when the sun bathed the beaches in a golden glow. The day approached when the village feast should have been held but since that last disastrous time it seemed to have been forgotten. And yet, just as when I had first come to live in Tregaran, I felt unease smouldering.

Nervousness, a whiff of danger to make the senses

flare – that was partly why I had returned. Rumours and counter-rumours trailed their restlessness everywhere. The countries I had visited seemed wound up with war, the Austro-Hungarian empire tied like a ball: loosen one thread and you loosened all. By contrast with the wider world Tregaran appeared a haven of peace. But the tension was there, in the streets as well as behind closed doors.

I made no attempt to contact Tregaran House and its inhabitants made no attempt to contact me. Occasionally I saw the Colonel striding through the village, pipe in hand, despite the heat dressed in his usual country tweeds. Evelyn Tregaran was abroad herself, visiting her son Nigel who was now stationed overseas. John was reported in his last term at school, with a traditional army career ahead of him. I often wondered about him as I strolled along those cliffs which once had so fascinated me. He must have grown up in those months that I had been away, would be . . . what, eighteen? . . . a man. And Alice would have grown to womanhood.

But I found myself thinking of them in a vague way as one might of persons whose lives had briefly touched one's own, minor characters in some other play. I had achieved my aim, distanced myself from them and all they had begun to mean to me.

As for the Tregarns, sometimes Hodges brought home titbits of gossip about the two brothers. Alice too seemed lost to view, or had my interest faded? When I heard that John had come back for the summer, I barely gave the news a second thought. What was it to me if he went out in Tom's boat, or if Alice went with him? I was no longer interested.

I suppose I was like a man who has had a brush with some disease and, in his curing, has had the life leached out of him with his medications. The more I felt myself inoculated against the world the more I knew myself complacent, self-serving, self-satisfied; the more I knew myself the loser.

A knock on my door very late one night reversed my selfish detachment. This was the early summer of 1914. Complacency died in that summer, detachment was lost for ever.

It was the sort of night that Tregaran was famous for, without moon, and yet with a silver glow that put a light where there was none. It was well past midnight, and I couldn't sleep. I had gone to bed, got up again, and had been reading by the window. The sea was like a distant wood full of mysterious rustlings; that strange vibrancy made me restless too, I felt pinpricks along the spine. The knock was loud enough to wake the dead, and when I opened the door I found John standing there.

Even in the dimness I could see the state he was in, clothes torn and dirty, face scored with lines as if brambles had ripped the skin. But his expression was what shocked me most.

He made no bones about his request. Like Tom he went straight to the essential. 'We need your help,' he panted. 'They've got Tom.' And when I suppose I did not react fast enough, 'He'll go to jail. We need a lawyer. You.'

I got him inside, gave him a drink, calmed him down so that he could explain. Out came the story in a rush. The first part was quickly told, the rest came later. I tell it here all of a piece to keep it intact. Funnily enough, at the time it didn't seem to matter that we had only met formally once, that as far as John was concerned I was an outsider who, at best, had taken too much interest in his affairs, at worst was what his mother had called a 'Peeping Tom'. I cannot vouch for all the nuances, distortions that may have crept in afterwards. But I can swear that whatever lies were told later, this was truth as he told it that night.

He had come home in a rebellious mood, to find his mother absent, and his father his usual disinterested self. As a gesture of defiance to his parents, perhaps to convince Zack that he was as good as any Tregarn, he had taken to going with Tom on his nightly poaching rounds. That Tom was a poacher I already knew, albeit a discreet one. And poaching is a countryman's delight, a sport at which he excels; I don't know any villager who hasn't knocked off a rabbit or two when he has had a chance. But the laws against it are severe, almost as harsh as medieval ones when lords kept their forests inviolate for their own use. For many years a city man, I'd forgotten this gentlemanly obsession with preserving pheasants and grouse. I appreciated, though, that it wasn't often a landowner's son allied himself with poachers against his father's land. But that is what John had done.

As a gesture it wasn't wise, especially since his mother had found him out.

Her unexpected return the previous night had caught everyone off guard. Somehow someone must have warned her, John didn't know who, her personal maid, Em, perhaps, that was the sort of thing Em would do. And Em's beau was Jim Polwren, the estate steward.

'Not much Jim doesn't know,' John said, 'but he's a decent chap. When times are hard he turns a blind eye. He wouldn't tell to make trouble like Em does. But he's no match for Em. She could worm blood from a stone. She thinks the world of my mother, do anything for her. And I'm the black sheep.'

He was sitting now, glass in hand, twirling it round and round without drinking, as if its contents were more important than his words. It was his own life he was spilling out to a stranger whom he could not even rely on to take his side. And yet perhaps that was why he talked. He would not have been so free if I had been

71

someone he knew. And sympathy might have inhibited him. Pride doesn't like sympathy.

'You've got to picture her,' he said, 'returned to the bosom of her family, all joy and light. I'm prepared for hours of Nigel talk, Nigel this, Nigel that, Nigel in India saving the British Empire. Instead she starts in about the woods.'

It was easy to imagine her arguments. The woods were overgrown, were a menace, were unused capital, why weren't they being cut down? It was sheer rot to talk of sentimental value. As for the deer, what good were they if others made a profit from them? On and on and on, until Michael Tregaran had had enough and promised to hire more men. Then, 'Good,' she said, 'you can begin at once. I hear there's a "party" planned tomorrow night and venison's on the menu.'

She'd spent the rest of the evening making lists, lists of people who would help, places where the fences were broken down, where the guards should stand, where Jim Polwren should position himself. Wasn't Archie Penquire waiting for her phone call, hadn't he offered to lend his men? Before dinner was served she'd arranged it all, rung up people, cajoled them into organizing a little army while her husband had sat back glowering helplessly. And then, when they were ready to dine, she leaned across the expanse of tablecloth and looked directly at her younger son. 'So, John,' she said, 'now tell me about yourself.'

Here was where he faltered. For there was something she couldn't know, no one did, not even Tom. And yet he could have sworn that night she had guessed his secret.

It seemed he had returned to Tregaran with a single intention in mind: never to leave again. Having lived through, 'endured' is the word I'd have used, one exile was sufficient, he would not endure a second one. He told me he would refuse to take up soldiering, he hated military life with a passion, was willing to work at anything to earn a living. And when he had made a 'go of things', he would marry Alice.

He never described how he and Alice had kept in touch, if in fact he had written and she replied, or if by mutual consent they had decided to keep apart, 'lying low' to disarm suspicion. None of that mattered now.

The decision must have been a difficult one; as he had pointed out, he was a second son without income of his own. It was too late for the university career he would have liked, but there were things he was good at that the army hadn't knocked out of him, farming for one. Since fishing was becoming difficult, the idea of working on a farm appealed to him, it was better than working at destruction. There was enough destruction in this world as it was. Destruction and violence were abhorrent to him.

He had hesitated to break this news, but now his mother seemed to challenge him for it. Suddenly his expedition with Tom the following night became the symbol of this greater purpose, was turned into a contest of wills he couldn't honourably refuse, a private battle between him and her, outweighing common sense. So, against all Tom's advice, against all reason, he had insisted on going through with the plan.

Tom had been worried. Not for himself, but for John. Tom was used to trouble, could wriggle out of most things but this organized defence would be formidable. Tom had counselled postponement. That too had irritated John, as if he wasn't good enough. Again he had insisted. And no sooner were they in the woods, than the trap had closed about them.

The hour was right, there was no moon, only silver

darkness. Under the trees the deer were feeding peace-
fully. He and Tom were on their knees crawling side by
side. Suddenly Tom had stopped and pointed. At first
John hadn't seen anything, only the darkness with its
faint metallic glitter, but then as Tom had continued to
point he had realized that that strange glitter, that metal
glint, had some other cause.

'We were looking at a gun barrel,' he said. 'And behind
us, along the fence we had just crawled through, we
heard twigs snap, as if people were stepping on them.'

He knew they were trapped, men behind, God knows
how many in front, Evelyn's army out in force, no way
round or past, nowhere to hide, caught in light cover
between open spaces. Once the moon came out they
would be sitting ducks.

Tom had remained calm. That was typical of him, slow
and steady, summing up a situation, pondering various
possibilities then making the best of the worst. Had he
been alone he could have slithered past as easily as a
snake down a hole. But he was burdened with John. And
John knew he had been a fool. He knew he had risked
his best friend to gratify himself. And he thought, damn
my mother to hell for setting me up like this.

There was a sudden stirring in the thickets to the right,
westward, close to the house. They couldn't see what it
was, too big for an animal, too small for a man, and they
had looked at each other in alarm. A figure darted into
the clearing in front of them. It was dressed in white,
something light and fluttery, and paused for a moment
there in that silver dark before turning to dart back again
out of sight.

The gamekeepers saw it too. Men shouted to each other,
Polwren bellowing at them to stand firm. Torches flickered, a few guns went off. Then everyone was crying at
once, ''Tis a woman. By damn 'tis a woman. Hold fire.'

In the confusion that followed Tom moved fast. The noise, the shouts and gunshots had told him what he needed to know, had showed him where everyone was. Run, he had said, now or never. And taking off himself like a deer he bounded into the open space where the figure had been, into the gap she had made for them.

'I couldn't move,' John said. 'I couldn't speak. My tongue stuck to the roof of my mouth. I couldn't even say, "That was Alice." All I knew was I wouldn't go and leave her behind. But she'd gone. They'd both gone, quick as a flash, leaving me stranded there. So I turned round and began to stumble back towards the fence and the men waiting there. They couldn't have missed,' he said, 'they'd have had me sure if Tom hadn't veered again, pushed me flat and charged out towards them himself.'

And so that was how Tom had been caught. And how John had escaped. And Alice had tried to help them both.

For a while he had lain there stunned until the noise had died away and he knew the fence was unguarded. Then he had got through it again, stuck his gun in a hollow tree in approved fashion, turned back along the cliffs, half expecting Tom to catch up with him. His one coherent thought had been to find Alice; Alice would know where Tom was. But when he passed in front of Tregaran House and saw it lit up like a Christmas tree, the thought suddenly came to him that perhaps she had been caught as well, both she and Tom. And somewhere inside that house Evelyn would be sitting gloating. And he had begun to run like a mad man.

Halfway along the cliff on the village side was a sort of semicircle of trees crowning what had once been an old hill fort, overgrown now but with the surrounding ditch and wall still intact. If they had gone anywhere that was where they would be. But when he had reached it he stopped, afraid to go on, afraid of finding no one.

His relief on seeing Alice had made him vomit; he had to lean on a tree to get his breath. She was standing by the hedge, her dress gleaming. But her smile had faded when he came up. He sensed she had taken him for Tom in the dark, and a terrible coldness seized him. He felt he almost hated Tom, hated Tom for rescuing him, hated himself for letting himself be rescued. And hated her for her devotion to her brother.

'I was wild with envy, see,' he said in a monotone. 'Even of him. I thought, she'll never feel that way about me, not in a million years. When the chips are down, like her brother Zack, she won't have faith in me. I'm a Tregaran. That, and that alone matters. And the fact I am to blame.'

As he approached Alice he realized it was her best dress she was wearing, the white one with the ruffles, and it was torn. When she moved it trailed in the dirt. He knew now why she had put it on, so that she could be more clearly seen among the trees. That thought too had burned in him, that she had made an effort to help him while he had lain there in the grass, unable to help himself.

When he tried to question her, how she had found out, why she had come, 'Jeb Miller, one of Tom's pals told me,' was all she would say. 'Taken on special like, as a guard, and so knew 'twasn't safe. Where's Tom?'

That's all she cares about, he'd thought, Tom, Tom, Tom.

'And what do you think you're doing, wearing that?' he had shouted suddenly, pulled at the skirt of her dress with a ripping sound. 'Dance at my funeral? Well here I am. Just like old times. You and Tom to the rescue, and me safe and sound. Except for once it hasn't worked, the magic's gone.

'There was a stillness to her then,' John said, 'a kind of finality, as if she had gone somewhere away inside herself, far away where I couldn't follow, as if she had sealed away some awful part and was steeling herself to endure a second. I thought, that's how it must have been all those months when I left her alone. Yet God help me, even then, I still wished that she hadn't interfered, that if she had these feelings they were only for me. And then, as suddenly she seemed to come back to herself. She looked at me and tried to smile but her eyes were so sad I was ashamed.

'I offered to go back to find Tom, had actually started up the path towards the house but she ran after me. She asked me what use that was, it'd only make things worse. They'd have the two of us, just as they'd wanted. No, not two, the three of us. She'd come too. She wouldn't let the Tregarans triumph over us. And then she'd said a curious thing.

'"You shan't go alone. Don't you know, my dear, you'll never be alone again."'

She had stood there in that long, torn dress as if entering a ballroom, scrubbing at her cheeks furiously. There were streaks of tears, but she didn't seem to know she had been crying.

'Loving him doesn't mean not loving you,' she'd said. 'There's room for both. But they mustn't shut him up.' Her voice had a break in it. 'He'll die. He'll fight like a lion. I can't bear it for him.

'Beneath that flimsy dress she was trembling,' John said. 'She was like one of those trees along the cliff, that bows before a storm and won't break. But that's what Alice is. She never wavers. And if you're in trouble, you'll never have a more loyal friend. Sometimes I think the way to her heart is to be in trouble. And that makes me afraid.'

After that there was silence in my comfortable room. The silver light streamed in, the sea murmured. We sat in thought, as if something strange and fearful had touched our lives.

Then John stirred. 'There you have it,' he said simply. 'The three of us, she wanting to save me, me wanting to save her, Tom saving all of us, as it always was. To satisfy her I ran back with her to look at Tregaran House. It was still bright and men were moving in and out. They wouldn't have been there if Tom was still at large. So I took her home, down the cliff through the village to her own house.'

He gave a sudden smile that lit up his face. 'It was dark, no one was sitting there to celebrate. And when I had taken my leave of her, when I was sure all was right between us and she was safely inside, back I came the third time, straight here, to ask your advice.'

And just as when Tom had come to me about the will, John's direct approach hit some nerve and I was unable to resist.

I folded my hands and put my legal mind to work. How much did his mother really know? Did she have proof that her son was involved, or was she only guessing? Could he or Alice have been recognized? Was it possible that Tom was lying somewhere hurt? And if Tom had been caught, would he win freedom by telling the truth? Why should he protect John? Why should John suppose he would?

I didn't have to go through all these possibilities, John was shrewd enough to think of them himself. He answered my questions one by one, except the last which he dismissed contemptuously. 'Everyone likes Tom,' he said at last. 'Look what Jeb Miller did. They'd give him the benefit of the doubt if they could. And who would want to involve Alice? Tom wasn't hurt when he pushed me over; he could have got away even then. But if he's caught I know where he'll be, in Tregaran cellars, at my mother's mercy. It was Tregaran lands he was on. And my father is Chief Magistrate.'

He looked better now with the drink inside him, but he kept wiping his face as if these thoughts made him sweat. 'My guess is that some time tomorrow, early on, they'll haul him out for justice. And if my mother has her way my father'll be forced to imprison him. But I know where the key of the cellars is kept. I could . . .'

'And make him a fugitive?' I kept my own voice nonchalant. 'Make yourself one? You've caused enough trouble as it is.'

Again I sat back, fingertips touching, considering. Taken red-handed Tom did not have much of a chance unless there were extenuating circumstances. I guessed he would never use them to plead on his own behalf; John would have to do so for him.

A court of law is like a battlefield. One has to marshal one's troops, decide on one's tactics – whether to attack or defend, what guns to bring to bear, what weaknesses to exploit. I decided to take the initiative.

'Climb into the house the way you climbed out,' I instructed John, briskly authoritative, not giving him time to argue. 'If anyone asks, say you were asleep all night. Unless they broke down your door, what proof is there that you didn't? Tidy yourself up, lie all you like, but get to your father before your mother does.'

I remembered the night of the dinner, and the look on the Colonel's face. I remembered his attempts to defend his son. 'It's just a hunch I have,' I said. 'But it may succeed. I think your father's fairer than you give him credit for. Tell him the whole story as you've just told it to me; ask him to give Tom a second chance. And if he won't . . .' I took a breath, 'Tell him I will defend, using you as witness.'

He still looked doubtful. 'Your best card is you yourself,' I told him bluntly. 'Your father won't want you disgraced. He'd never have set a trap like that if he thought you were involved. She may have known but I'll swear he didn't.'

And with the use of that 'she', he knew which side I had chosen.

'Your father likes you,' I said, 'more than you think. So give him an opportunity to prove it.'

And for the first time in years I put my hand out to a fellow creature in partnership.

When he was gone, I sat down once more and took a drink myself. The dawn would be breaking in a while, already the eastern sky was red, heralding another fine day. I thought, I've taken a step I swore I would never take; I've made an enemy who won't forget, I've forced John to make a stand he might regret, but as God is in Heaven, I swear she shan't get the better of us.

By that time the household was stirring, and rumour was spreading in that country way that makes you think you are living in a jungle. The maid, Doreen, who brought the early morning tea was too full of news to notice that I was up and dressed.

'Tom Tregarn's been took,' she said, her eyes filling with sympathy. 'Poor handsome lad, half the squire's men on his track and he unarmed. No way he could shake them off, though 'twas the squire himself that caught him. Said he was dangerous. That's a lie. Tom didn't even have his gun on him. Threw it away. One of the men found it afterwards. They say the squire'll make an example of 'un.'

She leaned forward, confidingly. 'Bodmin Jail for 'un,' she said. 'They'll book 'un good. Twenty years if 'tis a day.' She sniffed afresh. ''Tis true,' she said. 'When the Tregarans be out for blood there be no stopping 'un.'

Even discounting her exaggeration, the severity of the law startled me. True, my dealings had never been with woodland crimes. But then, less than a century ago, a man could be hanged for stealing sheep. I thought, there's more to this than hunting laws, to put a man away, rob him of health and youth, just for poaching a deer. To my surprise, my anger grew in a most unlawyer-like way. I didn't believe Michael Tregaran was capable of such revenge, but Evelyn certainly was. And if I took her on in open court, it was not the legal verdict that bothered me. It was her judgement of me that would count.

All that hot morning the village waited, subdued and anxious. And, for once, united. It was not that they liked the Tregarns as such, but, when faced with a choice, they preferred their own against the Tregarans. Besides it was true that Tom was popular, especially with the girls. The kitchen buzzed. The life history of Tom, of Zack, of Alice's unexpected birth after so long a gap, of mother, father, grandparents, gossip thirty years old was dragged out and rehashed. And Tom always spoken of in the past tense, as if he were already dead, not merely stewing in Tregaran cellars. But I remembered what Alice had said. 'He'll die.' I thought, he might, if they shut him up for twenty years.

Finally at noon the message came, a note, written hastily by John. 'Compromise. Booked for first offence, let off for good behaviour.' And then, as a postscript, the laconic words, 'You were right.'

I sighed in relief and retired to bed more than thankful that the affair had been settled without my help. But I was not right at all. In the end Tom didn't get off. And the consequences were only just beginning.

I didn't see John again for several weeks, not until the funeral. What happened during this time is pieced

together, partly guessed at from later events, partly inter-
preted from what he told me. This part of the story came
in snatches, not as a whole, but I tell it here as best I can,
using his own words where I am able. He himself was
still in shock and may have muddled cause and effect.
I take the liberty of presenting the case as it seems to
me it should be read, in order, coherently, from start
to finish.

Well then, to begin. As I had guessed, he had had
no trouble getting back into his house, for all that the
men were gathered on the front porch, drinking off their
night's work. They were not exactly jubilant, most in
fact seemed subdued. No one wanted Tom to be made a
scapegoat; who and where was his companion? As for
the woman in white, was she real or a ghost? Wasn't there
some old tale of a Tregaran maid who had run in front of
troops to let her lover escape? They liked the story of a
ghost, a ghost went down well with beer in a summer's
dawn; better a ghost than real flesh and blood; a real girl
presented too many difficulties.

Meanwhile Tom was caught all right; he could be heard
stamping up and down beneath their feet and his ham-
mering on the cellar door shook the beams. His bellowing
echoed through the house which his ancestors had built
and an occasional breaking of glass suggested that he was
raiding the Colonel's wine cellar. It was the thought of his
wine as much as of his deer that made the Colonel decide
to take a stand. He'd have Tom up before first light, and
be done with it, that would show who was master, that
would prove who was in charge.

Until that moment John had not realized that it was his
father who had actually caught Tom, that he had been
one of the men along the fence. The Colonel's presence
there was typical of him, a sudden impulse, without logic
or reason, as if, having at last given in to his wife and

82

engaged more men, he had to do their work for them. In fact, as far as could be ascertained, Tom had easily taken the others by surprise and would have burst through them if the Colonel hadn't stepped out from behind a bush. And although Tom wriggled like an eel, and left his coat in shreds, the older man was stubborn too, and held on tight until help arrived.

It had taken three wardens to hold Tom then and drag him back towards the house. Tom himself was not much hurt, a cut lip and blackened eye caused mostly by his own exertions. But the Colonel had been shaken up, and angered. Not so much on his own account but because his wife had been proved right. He shut himself up in his study to brood. And there John found him in his blackest mood.

'I didn't stop but went straight there,' John explained afterwards. 'He was sitting in his room with the door closed, just sitting without moving, eyes open, staring out towards the sea. Even when I came in he didn't look up. His face was mottled red. If it had been anyone else,' he hesitated, then blurted out, 'if it had been anyone else you'd have thought he had been crying. He let me stand there for the longest while. I don't think he realized who I was. "Father," I said at last. I had to repeat myself several times. "Father, there's something you should know. By rights it should be me you caught. It's me, not Tom, you should be passing judgement on."'

When his father didn't stir, John, suddenly angry, had cried, 'Listen for once. I planned it all. I meant to cock my nose at you. And then tomorrow, today, tell you I'm finished with the army. I was sent there for revenge, just for being friendly with someone you didn't like. There never was any sense to it. I don't intend to leave Cornwall again. Unless I take Alice with me!'

His father had sat there like an old man, too old to be

surprised. Then he looked up. John had never noticed before how blue his eyes were, how like Alice's. 'No need,' he'd said. 'I've already been told.'

He put his hands on the desk as if to lumber up. John had never noticed before how the veins stood out, nor how the backs were covered with liver spots, nor how thin the wrists were, supple, fine-boned, good horseman's wrists. Michael Tregaran spoke quietly then. 'At least your mother told me about you and Tregarn,' he said. 'Although not till we brought him back. Made a fool of me over that, didn't she? And you played into her hands. And she suspected the rest. Isn't it a bit late to change your mind?'

John said, 'I've done my time, two years of it. And so has Alice. Now we're out, there's no way you can shut us in again.'

He could feel his father thinking. He'd always known his father was a strange man. Except for those irrational outbursts he'd be quiet, one of those strong silent sorts who holds everything in. Like John himself. Funny, wasn't it, John had thought, that in all these years he had never imagined his father thinking anything; had never really looked at his father, never wondered about him. Now he was surprised when his father said, 'Always was amazed you agreed; always wondered why you didn't dig in your heels back then. I know of course she wanted it. And she's hard to resist. But doing what she wants doesn't mean she'll be pleased. Sometimes it's the opposite.'

He was standing now, his clothes rumpled. John had never seen his father so dishevelled, unwashed, unshaved. He'd always ridiculed the Colonel's pride in his military appearance. Now Colonel Tregaran was saying, 'I didn't want to catch you, boy. Nor him. Bloody young fools. Why didn't you back off? No deer's worth the price.'

He jerked his head. Far away, down in the bowels of the house, they could hear a rumbling. 'That's him,' the Colonel said. 'I've been sitting here, listening. Like the roaring of the past, like the outrage of the years, rising out of the ground.'

He said, 'We did them wrong, boy, a hundred times, centuries of wrong. We stole this place, bit by bit; we stole their land; we stole their name. And yet we're bound to them and they to us, flesh and blood and bone.'

He went on, 'We've been mating for centuries and all for hate, for revenge, for lust, never for love. Perhaps it's time we did something right.'

Now the Colonel was speaking to himself, or rather using John as a sounding board for his words. His son had never heard him say so much, never all at one time. 'They did me wrong as well,' Michael Tregaran was continuing. 'But most of all we wronged you to make you suffer for it. I never hated you, boy; she did. But I loved her still, you see, and love makes you do strange things.'

He said, 'It didn't work. Not for her, not for me, not for you. And I owe it to you, to explain and apologize.'

CHAPTER FIVE

It seemed very close in that little room which the Colonel called his study. He never studied anything in there, just sat and smoked. He knew a lot about Tregaran though, John said, he knew the history of the house, the architectural changes, details of that sort, but not the expenses and accounts which he was always being nagged about. When John had been a child his father used to tell stories about those people whose portraits hung in the upstairs gallery. John couldn't remember his father ever before speaking of any shared Tregarn ancestry, and if Tom knew he had never said. But Tom must have known. Zack would have made sure of that. Somehow, realizing now how the two families had been intertwined, had made John happier, as if he were discovering his true roots.

But his father was not finished; perhaps he had never dared begin before. To John it had seemed as if he were hearing something he had always known but never understood; as if thoughts that he hadn't been able to put into words now made sense, as if at last things were dropping into place. 'It was a day like this,' his father was saying, 'when I found out. In one way I'd already known; one always does, and she'd never tried to hide. She'd flaunted it. I'd turned away out of fear, pretending otherwise. But all the signs were there, if I had let myself look. It was Zack of course who accosted me. Mad with grief, rage, inspired by some strange chivalry, he came in here just as you did, and told me a tale of lust and greed that made me sick.

'And yet, you know,' he had gone on slowly as if discovering things about himself, 'I couldn't fault him although I tried. It was as if part of me was standing there, listening to my own self speak. And what he said had a ring of truth, however unpalatable. I remember thinking at the end, yes, that was how it must have been, and almost nodding in agreement. It was only afterwards the pain began.

'Zack was a handsome man,' the Colonel had said, reminiscently. 'Younger than me. He had a force to him that I can't explain. I used to think Nigel would have it too, a quality that makes a man stand out, but he's lost it somehow. His mother spoiled him, somewhere there's a rottenness inside. There, I've never said that before, but it's true. And now I don't believe he inherited anything from Zack. Once I did. That day Zack swore Nigel was his son. "Let him go," he said. I remember how tall he seemed, how forthright, arrogant. "Let Nigel go and her with 'un. I'll take care of both." And he looked at me, deliberately defying me to deny his right.

'And when I remained struck dumb, "She stays with 'ee out of pity," he said. "'Tis me she loves. And I love her. She never should have married 'ee."'

Michael Tregaran had believed him at first. It wasn't like Zack to lie. It was she who had told the lies, and had filled him full of them.

After Zack had gone he had sat on in his room, thinking. In those days he used to drink a lot but nothing seemed to drown the hurt. Over and over again Zack's claims spun in his head. And gradually it seemed to him that what Zack had said explained Zack's part, but not hers. It suddenly dawned on him that she had no feelings for either of them, had conned them both. Zack hadn't meant to give her away but through his own words he had damned her. It was she who had been the one to start, to pursue, even pester Zack, a lady playing with an underling. And when she had him caught, she had dropped him like a glove, had backed away, dangling her pregnancy as an excuse, pretending her husband wouldn't give the child up, never saying outright whose it was – Zack thought it his, but it could as well be her husband's as not. Looked at dispassionately the tale was a sordid one made up of sordid lies, depending on whom she was speaking to. And Zack as besotted as the husband was, both men blinded to her inconsistencies.

In the evening, after the child had been put to bed, he had got up, unlocked the door, and gone to find her.

She was in the drawing room where she always sat, by the veranda overlooking the park. She used to say that it was the only place in the house that didn't stifle her, that it was the sea that gave her life. It must have startled her to see him there and yet perhaps she had been expecting him. She must have guessed why Zack had come to see him. Yet she wouldn't speak of Zack until her husband did, just looked with those great dark eyes as if passing judgement.

'I remember wondering if she saw me at all,' the Colonel said. 'Or if I were just a blank she looked through. And when I said at last, standing there like a dolt, bottle in hand, "Why stay with me when you've got him?" she never bothered to answer, turned away and leaned out the window to pick a rose. I remember how she shredded it, stripping the petals off. And then she shrugged.'

She would have been younger then, in her full flush of beauty. Her husband was aware of her as never before. Her shoulders were white in the dusk. Close to, he could smell the perfume she wore, as if all the heat of the day were distilled in it. When she gestured with her hand, taking in the house, the park, the woods, 'You had all this,' the gesture said. 'That's all there was to it.' And he knew that had it been another age, another time, and Zack Tregarn had owned it in his turn, she would have stayed with him instead. So much for love and loving.

He remembered asking, 'What about the boy? Zack says he's his,' but she'd laughed. 'Zack'd like to think so,' she said. 'But neither of you have a claim on him.' She had suddenly turned, fierce as a cat, 'He's mine,' she said.

'There was something about her then,' the Colonel continued, 'I don't know what, some secret triumph, some private joke that made my blood run cold. But as I came up close, "Stand back," she cried. Her lips curled in undisguised disgust. "I can't bear your touch." And as I hesitated, "Look at you," she cried. "Compared to him, what are you? A shell, a husk, a hollow reed. He's twice the man of you. But I won't disgrace your precious name, nor your precious house. And your precious son shall be your heir." She gave another laugh. "I'll be a faithful wife," she said, "if only you leave me alone."

'I remember looking at my hands. They seemed to stretch out of their own accord, they seemed to grow to twice their size. I don't excuse what happened next. But it seemed to me that as I bore her to the ground she lay there laughing up at me. "You'll never tame me, Michael Tregaran," I thought she said. "You'll never make me yours."'

He finished speaking, was silent, all the violence gone. And the house was quiet, even the noise of Tom below had died away. John himself had felt strangely at peace, although what his father had said should never have been told.

'I felt,' John said, 'as if a sore had been lanced, as if years of poison were draining out. And in a strange way

I admired my father for doing it. I felt I had never liked him better than when he gave himself away; it seemed, I don't know how, as if a whole new aspect had opened up, as if I was on the brink of things. And I think he thought so too, although he never said so. He just went on in his old way as if nothing extraordinary had happened. And for the first time in our lives, at least in mine, I felt free of her.'

Having had his say, the Colonel became his abrupt self. 'So now here's a new twist to an old quarrel,' he said. 'Bugger it. I'd have looked the other way, but Tom ran straight into me. And I never dreamed you were there, never thought you'd have the gall. No offence meant, boy, just speaking straight. But hear that.' He cocked his head again.

Tom had started up once more. 'Like a bull in a maze, a minotaur.' The Colonel smiled his rare smile. 'First things first. See if you can quiet him down. We'll do what we can for him, then take care of you. Get it over with fast, boy, before others interfere. Old Penquire's bursting his breeches to poke his nose in.'

Normally that word 'boy' would have angered John. Now he saw it as affection. And he appreciated the need for haste, although it was Evelyn they wanted to avoid, not Sir Archibald. But when Tom was brought up, John was shocked. He'd never seen his friend like this before. Tom's clothes were flecked with blood, his face bloodstained and bruised, but it was the look in his eyes that was alarming, the whites showing like a wild animal.

The Colonel noticed at once. 'Hold tight,' he said in an undertone. 'He'll break like an unbridled horse.' And to Tom, loudly, authoritatively, making him listen, 'Look here, Tregarn, you've made a right old mess of things. Can't let you off, not with half the county looking on.'

He and John had gone into the morning room by now and he was standing with his back to the mantelpiece, staring from one to the other. When Tom said, through thick lips, 'What be 'ee here fer, no call fer that?' and pointed to John, while John himself, ignoring his father's advice, began to argue that it was all his fault, the older man nodded, as if pleased.

He cut them short. 'You know the law,' he said. 'If you plead innocent it'll be long-drawn-out, a county Assize Court, probable imprisonment, no way of avoiding it, not with the mood the landowners are in. If I deal with it myself, and you plead guilty, I'll give you both three months, suspended sentence.' And as hope dawned in their eyes, 'But don't push your luck a second time.'

He stared again at Tom. 'Just say I've paid a debt,' he said. 'Not for my son, for myself. Now get out of here quick in case I change my mind.'

Before either of them could protest Jim Polwren had whisked Tom out of the house, out of Evelyn's way, out of harm. Only then did the Colonel relax.

'That's done,' he said, almost satisfied. 'A good morning's work. Thanks to you, boy. Now your turn. But first we'll eat.'

He grinned again. 'Isn't often at my age that I run around all night,' he said. 'Thought I'd lost the knack.' He flexed his arms. 'Almost tore them off,' he said, referring back to Tom. 'Strong as an ox. A good-tempered chap, I hear. Charm, like the older one. That's something the Tregarns have got in full, charm, and we haven't. You and I, I mean, we missed out of that at birth.'

And strangely, for the first time ever, that too was a bond between them.

So while they seated themselves at the table in companionable ease, waiting for the breakfast to be brought (which his father wolfed down in considerable quantities), John began to explain, hesitatingly at first, then with growing confidence, what he had in mind for himself and Alice.

His father listened in silence. 'You're too young to marry,' he said at the end, mopping up his eggs with bread. He took a gulp of tea. 'But if you want to try your wings and grow a bit, prove you're not afraid of hard work, and I'm sure you're not, there's an estate farm coming vacant. A bit run-down, the cottage falling into ruin, that sort of thing. You can start with that.'

He set down his cup. 'And if Alice is a true Tregarn you'll have difficulty in losing her,' he said. 'That's another quality they have; they stick. Knew a Tregarn myself once, another Alice. I was your age and she was young. Some sort of cousin to this one. Nothing came of it. She was Methodist and strictly reared. And I went off soldiering, too cautious to take risks.'

He sighed. 'That was my fault,' he said. 'Always too careful, too cautious, then overreacting. Proportion, that's what counts in life, like the painting of a picture or the building of a house. Take this one, for example, the Tregarns knew what proportion was.'

It was the only piece of advice he ever gave his son. The door of the room burst open and Evelyn Tregaran swept in.

She must not have gone to bed either for she still wore her green evening gown. Its ruffles trailed across the floor, reminding John of Alice's white ones. Her hair was combed, not a wisp out of place; she looked as fresh as a girl. But behind the freshness was venom lying curled. 'Don't tell me,' she said, her voice ice-cold, 'that you've let him off?'

She closed the door behind her with a snap. 'Not after

all the trouble I took,' she said, 'not after all the help you got! I'll never raise my head again.'

John felt his father stiffen like a man braced for a blow.

'And what about him?' She was pointing now to John. 'What's happening to him?'

Colonel Tregaran answered her slowly, enunciating every word. 'You're speaking of your son, Evelyn, your son and mine. Do you want to see him in jail? I can't convict the one without the other, or let the one go free and not them both.'

'Fiddlesticks,' she said, her expression sharpening. 'Tregarns deserve what they get. My friends will take it hard that you don't make an example of them.'

'Not without evidence.' Colonel Tregaran was equally brusque. 'I'll swear that I mistook Tom, and John was safely home in bed. I'll swear so in court even if I perjure myself. So leave well alone.'

That familiar expression threw Evelyn into a rage. 'That's what you always say,' she cried. 'And see what it brings you, a son who makes a fool of you and neighbours who despise you. I'd have more pride myself.'

When the Colonel did not reply her eyes narrowed. 'What's he been telling you?' she asked. She pulled out a chair and sat down as if her legs were trembling. 'And what've you been telling him to make you suddenly such pals?'

She tried to pour herself some tea from the silver urn but her hand shook so that the contents slopped over the tablecloth. 'It's all lies.' Her voice had begun to tremble too. 'Lies, I say, lies, lies. My life has been destroyed by lies.'

'Lies,' her husband's voice was mocking. 'Depends on the point of view.'

She ignored him, turned to her son. 'He hates you, you

know,' she said, addressing herself to John. 'You'd be an idiot to count on him.' And then to her husband, attacking fiercely now, 'You agreed to sending him away to avoid all this. I suppose he's talked you round to his side. How's he to live? And who's going to live with him?'

And when they didn't answer, 'So I did guess right. So he will give up his career after all that money spent. But if he thinks he can stay here I won't have him in the house. Not a thief and a ruffian, marrying beneath him to make us a laughing stock.'

'You sent him.' Again the Colonel emphasized the words. 'You tried to change him. I only let you, more's the pity. This time I don't. The Sawer place is vacant. He can have that.'

Her face became white, as if all the colour had drained out of it. 'He can't,' she said. 'The Sawer farm is part of Tregaran estate, that's Nigel's land.'

She stood up, facing them, while slowly they too rose to their feet. Beside them she seemed slight, a slip of a thing in her spring-green gown, balancing on her small green-slippered feet. 'I'll not have Nigel robbed,' she cried. 'That's part of his inheritance.'

'Not while I live.' The Colonel's face grew red where hers was pale, the veins stood out on his neck. 'It's mine to give or not, as I choose. And I remember I have two sons, even if you don't.'

His words seemed to jolt her. Perhaps she had not expected resistance. Perhaps it was the first time in years he had stood up to her. Surprise turned quickly to resentment. A crafty look crossed her face and was as quickly hidden. 'You might have remembered that earlier,' she said. Her voice was gentle now, low-pitched, but the anger was there beneath the sweetness. 'Before he was born, in fact.'

She said to John, conversationally, 'You know you were

94

an afterthought, or did your father forget to tell you that? Perhaps he forgot to mention that the doctors said I should never have a second child, that having a second child could kill me.'

Then, quick as a snake, to her husband, 'The land's entailed.'

Son and husband answered at once: 'I don't want Nigel's share,' from John, and 'Not Sawer's place. I'll have the lawyers out to exclude it; I'll have it all written down.'

Now anger did break out; she started towards them wildly. 'Thick as thieves, aren't we,' she sneered. 'Is that what you have in common? Well, remember he didn't want you, John Tregaran, that he's ashamed of you.'

She gave a laugh, mirthless, full of loathing. 'If you don't believe me, ask him how you were conceived, ask him who wanted to get rid of you.'

She said, as slowly and distinctly as he had done, each word a separate blow, each word a curse, 'All the harm in this house came from your birth. You were born from rape itself. Ask Em. She saw the state I was in that night. I'm sure he never told you how he beat me and forced me to prove himself a man. And when he was done wasn't he proud, the first time in years.'

She laughed again. 'That's what he is, that father you think so much of, only an impotent old man who once took his jealousy out in rape.'

She said, 'Oh, you're his son, no mistake about that. Look at you, the pair of you, standing there afraid to say boo to a goose. You'll never make anything of yourself, like him. Marry Alice Tregarn for all I care. You deserve each other. Drag yourself down to her level, why should you feel family pride? No one needs you; I've some-one else.'

Her voice had a break in it and for a moment, just a

moment, John felt the old touch of guilt, as if he was at fault, as if somehow he had let her down.

He heard his father clear his throat, the Colonel was not impervious either. But they held their ground.

'All right,' she cried then, glinting at them dangerously, 'I'll fight both of you. Thank God, I have Nigel to depend on. Thank God, Nigel is a gentleman.'

The Colonel slammed his fist against the wall, so that the pictures rattled. 'By God,' he shouted, 'you go too far.' He was panting heavily, and his eyes were starting from his head. 'I've been quiet long enough, twenty years of keeping quiet. You spoiled my life, you spoiled Zack's. But you shan't spoil his.' He turned to John. 'She's done with ruining you, boy,' he said. 'Tomorrow I change my will to prove it.'

But tomorrow was too late. 'That evening,' John said, 'he had the stroke that killed him.'

So it was that, as the summer wore on, Michael Tregaran fought his last fight, lying like a great still hump under the heavy coverlets, only his raucous breathing showing he was alive. And as doctors and nurses hovered and Nigel was hastily sent for, the village waited anxiously for the outcome. Outside, the greater world moved as inexorably towards disaster.

On receiving John's note my original feeling had been of relief, selfish relief that Tom had been spared and so had I. I still wasn't ready for a complete break with the Tregarans. The Colonel's illness changed all that. In the first place his incapacity allowed Evelyn to reopen the case against Tom, forcing Jim Polwren to give evidence (an obligation he could not refuse although it broke his courtship with Em). Tom was arrested and brought before Sir Archibald who was more than happy to take the Colonel's place. But even he did not dare alter the sentence too much or make it harsher than it had been, although to Tom three months must have seemed like eternity. Nor did Evelyn move against her son, the arrest and sentencing over before John had wind of it. Perhaps Sir Archibald balked at that; perhaps she thought it would hurt John worse. Certainly it would discredit him with the Tregarns. Whatever the reason, Tom went to prison, John didn't; yet another score for the Tregarns to settle. And to the extent that it alienated village opinion Evelyn had for once made a disastrous move.

"Taint fair,' the little maid, Doreen, wept, and she was right. By rights John Tregaran should have been in prison with Tom; by rights so should every other villager who had taken a shot at a pheasant or fished in a stream. The age-old quarrel between landlord and peasant was revealing itself in a new light; useless for Vicar Trevenn, at Evelyn's behest, to preach about the duty of obedience. The poor get poorer; the rich richer; to him who has shall more be given; one law for the gentleman one for the worker, that was the sermon the village heard. God help the underdog . . . and God help Tom, who in this way became the victim.

But it was not only Tom's sentencing that rocked the village. The year had been hard in many ways. The price of copper had fallen; many mines had closed; miners were laid off. There was an unexpected glut of corn which led to the sacking of farmhands. An even crueller blow, the fishing had dropped off. The scarcity of fish was so bad the boats were in harbour more often than not. Some blamed the weather, unusually hot and dry; some the shift of tides. Others complained of former greed, which had "fished out" the sea, criticizing their traditional rivals, the Breton fishing fleet. No one spoke openly of the contrast with last year's feast but they must have thought of it.

A strange thing had happened on the day on which the feast was usually held. I have not mentioned it before, having taken it for a silliness. The Colonel's embargo had been still in force of course, but on the actual day the village had been unnaturally quiet, like a Sunday in Lent. I missed the familiar morning sounds myself and wondered where the milkman was, where the butcher boy with his infuriating whistle, where the tradesman's cart with his horse's slow ambling trot. Normal services seemed to have ceased; when Hodges returned from the village to report a strike, a 'suspension of work', that closed the village shops and left people milling in the streets I was irritated. A few houses surreptitiously stuck out wreaths which soon looked bedraggled and forlorn, turning brown in the relentless heat. And on the cliffs where boys as surreptitiously kept watch no shoals of pilchards were reported. Now, in retrospect, that half-hearted protest took on another aspect. Like the soughing of a wind long before the storm begins I heard its stirring.

Perhaps Evelyn sensed it too. As if to emphasize her power and the village's lack of it, in her husband's name she first decreed that henceforth all village matters were to be approved by her in his place. Not waiting for resentment to cool, for this ordinance roused resentment, she next ordered the parks and gardens to be fenced off. Finally, just before Nigel's return, she stopped all access to the cliffs.

As I have explained, for the village the cliff path was a kind of short cut; rough and hilly though it was, most preferred it to the long way round by road. Closing it added several miles for the women on their way to Truro market. Worse, the few remaining miners were cut off from their mines, otherwise reached by sea and sometimes then only at low tide. Anger spread at this example of Evelyn's highhandedness. In fact, I was angry myself, having come to regard the path as my own.

The village, which had been accustomed since time unknown to free passage along the cliffs, had every right to feel wronged. The night Mrs Tregaran's decision was announced was the first night a rick was fired.

The fire was small, easily contained. By the time the old fire engine had wheezed to the site the worst of the blaze was out. The next night a second fire burned down a barn. These two were followed by a third and fourth, each closer to Tregaran House. A splatter of eggs struck the windshield of Evelyn's car and mysteriously a banner appeared across the village square, printed in home-made letters, proclaiming village autonomy. This growing unrest between Tregaran village and Tregaran House came to a head on the day of Nigel's return.

It seemed that Nigel had asked for leave when the Colonel had first been taken ill, and since, owing to the state of the world affairs, his regiment had been ordered home, he had been granted it. The young subaltern who had left two years ago had grown into a handsome young man, with all his mother's energy and his father's looks, and a bullish obstinacy that was his own. Alerted to all that had taken place, presumably given his mother's version, under her eagle eye he took up the reins of government as firmly as she could have wished.

He ordered Tregaran woods and fences patrolled by local police, he spoke of searching for arsonists, and under pretence of 'national' security took steps to close off the cliff with wire, bales of barbed wire, to ensure his mother's orders were obeyed. 'And to shut me out,' John said, 'he revoked the lease to the Sawer place.'

He did not add that since his father's stroke he had been working there, with Alice's help trying to put the fields and house to rights. His brother's decision hit him hard, as hard as it did the villagers. The Colonel's death was the last blow. John mourned for him more genuinely than the rest of the family. But it released him too, released him from any lingering loyalty to people he despised and who now did everything in their power to ruin him.

Colonel Tregaran's funeral took place on 28 June 1914. I find it an irony of sorts that at the very moment when the Archduke Ferdinand was stepping out of his car at Sarajevo, half a continent away, the Colonel was being laid to rest with his forefathers. In both cases a way of life was about to come to an end. True the Colonel's empire was tiny compared with the one the Archduke would have had and his entourage certainly not as large as the Archduke's. I felt he had been killed as surely as the Archduke was, but slowly, over several years.

The service was well attended by friends and foes; all the neighbouring Cornish aristocracy was out in force, representatives of a class that was soon to disappear in the battlefields of France. There was the usual sprinkling of local dignitaries who edged together nervously, awed by the occasion; the rest of the village paid its respects in silence, the men dressed in black, the women in their best clothes, with black shawls over their heads. They turned their backs and the men took off their hats as the plain oak casket was carried into the church. But the younger men kept a sullen watch and a murmuring began, not exactly a rumbling, but a faint far-off sound, like a swarm of bees.

I was present myself and can confirm that perhaps no real confrontation was meant. In fact at the time, not knowing, of course, all that John was later to reveal, I actually admired the widow's composure as, heavily veiled, leaning on Nigel's arm, she walked from the church to the burial plot. The black silk became her; she seemed to embody grief. ('She told me I was to blame,'

John said. "You've killed your father," she said. "Silly old man, gadding about like a youngster. All that effort was too much for him. And I hold you accountable."')

All went smoothly until the mourners were returning from the graveyard. It lay a few paces beyond the church, a tranquil place shaded with firs and elms, dominated by the Tregaran monument, an elaborate eighteenth-century stone edifice placed above a simpler brick Tudor crypt. The service had been brief but poignant, for once Vicar Trevenn speaking to the point. Everyone seemed to realize that the Colonel's passing marked a change, although uncertain of the extent. I myself was just reflecting that there could be worse fates than being laid to rest among ancestors whose lives had been lived along similar lines, in the same place, for centuries, when a scuffling at the churchyard gates broke the calm.

Nigel and his mother were leading the party, with John and the vicar a step behind. The village boy who had been hired to hold the gates ajar had fled, and in his place a score of men stood athwart the road.

These were not young hotheads, wild for trouble, but hard-working men, not given to rashness. Several of them I recognized; most of them were miners, a few were fishermen. All had a look that those Serbian revolutionaries would have appreciated: resolution, born out of despair, and they waited stoically until the procession drew up. In the rear was Zack Tregarn. I was not so much surprised to see him as puzzled why he was not in front. He seemed a natural ring-leader. He had always accused the Tregarans of injustice, now he had a genuine grievance to air.

However he remained in the background, not exactly out of sight but more like an observer than an instigator. Afterwards I decided that this reticence, although unlike him, was deliberate. I think he wanted to let his companions speak without cramping their style or drawing attention to himself. I think too that he was determined not to be accused of disrespect; after all, he had had a bond of sorts with Michael Tregaran and perhaps felt his death more keenly than he liked to admit. And perhaps he did not want to embarrass the new squire, this young man whom once he had felt the right to claim as son. There must have been a feeling for Nigel as well, stronger than he knew. In any case he kept quiet at first, revealing an unexpected sensitivity, and let his friends do the talking for him.

The group addressed Nigel, hats in hand, their comments apt and sensible, as forthright as themselves. They might have been a political deputation except for the choice of time and place. But I think they chose these deliberately, fearful that if they did not strike while the iron was hot they would be refused access to their new landlord.

'Beg pardon, sur,' they said. 'We've come to know our rights. Squire Tregaran were a just man and in his way he knowed us well.' They ignored the vicar's flustered shooing and continued, 'But now he'm gone and you'm in charge, what do 'ee mean to do by us?'

Given the previous circumstances, the question was a fair one. If Nigel had had any sense he would have answered as fairly. Instead he tried to bluster.

'Out of the way,' he snapped. 'You're blocking the path.' An unfortunate choice of expression that raised village hackles.

'Like the cliff's been blocked?' the spokesman insisted. 'What we'm to think of that?'

'If you've fault to find,' Nigel became pompous, attempting to push past, 'complain to my steward. But be careful. The more you want things changed, the more response you'll get. There're the harbour dues, for example, they're ridiculously low, do you want them raised? Most of the cottages belong to the estate; it's time the rents were reviewed. If it's war you want, I warn you I'll fight back.'

He had gone red in the face; for a second he revealed his father, the unfortunate blustering side of poor Michael Tregaran. Then he grew calm. 'No need for us to quarrel,' he said. 'Come and see me some other time. I'm sure we can work things out.'

He smiled, began to walk on. From the rear Zack said, mildly for him, 'Now look 'ee here, we're not here to make things worse, just to protect ourselves. Men out of work can't pay rent as 'tis; if there's no fish there's no call to raise the dues. But the cliff path's ours as much as yours, more ours, since we do use it. You go outside the law yerself to bar us from ut.'

All this seemed reasonable to me; in fact, Nigel appeared mad not to back down when he had the chance. But he had his mother's stubbornness. And perhaps the Colonel had been right, there was something weak about him that turned him to a bully. He stopped and shook his fist. 'As for you,' he cried, 'I'll have you shut up where you belong, you and your brother both.'

That too was an unfortunate remark. It must have jarred the older man to be addressed like that in public by this particular member of the Tregaran family. Zack's face grew dark, his hands clenched. And from the crowd behind him came the same angry hum. It spread along the village street, and, hearing it, Nigel looked startled.

A frown creased that splendid forehead; his eyes widened in alarm. You could almost see him feeling for his pistol as if faced with a riot in Afghanistan. In a moment the funeral would have ended in a brawl had not the other guests come crowding round, Sir Archibald to the rescue, whispering in Nigel's ear. Sir Archibald was all for keeping villagers in their place but propriety was more important at this time, he'd not be involved in a common riot at a funeral.

So while the vicar flapped like a frightened hen, and while the rest of the mourners came trooping past, the deputation withdrew, disappointment in every line.

It was this last incident that had brought John round to my house the day after the funeral. 'It's stupid,' he said now, having told me the main gist of the tale which I, in turn, have recorded. He looked tired, having spent most of the day arguing with his brother. 'Although Nigel has to leave again, ordered back to the regiment, he's determined not to give in. And Mother's backing him. There's nothing I can do to make them change their minds.

'But the village won't back down either,' he burst out. 'They can't. Take Zack, for example. Close off the path and his mine is closed. Oh, I know it's old, and doesn't yield much, but it's a source of income if the fishing's gone. And it *is* his, for all that my mother says. And if the village resists, then Nigel'll use stronger means.'

I knew that hitherto the local policeman had been put in charge. Hodges had told me he was the one who caught the egg-throwers and had endured the children's taunts while he patrolled the boundaries. But he was Cornish born, not trained to control real rioters, and probably at heart he was in sympathy with the villagers. 'I can't stop Nigel,' John was repeating. He sounded worried. 'Nor can Zack. If Nigel calls out troops there's bound to be a clash. Someone'll be hurt. I don't want that.'

We were again in my study and he was speaking as to a friend. His confidences both pleased and irritated me. I didn't want to be drawn further into this quarrel, much less this intimacy. And yet I was. The story he'd just related about his father and mother, for example, revealed more compassion than I would have been capable of in a similar position. His father's illness and death had given him unexpected strength. I thought, if worst comes to worst he'll stand up to his brother himself. That too was something new; John had been taught to think himself inferior.

Speaking of Zack's mine had released another line of thought. The boy began to talk of mining with a depth of knowledge I didn't realize he had. But scratch a Cornishman, they say, and you'll find veins of tin. After a storm in these parts the streams often ran red with tin or copper from their workings, and sometimes on a headland I had discovered ruined towers, like Moorish fortresses, parts of the old engine-houses. 'They're not really large, these mines,' John now explained, 'just room for one or two men. The right to work them has passed down for generations; I doubt if anyone knows who really owns them. Or cares. Probably it's claim to his that makes Zack Tregarn feel the cliffs are his. If Tom were here I'd be more comfortable. Tom has a soothing effect on him.'

I had to agree with that. Which is why I did what I had sworn never to do and went with him openly to the Tregarn house to talk Zack round.

We took the long way by road, driving in a pony trap. The Tregarns lived on the western side of the village in another little cove which bore their name. As we trotted along I recognized many of the places from the names Tom had written on his map, little clusters of houses built round a church, scarcely meriting the title of village. The road wound inland before doubling back. I thought the fields had never looked so lush nor the corn so ripe, nor the meadows so thick with Queen Anne's lace, as if nature was pouring all its bounty out. From the highest point we could see Tregaran Bay spread beneath us in a great loop, the slate headlands jutting out on either side like fingers clasping it. As we approached Zack's house the road narrowed, dropping sharply down between deep hedges lined with elms. There was a stream which trickled under a bridge before opening out on to the beach. Birds chirped sleepily in the warm afternoon; the sun sent splashes of gold between the leaves; it seemed a perfect Cornish day, a day for being without a care in the world.

During the ride I heard many of the details which fleshed out the story I have just written down. And again it occurred to me that the Colonel's death had released some hold on John, breaking down his reserve. I sensed a determination that his younger self had striven for but never achieved. And I listened to him with growing apprehension. I felt, more strongly than ever, the relentless escalation of this feud. Like the consequences of that incident in Bosnia, there was a powder chain. Each event was fuelled by the one before, each sparked the next; in the end the whole would be ignited in an all-enveloping flame.

The Tregarns' house lay just behind the bridge, close to the beach. The contrast of sun and sea was blinding after the dimness of the road, but the house itself blended into the background, as if it had always been there, a long low house made of bleached stone, so old its slate roof was lichen covered and its front door sagged. I found it more to my taste than Tregaran, for all that it was small. The mullioned windows were open and white curtains fluttered in the breeze; fuchsia bushes were trained against the fence; there was a smell of baking; all that was homely in Cornish life seemed enclosed within its walls. And yet it was a house that in its long history had known sadness too, and deceit, and despair.

The door opened. Alice ran out. I shall never recapture in words how she moved, unless to liken it to wind over grass, or sun before rain. She ran barefoot along the garden path edged with snapdragons and sea thrift, and stood by the gate, arms outstretched, as John jumped down. Nor shall I ever forget how they met, fitted together like two things meant. Whatever shadow had fallen over them when Tom was caught had passed. There was affection, understanding, in the way she twined her arm in his, and he wrapped his arm around her waist. I have never seen, nor felt, two people so lost for a moment in their own private world.

When she turned back to me there was no trace of embarrassment. Gone was the shyness she had previously shown; this was a woman, wholeheartedly in love. It showed her pride, she exalted in it. Yet in her speech she was as simple and direct as before. 'I'm glad 'ee comed,' she said. 'Many's the day I've asked John about 'ee. You were some kind to 'un and Tom. I'm sorry like that here's new trouble come.'

It was the first time she had spoken directly to me, the first time we had actually met. Not a day since has passed when I have not thought of it, have not felt the breeze, smelled the bread, touched her cool hand with mine.

Close to, her eyes were more startling than I had thought, were flecked with light, changing as the sea does from blue to green to slate. She was wearing her old blue dress with the salt stains and her hair was blown into ringlets. Once more I had the feeling that she might have stepped from some ancient world that had no part of ours.

She was speaking to John, quickly now, urgently. 'Zack's gone,' she said. 'He and the others went to Gransters. The tide be out so they walked across the flats. I do fear fer 'un. They'm in some state.'

And then to me, 'I'd ask 'ee in, but there's no time. If we'm to catch 'em we've got to go afore the tide turns.'

She snatched up a miner's lantern which she had left beside the gate. Then she was speaking once more to

John. I caught only a few words before she began to run across the bridge and down to the beach. She ran without stopping or looking back, as if she expected us to follow. Or as if she would go on whether we came or not.

John hesitated for a moment. 'There's been wild talk,' he said unhappily. 'Zack's planned a meeting in the mine. God knows what he's thinking of. She's gone to stop him, and I must go with her.'

He took off after her, catching up with her almost at once and taking the lantern. Together they began to splash through the stream which had spread out into a mesh of rivulets across the beach. And after a moment's hesitation I followed them. I can't explain why. I couldn't then, and I still can't. It was a foolishness, so unlike me I might have been another man. Yet at the time it didn't feel so foolish, it seemed right and natural.

The water glistened in the sun. Gingerly I waded through it, not noticing that I was ruining my boots. Sometimes I had to jump where the sand was soft and squelchy underfoot. Soon the house was left far behind, its grey-gold stone blended into the background. Ahead, the sea receded into haze. The sound of the waves curling in was soft and lazy. No one else was in sight except those two hurrying figures, and a score of gulls that flapped noisily away leaving a line of prints in the wet sand.

I had never seen the tide so far out; when I drew level with the harbour the walls were dry, the green base of the pier rising like a fortress wall. A sluggish trickle came from its mouth where the boats were lying like beached whales, and the heat reflected off the whitewashed cottages, no doubt turning them to ovens.

On the other side of the harbour Alice and John waited for me. The sand was drier here above the high-water mark, and littered with brown seaweed that crackled underfoot. A trail of prints, human ones this time, led along the edge of the cliff. 'That's where they went,' Alice pointed to the tracks. 'And the others be overhead, so keep close out of sight. You can hear 'em if you listen.'

We were under the cliffs by now and from above came a rattling sound, a scrape of metal over stone, an occasional shout. We paused. Alice was frowning, a faint line of worry between the eyes, and even John looked surprised. I don't think he had realized her brother meant to be so thorough, or begin so soon. 'They'm started then,' Alice said. 'Zack warned 'twould be so. And if we don't stop 'un he's sworn to blow 'em to kingdom come.'

And she began to run again.

The sun was very hot here, trapped by the cliffs. The tide had flushed out all those little coves I used to spy down upon, merging them into one long sand bar dotted with rocks where the fishermen used to drop their lobster pots. In an hour or so when the tide turned, once again each cove would be cut off and isolated from its neighbour, its own secret world once more. I thought, suddenly angry with myself, this is ridiculous, racing along like a madman, me with my weak heart, trying to stop other madmen from blowing themselves up. But I plodded on. I had no idea where we were. From below, the cliffs looked all the same, but Alice must have recognized the place for suddenly she stopped, set her lamp down upon the rocks and tried to light it. As I approached she held her finger to her lips to silence me, beckoning to me to approach.

Still, no one was in sight, just a pair of terns watching disinterestedly, a trickle of water dripping reddish as if full of rust. 'Up there,' she said.

John had already scrambled on to a ledge; Alice sprang as quickly beside him, I lumbered up more carefully. We found ourselves in a narrow slit that sloped backwards towards the cliff into a darkness more absolute by contrast. From outside, the opening seemed hardly wide enough for one man to squeeze through, yet John passed easily and we followed.

Once inside, Alice went ahead; again reluctantly I came next; John brought up the rear. The passage wound around the cliff. Except for the flicker of light in front we seemed to have no substance, might have been floating on air. The air itself was warm and moist and when I put out my hands to touch the walls they were wet. But as our eyes became accustomed to the dark we picked out the passage easily. Carpeted with fine white sand and quartz, it resembled a gallery braced with planks. From time to time an open space between these struts gave a glimpse to the outside, a strange fleeting look at sea or sky seen out of perspective. Then the path would wind inwards again, crossing other similar paths. It would have been easy to be lost, but Alice never hesitated.

'Used to bring Zack his dinner pasty,' she whispered once, her mouth close to my ear. I caught a fragrance of hair or breath, like the scent of her garden flowers. 'Walk careful now, we'm almost there.'

Far away in the depths of the mine there came a booming sound, then a rattle of shingle and the shush of water as the wave withdrew. 'This mine's really old,' John said, 'the ore runs into the sea. The tin's still there, or so they say. It's getting to it that's difficult.'

The path began to rise. Sometimes now it turned sharply right or left as if it had been hacked by hand. And when we paused to peer ahead, I felt as hot as if I had been running in a Turkish bath.

We were looking into a wider place or cave that must have been still used as a mine for there was a litter of wood and planks, and a pile of new pit-props with their pungent smell. At one side ran a line of metal tracks, upon which a wooden trolley was precariously perched. There was a mass of rope and cables, a line of pulley wires, great heaps of red-coloured stone. And beyond all this, in the central open space, a group of men.

They wore little lamps attached to their caps, or carried them, and the flickering lights emphasized the shadows on their faces as they leaned anxiously forward, listening to Zack. Beside them was a pile of crates. Even in the dim light I knew what these were before I read the red letters stamped upon them. Lawyer-like, I averted my eyes. No need to incriminate myself more than I had to. Enough dynamite there to blow us all to 'kingdom come'.

I recognized the men immediately, the same group who had confronted Nigel at the churchyard gates. They were speaking in whispers but because sounds magnified in these caves, and were funnelled out, we could hear them clearly. And we could again hear movements overhead, the same metallic sound of wire being dragged, being wound out over bush and hedge, creating a barrier, a barrier of class and privilege and rank that shut one side in and the other out.

'We're at the eastern end,' John was whispering also. 'They're unwinding the wire there now. Damn great spikes on it, tear a man's hands off.'

Movement above, movement beneath – the thought of all those tons of earth, those fathoms of sea, brought fresh panic. I could feel the sweat trickling down my shoulderblades. I had to swallow hard.

Alice made a sign for us to stop where we were. She herself slid down the rock and began to cross the cave. Her bare feet made crunching sounds on the sand, causing the men in the middle to start up. Seeing her they sank down again, waiting for Zack to speak. But when he did, he didn't sound displeased, only preoccupied.

'Go home,' he said, 'don't need 'ee here. This be men's work.'

'I've brought 'ee two more then,' she said. She gestured

towards us. 'And afore 'ee go on perhaps 'ee'd better listen to 'em. That'll do more good than going blind like a bull in a china shop.'

John and I exchanged quick glances. It had obviously dawned on him, as it now dawned on me, that he had no plan, that we'd come all this way just because she had asked us to, without thought, without consideration of place or consequence. And it struck me for the first time that again I was interfering. John had merely invited me to Tregarn, nothing more. Like an old fool I had followed them, as if I were part of the conspiracy, as if I belonged with them. I had nothing to say, and the thought of 'talking to' Zack in these circumstances wasn't exactly appealing. I was sure John felt the same. Yet, I would swear to this, Alice hadn't planned to use us; there was no subterfuge as Evelyn Tregaran would have shown.

The crouching men turned expectantly. They were quiet men, family men, law-abiding by nature and upbringing. Quickly I tried to think of ways to influence them. I was tired, more weary than I liked to admit. But the truth was, whichever way I looked, by simply being there I was involved, almost as involved as they, accessory before the fact if not after it. It was in my interest, as well as theirs, to stop them from spinning out of hand.

I began to consider ways by which the situation could be defused. That Nigel Tregaran had overstepped himself was unquestionable but if Zack and his companions attempted what I thought they meant to do, they would be even more in the wrong. If they used that gunpowder as they planned, they'd need more than my advice to save them.

Feelings had gone too far for them just to disperse quietly. They looked for leadership from Zack, and were angry enough to follow him. On the other hand, beneath his belligerence I sensed that Zack himself was a rational man. If he were offered a solution that would save face, he would surely take it.

Zack's reply to his sister was not encouraging. 'That be that old lawyer chap who helped put Tom away,' he said, peering at me across the cave. 'He's no use to we. And t'other be a Tregaran spy. I've already forbid 'ee to see 'un, so what's he doing in yer company?'

I thought, he doesn't sound as angry as he might, just pointing out facts. That gave me heart. From experience I knew that the hardest men to deal with are those whose anger stops them thinking.

'Blowing up people isn't exactly what I care for,' I said, stepping into the open. 'That's anarchists' work. And that's how you'll be judged when you're caught.'

I spoke in my best courtroom manner, dry, precise, to get attention. If they began to consider, perhaps they could be diverted. But fatigue was catching up with me; I didn't know how much longer I could keep going, and my tolerance was wearing thin.

'Gentlemen,' I said, 'Mr Tregarn, you feel hard done by. And I agree. So will any legal court that hears your case. But this way,' I waved my hand at the barrels, 'you'll get no sympathy. If you use force, you'll alienate family and friends, all that you hold dear. All you'll get out of it is a hole twice as big as the one we're in now, room to bury them, and yourselves along with them when they hang you for murder. It's not the cliffs that need blowing up, it's the wire on top of them.'

'That's the truth.' Zack's face wore a familiar frown, a family trait; his forehead was deeply lined as if years of worry had left an imprint. 'But that wire's some thick. 'Twould be a devil to cut.'

'It's not that thick.' John's voice held a ripple of excitement. 'And it's not spread the whole way, it just blocks

113

both ends. They mean to patrol the fields along the road to stop anyone slipping in between. But with clippers it could be cut, special clippers, that is. Tonight. A group of us to cut, while the others create a diversion.

'I'll volunteer to help,' he said. 'Draw attention away. Like Tom did.'

It was an open invitation. And a brave one. Well done, I thought. Let's see how Zack reacts.

John said, 'Tom got put in jail on my account, the least I can do is make amends. Besides,' he gave a grin, 'I'd rather like being on the same side. And if those clippers work well then we'll hack Tom out of jail with them.'

He used words like 'we' and 'they' deliberately, making them feel he was on their side. The other men began to laugh, talking softly among themselves, nodding their heads. It was hard to believe men so mild would resort to such rashness. Yet that of itself was proof of how strongly they felt.

Zack didn't laugh. He stood sizing up the younger man. 'I don't like 'ee,' he said at last. 'I don't trust 'ee neither. Why should 'ee do anything for us?'

'Because this time you're right.' John was firm. 'My brother's no call to be vindictive. And because I want to prove myself. What've you to lose? If I'm caught there'll be nothing to link me to you; they'll think I acted on my own. Give me a chance, that's all I ask.'

'Unless 'ee talk.' Zack was brutal. 'What's to stop 'ee giving us away? What's to prove ee've not come here to find out what we'm up to, bringing t'other with you as your witness?'

Before John could say anything in his defence, Alice cried, 'I am.'

She turned on Zack. 'Do 'ee think I'm that mean,' she cried, 'to love a man who'd betray us? Why, Zack Tregarn, you'm touched in the head. And him and Tom that been

114

such friends. Tom's capture took him hard as well, he's dying to make amends.'

During this exchange the other men had drifted apart, letting this family squabble work itself out. I noticed how they had skilfully concealed the crates by pushing them quickly to one side so that the lettering was hidden. Now they conferred together in a businesslike way. I'd heard rumours before of the miners' Stannary Parliament, now I saw it in action. After a while, one by one they stepped forward to give their vote, a nod of the head, a half-lifted hand, to indicate their acceptance of the plan.

Their decision made, they returned, listened intently to John and Zack's suggestions, approved or amended them, with cautious optimism. They certainly seemed more enthusiastic than when we'd arrived. By common consent they divided into two groups, one under John, one under Zack. Time and place of rendezvous, method of diversion, all were discussed with military precision. When it came to the question of buying wire-clippers there was a pause, money being a problem. I offered some, I don't know why, it was unlike anything I'd done before, but the excitement was infectious. At the end, when the rest had gone, disappearing silently, again one by one to avoid detection, Zack turned to us.

'Well, girl,' he said to Alice, 'for once it seems 'ee've done us good. They've more confidence in young Tregaran than I have. But if 'ee,' he was speaking to John now, 'stand by us, then fair and fair 'like, I'll stand by 'ee. As for him,' a jerk of the thumb, 'let's give him thanks and get him home before things hot up. The tide'll have turned, but there's a boat at Coombe left tied. Use it.'

He too strode off. I thought, suddenly grieved for him, what a waste. If he had been in any other place, if some canker had not eaten him, what a different person he could have been, what a success he might have made of his life.

Most of the miners risked the tide, able to scramble over the rocks before it. The older men, like me, were grateful for an easier passage. We followed behind them through one of the honeycomb tunnels to a small beach where a rowing boat had been dragged above the high-water mark. They ran it down the shingle and we clambered on board. Alice and John were in the prow, I sat in the stern. The rowers pushed us out through the surf and swung themselves over the gunwales. Two to an oar they bent their backs, sending us shooting over the water. But as we rounded the point we heard a shout. We had forgotten that out to sea the boat would be more obvious than closer in. 'That be Master John Tregaran,' came the cry, 'and the lawyer chap with 'un.' While another voice piped up, 'And there be Alice Tregarn.'

It was too late to duck although we tried. The shouts came echoing after us. John turned to me with a look that was part distress, part jubilation. 'Now the fat's in the fire,' he said. 'But I'm tired of hiding. Let them know which side I'm on. Me and Alice.'

I remember thinking, that's all very well for you. It's your quarrel. For I also had been marked. And I thought, whatever happens next my name will be on the list of Evelyn Tregaran's traitors.

I did not even have to wait that long. Before I reached home Evelyn Tregaran had called upon her friends to stand with her. And sent Em round to rope me in.

CHAPTER SIX

Em's intervention lent a touch of humour to a situation fraught with anxiety, although there was nothing humorous about her in those days. I had heard about her long ago, notorious for her devotion to the Tregarans, and her strict Methodist ways. She was a comely woman of about her mistress's age, and had come with her first as a lady's maid. Now housekeeper, she ruled the servants' hall at Tregaran House with a fist of iron, and the village stood in awe of her. In her long black skirt and high laced boots, with her hat perched on her head, she could be seen twice on Sundays in chapel, chaperoning the other servants. These hats, trimmed straw in summer, velour in winter, were her trademark. She wore them balanced on her plaits which were gathered over each ear in 'buns', like muffs. The village wags whispered that she never unbraided those plaits and even slept in them. 'That's why she's never married Jim Polwren,' they said. 'Them pins would stab a man to death.' Actually I think her long-drawn-out engagement, common to Cornish people of the time, had soured over her tale-bearing about Tom and John, and must have given added incentive to her dislike of the Tregarns. Now her lugubrious face with its stern lines had the masculine severity of a herald bearing bad news.

On seeing me she didn't move, merely delivered her

message through pursed lips as if I wasn't worthy of it. The message itself was simple, more or less as John had warned: Evelyn was asking for troops to guard the fields and expected her friends' support. An accompanying letter contained instructions: the name of the colonel at Bodmin barracks; where to wire, whom to telephone, what to say. Even folded, the black script was clearly visible; the writing flowed strident like Evelyn's voice. I tapped the paper as if deep in thought. It didn't take much thinking to know the real message behind the words: 'Stand and be counted.' Em was sent to count me.

It was not the contents of the note that troubled me as much as Em's unblinking stare. 'You know why I'm here,' that look said, 'to see, to listen and to condemn.' And in fact in her black hat and shawl she had the look of a presiding judge, capable of striking terror into the most hardened criminal. I felt there was no excuse I could give that would not immediately be torn to shreds.

'Mrs Tregaran do need a prompt reply.' Em attacked at once. 'Sir Archibald says they soldiers'll come only if everyone asks for 'em. There be enough trouble brewing elsewhere, can't waste valuable military time. But while Master Nigel be gone, Sir Archibald'll help out; he be a true family friend.'

She eyed my dishevelled state, looking pointedly at my rust-splashed boots. 'Of course we know you'm some fond of them cliffs. You'd not want them overrun, village riff-raff on the loose, what give 'em right to pester us.'

There was a mournful reproach in her voice which sharpened when I hesitated. 'And them Tregarns mean trouble, or my name's not Em Pelruan.'

I was dirty, tired and hot, in no mood for a fencing match. Yet I suppose, instinctively, I had still hoped to avoid offence. Weakly, I asked, 'Why blame Tregarns?'

'Knowed 'em since they was spawned,' she cried,

shaking her head so the pins flew on to the rug. (I've not explained that she had insisted on coming indoors and was sitting in my hall, hands crossed, basket on lap, as if she were in chapel.) Her sallow face flushed. 'Played with Tom when he were a lad, helped bring Alice into the world. Alice's Ma were a beauty, a saint, to bear ten children and have seven took. And of them three left, two like to break a woman's heart. But I don't have to tell 'ee this,' she added slyly. 'You do know all about 'em.'

Skilfully she slipped the next sentences in. 'Heard you was in their boat today,' she said. 'Heard you went a-visiting 'em. Heard you all be pally like, you and they and Master John.'

The accusatory tone made me angry. 'What the devil is that to you?' I cried.

She got up, shaking down her skirts as if brushing away crumbs. 'I'd best be moving then,' she said. 'Mrs Tregaran expects me back, no point in wasting time.'

And with that she left, her trim boots tapping out a sharp retreat. I watched her straw hat bob along the hedge with mixed regret. I knew I had just confirmed her suspicions, hers and Evelyn's, for as the mistress thought so did the maid. I tried to console myself. After this, I thought, perhaps Evelyn Tregaran will understand my position and give me some peace. I was partly right, partly wrong. I had made an enemy all right, who wasn't about to leave me alone. Just as in the outside world the lines of conflict were being drawn, so here in our little Cornish world neutrality had no place.

'Your hesitating threw Mother into a tizzy,' John told me some time afterwards. We were sitting on the terrace overlooking those famous cliffs, and he was stretched out in the sun. He looked well, brown from working out-of-doors. In profile his angular face had a Spanish look, which made me wonder if somewhere in the past his ancestors had been washed ashore from a wreck of the Armada. 'She wouldn't say so but she felt she had you tight. She thought you'd never stand against her any more than I would myself. She wasn't speaking to me by that time, but hourly she and Nigel conferred. The house was like a Brigade HQ with her in charge. She'd have made a splendid general. By nightfall she was sure she'd got her way. Sir Archibald to the rescue again. He knew someone on the General Staff who knew someone who knew a colonel, you know how it goes. And presto, strings are pulled, somehow Tregaran's front-line work, and she's got her armed guard.'

He grinned. 'The soldiers were embarrassed, chasing after yokels when there's a real flap on. I suppose someone had persuaded their CO it would be practice. They stood around hatchet-faced while their young lieutenant saluted and Mother gave orders, Queen Elizabeth addressing the army at Tilbury.' He grinned again. 'That could have been me,' he said cheerfully, 'that half-baked officer, I mean. And when he had positioned his men along the hedge, facing inland along the road, backs to the sea, we came round by boat and climbed up behind them.'

He laughed openly now. 'There they lay,' he said, 'rifles cocked in the wrong direction. Made them look real idiots. After dark, when the pubs let out, Tom's friends made a sortie. Came up the road as if drunk, laughing and carrying on like crazy. Their tipsy shouts could be heard for miles, really made the soldiers perk up.

'That was our diversion,' he said. 'Simple really. When they drew level with the fields they never stopped, just went reeling on up the road as if making for Truro. Near the cut-off to Tregaran House they pretended to get in a fight. One of them had brought a toy pistol and fired the blanks. The rest ran, leaving a "body" behind.

'It was Jeb Miller. Did a grand job. Rolled over on his back, turned up his toes, and "died". The shots brought out the military at the double. While some gave chase, others tried to revive poor Jeb. And when the confusion was complete, for some got lost and the officer panicked, Jeb sat up, brushed off his clothes, rolled down his sleeves (they'd been trying to find his pulse) and winked. "Bain't 'ee ever seen a man asleep afore?" he cried.

'They started back as if they'd seen a ghost. "Get on with 'ee," he told them with a smirk. "I bain't dead, not even drunk, just tired." And he stood up and walked away. There was nothing they could book him for,' John said. 'No law saying a man can't take a nap. And the others had disappeared. Right old balls-up it was. As for the rest of us, we ran the boats ashore, tied ropes to the boat-hooks and threw them up, scaled the cliffs at either end and cut the wire.

'Nothing to it,' he said. 'Once we were up we worked in pairs, one to cut and one to heave. I enjoyed myself. Better than lying in those woods with Tom waiting to be caught. I'd offered to go with the diversion group, but at the last moment Zack asked me to lead one of the beaching parties. First time he's trusted me with anything,' he added more soberly, 'so I agreed.'

He brooded for a moment. 'That wire's well named,' he said. 'Should have worn gloves.' He flexed his arms which were scored with cuts, as were his hands. 'Next time I will. But we were finished before the soldiers realized they'd been had; tore out the whole lot like Penelope's tapestry, sent bales of the stuff bouncing down the cliff into the sea.'

His face lit up with a sudden burst of triumph. 'You'd have thought we'd won a battle,' he said. 'That's what the newspapers called it, "The Battle for Tregaran Cliffs" or some such rubbish. When we got back, the whole village was out on the quay to greet us. How they cheered! Rolled out great barrels of beer, a heroes' welcome. If Tom's pals weren't drunk before they certainly were by morning. But I repeat, there was nothing to it. Over the top, through the wire and at 'em.'

Something about the way he said those words struck me. I was never to forget them. Nor his laughing face and triumphant look. They were to come back to haunt me.

'Alice gave me what for though,' he was continuing. 'Ripped into me herself. "What made 'ee do that?" she cried. "Turn your mother against you." But that was just her way of letting off steam, she must have known why I did it. And she was there when I offered to.'

He squinted out to sea, closing his eyes against the glare. In repose his expression still had a thoughtful cast, a slight melancholy, as if the future were stamped there along with his past. Even in his moment of triumph it was present, and that too I was to remember.

'Told her it was too late to worry,' he said, rousing himself. 'I've left home for good. Found a farm which'd take me on, let Nigel keep Sawer's. I'd as soon make my own way in the world, and so would Alice. "Better we aren't beholden to anyone," she said, "we'll manage."'

'God,' he burst out, and now the melancholy was gone, he was all young enthusiasm. 'It's good to be alive. I'm lucky. Good mates as friends, a job I like, the best girl in Cornwall, why, Paul, I feel in Paradise. What more could a man want to count his blessings?'

He was a third my age; he spoke of joys unknown to me, yet in my life he was the only one left to call me by my given name. Perhaps it was his happiness, perhaps the loss of my own, but in the region where my heart should have been I felt a twinge. And that too I was to remember.

He was speaking openly now of Alice, telling me their

plans in the way that, had his father lived, perhaps he would have felt free to tell him. Farming obviously agreed with him and he had always had a way with animals. He and Alice would marry when he had saved enough. Alice herself wanted to work but he didn't like her going into the cannery. As for Zack, well, he hesitated, Zack hadn't exactly given his blessing but he hadn't withheld it either. He rattled on excitedly, it did me good to hear him. And as a last gesture of defiance, an expression of unity, the village had decided to hold its customary annual feast.

'I know the time's passed,' he said, 'but we've got it planned.' He turned to me with the same bright look. 'They've told the tale of Tregaran's War,' he said, 'I'd prefer now to be remembered for something else. Real war's coming, Paul, it can't be avoided. It'd be fitting for Tregaran to look its best in this last peace-time summer.'

When I said I didn't like the idea, 'Why ever not?' he countered. 'The season's right. Anyway it's the villagers' decision, no one else's. Tregaran House doesn't rule them. My father never should have dictated what the village could or could not do in the first place.'

Perhaps not, I thought, but he owned it.

'Besides,' he went on, 'we don't need Big House spectators like a Roman circus. It'll be just ourselves. The village fleet will be out, and we'll have the boys on the headland, the pilchard watchers. Alice will be Queen again, it'll be just like old times, you'll see. Even Zack agrees, he's all for it.'

I thought, I'd be careful what Zack says. And last time was not that great a success. But again I held my tongue.

He was looking at me quizzically. 'You'll be an exception, of course,' he said. 'You're one of us, invited here and now.'

He used words like 'we' and 'us' unconsciously now,

not for effect but because he felt accepted. But there was still a gap, no, an abyss between him and the village – of tradition, privilege, class. It would take more than one small victory to bridge that gap. He meant well, and I was conscious of the compliment. Yet I felt an underlying unease, that Celtic sense of premonition.

His enthusiasm was infectious and for the moment he was popular. Public opinion is fickle. The village had rallied behind him once; they might not again, and he was vulnerable. Suddenly I felt afraid for him. When reserve is broken a man has nowhere left to hide. 'Be careful,' I wanted to say, but the moment passed, and then it was too late.

Meanwhile Tregaran House took its defeat calmly. I often wondered what Evelyn Tregaran thought. She'd not like losing face. The morning after, when in twos and threes the village women ventured out along the cliff path, did she watch them angrily? Or did she hold her peace waiting for Nigel to retaliate? The barbed wire was not replaced; when Nigel returned he kept out of sight; gradually the village relaxed, life went back to normal.

How Nigel remained at home was a mystery. His regiment must have been on full alert, part of the Old Army of regulars which was expected to hold any enemy. In the battles that autumn so many of its officers were to perish, so many lords and peers, that aristocratic records couldn't be kept straight. But perhaps Sir Archibald was still in the background, pulling strings, as every day now the real news grew darker, the world powers lurching out of control, declaring war like playing cards. Austria, Russia, Germany, France, one by one they made their bid. It was only a matter of days before England followed suit. In this time of crisis it seemed petty to persist with village vengeance, as Nigel did. His action was cruel, again showed a bullying streak. But it was clever. I sensed Evelyn's hand in it.

Divide and conquer – here is how he got revenge.

His father had relied upon Jim Polwren for company; Nigel hired a new steward, a North Country man, impervious to local feeling, eager to aid and abet the new squire, more than willing to accommodate. Soon his squat figure with its gaitered legs was seen stumping up the village streets, putting the fear of God into the tenants. The day before the feast he went from door to door, issuing the dreaded decisions. Rents were raised, leases revoked, repairs charged to occupants. But not for everyone.

That was the clever part. I saw Evelyn at work.

The choice was random, patently unfair and quite without logic. It tore the village apart. Those who were spared, rejoiced; those who were victimized, sulked. Old enmities flared, new ones sprang up, soon no one was speaking to his neighbour. And when word spread of Tregaran's financial distress, of the old squire's debts, of the possibility of selling the house, not surprisingly both sides rallied to its defence, those who had been hurt more loudly than those who hadn't. 'A fine old family,' they said, 'pity to see it go under.'

They hoped, of course, for a reprieve, loyalty like that deserved reward.

Popularity is as fickle as opinion. They would have said the same of the Tregarns, three hundred years ago.

The division in the village was enhanced by Vicar Trevenn's stance. Normally the vicarage was the rallying place for the participants in the feast-day parade, its large gardens the start of the procession; now he refused to let them be used. Although I offered mine instead, it wasn't the same, and I was an outsider. Then too, the customary tea had to be cancelled since the Tregarans usually paid for it. A feast day without a feast was like a pasty without meat. Finally, the crowning blow, other villagers refused to take part, not out of fear of the Tregarans, but to protect their own rights. Each village celebrated on a special day, it set a bad precedent for Tregaran to claim two. The group that gathered on my lawn on an afternoon in the first week of August was small and despondent, although they put on a brave face and tried to act cheerfully, bustling about importantly, arranging themselves in order, exhorting each other.

There were few of them but the streets themselves were crowded. It is difficult to say what the crowd's mood was, or what they expected. Attempts at decoration had petered out because the may trees were no longer in flower and the other garlands dried too quickly in the summer sun. Bits of string and dead petals littered the ground, a dismal contrast to the usual decorations. Being August, of course the children were out of school and there were some flags left over from Empire Day, celebrated in a fit of zealous patriotism. The cannery also was closed, but for lack of work, and the girls were not in their finery. Nor were the young men in the pub, there was no spare cash for that. And there was a nervous air, as if everyone was waiting for something to happen. With war clouds gathering it seemed wrong to be celebrating, and yet I sensed it wasn't the possibility of war that caused the nervousness.

I felt sorry for the village; the pitiless sunlight seemed to enhance its squalor. I felt sorry for the organizers of the fête. But I felt sorriest of all for Alice and John.

I had seen them only once in the intervening weeks, for John seldom came to Tregaran now and, although Zack appeared to mellow, somewhat surprisingly, I thought, he still kept a close watch on Alice and only allowed her out to visit Tom in Bodmin Jail. I had been amazed, therefore, one evening to see her pass along the bottom of my hedge,

John by her side. I have explained that a gate from my garden led into a lane which in turn gave way on to the cliffs; where it forked, one side led down to the village; the other joined with the main cliff path. By walking fast I could catch the young people up, so, leaving my hat but taking my stick, I hurried after them.

I needed that stick. The cliff path that John and others had worked to save was already choked with nettles and weeds. Great bramble thorns stretched from side to side. (Another irony. Once having opened it and staked their claim, the village had shunned the path, letting nature reclose it. It had become a sort of no-man's-land, an expression in itself which was soon to become hideously familiar.)

I could easily have overtaken them, perhaps I felt peeved that they had not called on me in passing, but my instinct told me that to continue would be intrusive. I wish I had heeded it. Although they were walking single file, John in the lead, there was that intimacy about them I had seen before, that cautioned others to back off. There was no way they could have seen me, for I was as yet too far behind for my progress to be heard and they never turned round. I knew I had no place in their company, yet I continued on, remaining out of sight but close enough to listen in.

I can only say that I felt compelled to follow, even more than at any other time; that I was drawn to them as moth to candle flame; that I warmed my spirit with the warmth of theirs. I did not pursue or listen to do harm; there was no malice in my intent. And if again I felt that double twinge of pleasure and pain, that was my burden alone; it had nothing to do with them.

I went on and on, the thick bushes and tall bracken, the winding path, shielding me, the evening sun strong enough to blind anyone who did turn back. In any case they were so engrossed they would not have noticed me. And so we continued for some distance, they not knowing I was there; I intent on eavesdropping. They say eavesdroppers hear no good of themselves. What I heard was to change my life.

Alice was speaking. Her tone was low and urgent, and from time to time she stood still and drew breath as if summoning up her strength for argument. The light was so vivid it seemed to make a halo round her body and her thin summer dress steamed behind her as if it were on fire. I noted at once how she was attempting to modify her speech, as if modelling it upon John's (although she had not lost her Cornish lilt, which grew more pronounced with every word) and I wanted to stop her trying, as if she were spoiling herself.

''Tain't fitting,' she was saying, ''Tain't right. 'Tis as if we'm . . . we're putting on a show for our own ends, showing disrespect for something that's not for altering.'

She was talking of the festival, specifically of her use of the traditional fishing cry. Her shoulders had tightened as if with effort to make him understand. ''Tain't something that can be used at whim,' she said, 'not just when you want.'

'That's superstitious rot.' John was blunt. 'I don't believe in it. Nor did you, last time. Last time you didn't mind trying it. What's made you change your mind?'

'I can't explain.' Again she sounded troubled. ''Tain't a thing to put into words, 'tis a feeling. Then it comed – came into my mind and felt right. Now it doesn't.'

'Right enough to save Zack's skin and Tom's,' John said angrily, 'not right to save mine.'

She put up her hand as if to stop him but she did not contradict him. 'It is just words,' he was insisting. 'What else could it be? You don't think that people believe that fish'll be conjured up just because you chant some gibberish.'

He smiled to take away the sting. 'Pilchards don't swim up on command,' he said.

'They did, last time,' she said.

He stopped and turned to face her. A rose briar had caught in her hair, scattering the petals like stars. It was her expression which transfixed him. He said wonderingly, 'My God, you do believe. But we can't stop now. Besides, you promised.'

She sighed. 'I shouldn't have done,' she said. 'What you're asking can't be asked for; it's given. Those words are as old as the hills, older; they come out of the heart of things.'

She was trying to make him understand, to coax him into compliance. 'If it bain't done right, well, then the fish do rise in a mighty wave, like the words say, a red wave of foam, to drown the village and sweep all the villagers under and carry the Queen back to the sea.'

She added as he digested this in silence, 'They do say a Queen is chosen only once. 'Tis bad luck a second time.'

'Right, wrong, good, bad.' John sounded exasperated. 'We're tied up in knots with rights and wrongs. I only know this. There's a war coming. Tomorrow perhaps we'll be at war, and then everything will be changed. Feast days, superstitions, magic (if you call it that) – war won't have a place for them. This may be the last time, Alice. It's worth doing properly.'

'Don't speak of war,' she cried. 'I can't bear you to speak of it.' She tore her hair loose from the bramble and began to push on forward. 'And I can't bear you to be disappointed.'

'Then don't argue,' he said, leading the way. 'Now, that's really wrong. Marry me, what are we waiting for,

for Zack to give his blessing, for Tom to come home? It's our lives, Alice, not theirs. And it's something too that you promised.'

His tone had quickened, grown deeper. He had forgotten the feast day completely, had slowed down so that she was treading on his heels. 'It's you I want,' he said, wheeling round again. 'It's you I cherish. "Come live with me and be my love." A poet wrote those words for us. Throw everything else up, to hell with home and family; leave them like I've done and then nothing else will matter; it'll just be us two as it always should have been.'

She regarded him with her clear luminous eyes. 'Love can't be bargained for,' she said. ''Tis like that old fishing cry, either it comes into your heart or it doesn't, you can't put it there, it can't be bought.'

She meant the word in the sense of 'being used', 'being manipulated', but he chose to take her literally. 'Who's talking of buying?' he asked. 'I'm greedy, that's all. I want you as a gift. I want you to give yourself, all of you, without my asking.'

The dusty thickness of the bushes shut them in; the feathered canopy of leaves cast light and shade. I could have stretched out my hand to touch them and they would still not have noticed.

'Don't,' she was whispering weakly now. 'Don't tempt me. God knows I need and miss you. But there's a rightness to that as well, there're still things to be finished with. And a time and a way for doing that makes it all of a piece.'

'That's Methodist morality,' he cried. 'God doesn't condemn us for loving. Loving's as right and natural as breathing. I've loved you all my life, Alice. Sometimes I think I must have loved you before, in other lives perhaps, when your ancestors and mine were one. And now we've been given a last chance to be together it would be wrong to lose it. Wrong and cruel and false.

'I'll not hurt you,' he was whispering. 'I'd never hurt you. I'll just hold you close, see, like this, what harm to this?'

The narrow path hindered her, his arms reached out to hold her, there was nowhere to escape. Somehow he had shrugged out of his coat and dropped it on the bracken so that the fronds bent like a bed. 'Here's where it's right,' he was telling her, 'where we first met, where we've always been together. And after the feast we'll go away, we'll never be apart; we've waited long enough, sweet Alice. The next day after, promise, we'll be married. I'll get a licence, we'll go to Plymouth. Then nothing can harm us, no one will ever come between us again.'

Each word was a caress, each word a blessing. On his knees he bore down, tucked her under him like a gosling, wrapping her like a coverlet. And trustingly she went with him.

I left them lying there, turned sharply about, the pang in my heart more bitter than a viper's tongue. Using my stick to thrash the nettles down I went back to my lonely house and life. I did not blame or censor them but I felt my loneliness like a menace.

John had remembered a line of poetry to celebrate love. I remembered another poet's words. They beat in my head for days: 'Aside the Devil turned for envy . . . with jealous leer malign.' I did not look malign or leer with jealousy, but I felt shut out of Paradise.

So that when I saw them in my garden on the day of the feast, my earlier interest in the preparations had faded. Suddenly what had before seemed mysterious became tawdry and commonplace. Two years ago I had sensed some ancient rite, transformed in Alice's person into some life-giving force; now I saw the event for what perhaps it had always been, an insignificant and bucolic village farce meant for bucolic fun.

The children capered, the bunting flapped, the musicians – what few there were of them – blew lustily, making up in noise for lack of village support; the Queen's chariot was pulled out and readied. It had been decked with carnations in place of the usual hawthorn, and the vivid pinks and reds, the cloying scents, were more reminiscent of the French Riviera than Celtic mysteries. And whereas once the Queen had reminded me of a Virgin Maiden, a sacrificial offering to the gods of spring and harvest, now she appeared in human form, a mortal girl trying to create an impossible miracle.

I left them to their final preparations and went slowly down towards the square. The air was hot, almost steamy, and the streets stank. Before, I remembered how the people had jostled and pushed good-naturedly, now they remained withdrawn and dubious. Only one or two boats stood out offshore, the fishermen stubbornly ignoring the jeers that accompanied them, pretending not to notice, although their nets were ready. But on the headland where the boys were supposed to be on guard to give the 'hevva' cry, there was no one.

Alice sat under a brilliant floral arch, her sea-blue eyes had lost their brilliance. Little curls of hair hung limply round her neck; she fanned herself with a large leaf and tried to smile when someone gave a muted cheer. The cheers were immediately hushed, her appearance largely greeted with silence, with blank stares, with incredulity. And this lack of response was strange and frightening.

It was when she reached the place where Zack had appeared that the sound began. It was not that familiar village hum, far off like a swarm of bees, but closer, sharper, like a hiss. Hearing it, Alice went white as chalk, whiter than her gown. Only two spots of hectic red stained her cheeks. But she did not look down; too courageous for that she simply stared ahead, her eyes fixed above the crowd as if searching the horizon. Behind her, John, who had been walking in Tom's place, stiffened in outrage. Then he pushed forward, not caring whom he knocked aside, blocking the cart so that it swayed and tipped in a curious repetition of the other time. I don't think she noticed. Once, years ago when I was young and wished to avoid the world, I travelled in the Middle East. I remember seeing there a young woman who was about to be stoned. I forget the crime, something trivial, but the look on her face when she was dragged to the execution ground showed that she had gone beyond reproach or fear into a kind of trance. So it was now with Alice. Suddenly I wanted to run and pick her up, shield her from that awful sound, cover her eyes, her ears, her mouth, so nothing could contaminate her. And perhaps I would have done had not John usurped the right.

'God damn you all,' he was crying, trying to push the crowds back, for once the cart had come to rest they pressed forward to surround it. One strange thing: the crowd consisted now only of women, most of them young, about Alice's age. The suppressed fury in their eyes was terrifying. As they moved closer the hissing increased, although how they made the sound through closed lips was a mystery. This was women's work, although men, in the background, still watched closely.

John gave a heave, dragging the shafts of the cart along the ground, and spilling the flowers in patches of red. He climbed up on it as once Zack had done, trying to comfort Alice. Her crown had gone askew and her veil was caught, she sat transfixed within that ring of hate. And when John tried to pull her off the cart, 'Let be,' she said, in a high strained voice. ''Tis too late.'

Under the hissing, now, words began to emerge,

random words, disjointed phrases, slowly building to a climax. Like a drum they beat, always to the same tune, and gradually making sense. A queen is chosen only once; the wrong choice brings ill luck; to vaunt oneself a second time means disaster; on the choice of the Queen rests the village's hopes; and so forth, a regular Greek chorus of troubles from the closing of the cliff path to the lack of fish. Until, in one final burst of spite, the final accusation. 'Only a maid can be a queen. Any other is forbidden. Shame and disgrace follow her who is no longer virgin.'

The voice that cried this last must have been some village harpy. She was tucked away on the chapel steps, keeping out of the limelight, her shawl thrown over her head, her insults as anonymous as those once hurled at Michael Tregaran.

John could not see her but I could. I reached behind me, searching for some weapon. Against the chapel wall ran a water pipe, a shaky affair of cast iron, covered with some trailing vines whose ends hung over the steps where she stood. I gave the pipe a vicious shake; the bolts gave way, the vine came loose. It fell about her neck, making her squeal and throw off the shawl. Bits of leaves and twigs showered over her plaits; she began to beat at earwigs. 'Hold your tongue, Em Pelruan,' I cried. 'There's enough evil in this world without inventing more. And there're other laws, like the law against libel.'

Em straightened up and shot me a look. I've seen men condemned to death, and been responsible for their sentencing. I've known that look before. I remember wondering at it in her. Like Zack's anger on the last occasion, it seemed greater than the moment warranted.

Taking advantage of this exchange John had pulled Alice away, and silent now, the women opened a path for her, their looks inscrutable. Disdainfully I released my hold on the pipe, for I had been gripping it as if to wrench it off the wall. My fingers were clenched, my hand shaking as I too prepared to leave.

'Off he shuffles,' Em's voice piped, 'like a sheep. Nothing's been right neither since he camed. Why don't he go back where he belongs? Not like 'un to interfere, might have to pay for ut.'

Her speech was broad, calculated to amuse, the timing perfect. The crowd leaned forward expectantly. She jammed her hat back on. 'But there, Mr Cradock, sur,' she said, addressing me directly, the 'sur' deliberately contemptuous, 'don't 'ee take on so. What is it to 'ee, as long as 'ee be all right? First things first and the devil take the hindmost, as long as 'ee bain't disturbed. But why do 'ee follow her, I wonder? Last I heard 'ee liked little boys.'

Cleverly she saved the punch line; cleverly she played the crowd. There was a gasp, then a titter which swelled into a howl. That was her parting shot. She stalked away, letting the others savour the joke. They whispered now among themselves, another victory of sorts. Overcome with shame and anger, and other emotions too complicated to explain, not anxious to be caught again by such hostility, I blundered off, at least having the sense not to seem to follow John and Alice, not caring where I went as long as I was out of reach of that wicked laughter. Em had spoken the words, it's true, but the thought that had framed them, the malice behind them, was Evelyn Tregaran's. And that's how she paid back those who betrayed her, that was her revenge.

I found myself at last on the quay where most of the fishing boats were moored. Today their decks were unnaturally clean, their nets dry. The only sign of life was the two boats drifting beyond the pier, the old fishermen drowsing in the sun. I watched the boats float with the tide, and as aimlessly float back again. The sea sparkled, the sea-birds swooped, like dreaming dogs the old seamen twitched. I thought, in a year or so I shall be like them, sleeping time away. And what have I to show for it, what has my life been, but an emptiness so barren that village gossip can brand me as an outcast?

It was very quiet, the sort of moment when one faces a truth about oneself. Then a clamour broke out, setting the seagulls flapping. It was the church bells ringing. For one wild instant I thought John had made good his word and married Alice, or that Zack had raised the alarm as perhaps in olden days his family would have had the right to do. The bells kept on ringing, until even the old men stirred. 'Be that for peace or war?' one croaked. No one answered him, but suddenly I knew the meaning. The sides were all lined up, England had made its bid.

That solemn realization accompanied me all the way home. Peace or war. We had chosen war. And in my personal life I was never to know peace again.

One other thing remains yet to be told, and I add it now, not as an afterthought but to round out this part of the story in a logical fashion. (I am speaking of this one day only, the end of this notorious day, not yet of all the events still to come.) For I too had to know what had happened to the principal actors, whether John had had his way and taken Alice off; perhaps, if he had had time, he would have persuaded her to go with him to Plymouth as he had planned. Perhaps had he married her then, their story would have been done with. And so would mine. He couldn't, or didn't, although he had come prepared for that very purpose. On the other hand, whether Alice would have eloped with him is a matter for conjecture. Overwhelmed by the treatment she had received, she might have. As they left the square certainly John still believed he would succeed. But he had forgotten

Zack. When the couple came up to the horse and trap which John had borrowed for the day (he had left them tethered close to the road near my house) he found Zack on watch.

'Thought 'ee'd need a hand,' Zack said. He was smoking, the sweet tobacco scent from his pipe drifted over the dusty hedge. He began to pull at the traces, his large hands deft with buckle and strap. 'Surprised I know how to manage a horse?' he asked. 'We Tregarns have always been gypsy-like.'

He spoke in ordinary tones, as if nothing were unusual; as if his sister were not leaning on John's arm, her white gown stained and crumpled; as if John were not still on edge, ready to come to blows at the slightest provocation. Nor did Zack say a word about the day's events, nor his sister's part in them, nor what he thought about the ending. He made no comment about the village attitude although it must have stung his pride. But what he did say put a stop to her leaving.

'Tom's back,' he said. 'Thought you should be the first to know. So I comed to tell 'ee he be asking after 'ee.'

'And that was that,' John was to say later, much later, when the years of bitterness were done and once more he saw his way clear to achieve his goal. (Not bitterness for this day only; this disappointment could be lived through, but for all the rest that it was prelude to.) 'Zack's perfect excuse for stopping her, better than forbidding it. No hope of my going against it, no hope of going against Tom.'

He mused for a moment in the silent way he had adopted since that time, as if trying to outwit fate before fate outwitted him. 'Clever, when you think of it,' he said. 'Wouldn't put it past Zack to have gone to Bodmin to get Tom out and produced him, pat, at the appropriate moment. Knew how to play on Alice's sympathies, you see. I told you the quickest way to her heart was to be in trouble. Don't suppose it was Tom's fault. Don't imagine Tom knew, or cared. All Tom wanted was to be let out.'

He mused again. 'Of course, Zack guessed what I had in mind,' he said after a while. 'Of course he hoped to prevent it. Just because I'd done one thing right hadn't meant he'd accepted me. I could have taken on the whole German army alone, I'd still be a Tregaran weakling.'

Again that brooding silence with which men grown accustomed to their own society communicate. 'Suppose you can't altogether fault him,' he said. 'Alice warned me often enough. Said he'd fight me all the way. Even if it meant using Em.

'He knew Em hated him,' he said. 'Some old tale there of jilted love. But, this once, it was worth having her on the same side. He wanted the day to fail as much as Evelyn did; he wanted to plant mistrust.

'Even when I was angriest, I felt sorry for Alice,' he said. 'But I admit I was angry. I felt, just for a moment, as I had done when Tom was captured and I was spared. And my pride was hurt, that again she seemed to prefer him to me. So I snatched up the reins, climbed into the trap and headed off without a backwards look.

'I never meant for anger to last,' he said. 'And it wasn't all resentment. Afterwards I thought it wasn't fair to her to bring pressure – not after that dreadful day, not when Tom needed her. And I didn't want to stir up more trouble with Zack. So I wrote to her saying I was busy on the farm, we should be patient, things like that. I didn't mean a word I wrote. I knew I never should have left her. That was my fault. I should have insisted then and there, damned Zack and married her.'

He had gone far away beyond me as he spoke, back to those days when things still hung in the balance, still were retrievable.

'But when I saw Tom,' he said then, rousing himself, 'I had to accept she acted for the best. How he had altered! The life gone out of him. Seen men like that since,' he said. 'Shell-shock they call it, out of their minds. That was how Tom was. And as far as Zack was concerned, since it was my family's fault, what did it matter if I paid in kind? Strange when you think of it, how his and Evelyn's minds worked, as if even in revenge they were in harmony.

'Alice warned that prison would kill Tom,' he said, 'and it did. "They let me out, old son," he said, "told me I was free. Time off for good behaviour, they said." He used the old endearments but the voice had changed, gone hoarse, as if the dampness had got inside. "Set me up proper too, didn't they? A neat exchange, out of one hell hole to the next, cannon fodder instead."

'They set us all up,' John said, in that cynical way the years were to give him. 'If not their cannon then our own, if not their gas then ours. Turn and turn about as the wind blows. If not my family then hers – like a coconut shy, see who can knock the dummies off their perch.'

But that was later, after the bitterness.

CHAPTER SEVEN

The aftermath of this disastrous day took months, no, years, of recovery. As I have said, divisions formed that probably lasted generations. A modern psychologist is no match for village scandal – the wheres and whyfores, the might-have-beens and should-nots are mulled over in cottage and pub, shouted over garden walls amid the washing, form the main topic of conversation for miles around. For all I know Tregaran House thrived on it.

No one escaped censure including myself, now made a public laughing stock. Em's comments went their merry round, were agreed with, sniggered at. Zack's intervention became a stroke of luck for John; didn't that get him off the hook, by gum, didn't that give him the perfect excuse to back out! Even Tom's unexpected return (which might have served as a fresh rallying point – after all, his unjust imprisonment had lit the first fuse), even Tom's return went virtually unnoticed. One name, however, was never mentioned and that was Alice's. It was as if, having already singled her out, the village decided to ignore her, to my mind compounding its original crime by the even greater one of ostracism.

There was only one thing that could compete with this delicious orgy of gossip, and that was the war in Europe. Every day now the papers were filled with details of the German advance through Belgium and France, of the

French and English retreat almost within sight of Paris. Even our rural isolation could not shut out the war. National fervour rose in Cornwall as elsewhere. 'Want a few of us out there,' the young men said, incensed at the failure to stop the enemy. 'We'd show 'em what's what.' At night you could hear them singing in the pubs, bellowing out their Cornish anthem. 'A hundred thousand Cornishmen will show the reason why,' they sang. And when the recruiting officers arrived (for, in the beginning, joining up was voluntary) the men of Tregaran signed up in droves.

They swaggered through the village in their new uniforms, sweltering in the late season sun, proudly displaying that regimental crest which a few weeks before they had such fun in mocking, finding nothing incongruous in the reversal. Hodges grumbled at them. 'A good way to see the world,' he said. 'Board and lodging at government expense, who'll be left to do the work while they're gallivanting abroad? How am I to run this house, we'll be more hard put than ever.'

Hodges' priority was my house, far too large for one man and chronically understaffed. But perhaps in his short-sighted way he had hit upon a point. To fishermen and miners out of work, bored by inactivity, the army might have seemed an adventure, a chance of escape. I couldn't help thinking of Pitt's response when in his day, bells rang for war. 'They ring them now for joy,' he is supposed to have said. 'Soon they'll be wringing their hands.' Thought of those handsome young men as 'cannon fodder' was more than I could bear, no adventure in that for them, no 'gallivanting' abroad.

Among the first to join up was Tom. I think of him as one of the real casualties, not so much of that Great War as they called it (if war can ever be called 'great', if size is determination of greatness), but of his own nature.

141

Having just been let out of jail it was ironic that he should enter another prison of his own free will. Of all the men I have ever known he had seemed the most medieval, by which I mean in tune with his village and surroundings, in harmony with its life. Yet he chose a regiment from far away (not the local county one), from 'up north' where everything was unfamiliar. To cut himself off from his home was like setting him adrift in a boat without a rudder. Somehow I couldn't imagine his knuckling down to army discipline, nor his basic gentleness adjusting to army life.

I suppose he 'swaggered' with the rest, if 'swaggered' is a word to use of him. I know before he left he took part in one of those Sunday parades with which the military now enlivened our days. (I never watched them myself but from the seclusion of my garden the music of fifes and the beat of drums rent the Sabbath stillness with martial insistence. And when the soldiers had quartered the village they doffed their caps, went into the church, sat and squirmed like naughty boys while the vicar preached victory and glory from the safety of his pulpit.)

That Sunday then, I caught a clue to Tom's behaviour, and glimpsed the underside of all that glory. A group of girls passed beneath my privet hedge. Dressed in their best they must have just come from church, although usually they would have been chapel-goers. Such is the allure of war and all that captive masculinity! Under their pert straw hats their heads were bent, they were deep in talk, too engrossed to notice where they were. The day was calm, the last flowers bloomed, the sea was tranquil under a cloudless sky, no trace anywhere of that carnage across the Channel.

'Twill be over by Christmas,' one was saying, repeating the common belief, but the others contradicted her.

'Them'll be some lucky,' a broad-faced cannery girl

rounded on her. 'And we'll be old afore they'm back. Christmas'll be a long way from here, and them homesick afore they reaches Paris.'

A third girl stopped and stared ahead of her. It was Doreen, the maid from my house, on her day off. 'Look at Tom Tregarn,' she said. 'Handsome as a lord in his new togs. Why do he want to leave the place where he belongs, 'cept they drove him to ut? Thinks he'll have a fresh chance, see. Thinks that uniform'll redeem 'un. Like all the rest, thinks 'twill raise 'em from the muck where they was born to make 'em heroes. Mark my words, won't be they that's counted heroes. They'll be driven in that muck deeper than afore.'

This comment came from a simple girl, one of those who had behaved so shamefully to Alice! That too was hard to reconcile. But I was to remember what she said. It came true for me every day of the war.

As for Alice, I could not forget her. Her face, her tear-wet eyes, her luminous smile began to haunt me. I grieved for her as a man grieves for an illusion he sees slipping from his grasp. All the feelings of my youth flooded back, my own unhappy love affair, my own long bachelorhood, my effeminate nature – there, I admit that much, nothing more. Em's accusation was false, yet it bore a hint of truth. In all that she and her mistress thought of as manhood, I was deficient, but I was never interested in boys. My affection for John was a blind; it was Alice herself who interested me, and at last I admitted it. I even considered going to Zack Tregarn, demanding to see her, although I knew it would be folly. I swear at that point I had no thought of supplanting John; I never expected returned affection. I was too old, too worn out, for desire; my thoughts were all platonic. Yet I also admit that I was 'in love' as much as my nature allowed, and, like a lovesick lad, I was bewitched by her.

I took to roaming again on the cliffs, forcing my way through that overgrown path. I found perverse pleasure in staring down at those empty coves which seemed to ring with hollow laughter. I slept badly, sitting up at night with my books, letting my thoughts wander. I blamed my anxiety upon the war; it was really anxiety for her. (At that time, of course, I did not know all the circumstances.) In my heart I began to blame John for leaving her here, as later he was to blame himself. And perhaps, too, I blamed her. Like Tom she had a medieval sense of place which kept her fixed to one spot where a modern girl would have rebelled. But the struggle she faced must have been hard, torn by loyalty to her brothers, divided by her fear of Zack and her love of John, frightened of making a wrong move, aware at last how deep and strong the enmity that kept them apart.

Tom's departure must have been the last blow. Used as she had become to his dependence upon her, used to those weekly visits to Bodmin Jail (which had saved his sanity), having relinquished her immediate chance of happiness for him, she had been repaid badly. And it is true that, had he stayed, he could have interceded for her with his brother. Left alone now for hours at a time, isolated in that house which had once seemed the essence of home, how endless time must have seemed.

She did not ask John to come, it was not her way to beg, and she had her own pride to counter his, but she pined, grew thin and wan, like a flower that lacks light. And in the end, Zack, remembering how his mother had died, must have grown alarmed for her.

Otherwise he never would have done what he did, and never consented to what I offered.

He was waiting for me one day at the edge of the fields where Evelyn Tregaran used to ride her horse and the army had set up its watch on the wrong side, backs to the sea. He was leaning on the stile, as if, knowing my habits, he had chosen time and place deliberately. Around him the stalks of stubble still showed gold, the brambles were weighted with blackberries; I was edging along the path, remembering fruit-picking expeditions in my youth, when, dressed in frilled skirts and velvet hats like the girl-child I had been supposed to be, I had trailed behind an older brother, a brother I had both adored and feared, the brother who in everything had overshadowed me.

Zack had his bag of tools strapped on his back and had dropped his pickaxe by the hedge. His boots, firmly planted on the stone stile, were stained red, the tin-coloured clay that had given me away to Em. He was wearing those workman's clothes that complimented his good looks and made the rest of us seem unmanly. I presumed he was returning from his mine, the one that I had visited with John. He certainly had not been out in the boat since Tom had left. I would have preferred to have avoided him and had begun to turn back when he hailed me loudly by name, and then beckoned me forward imperiously, as if indeed he was the owner of all this land and I was the interloper.

Somehow, seeing him like that, I couldn't imagine his working in a mine. He had the look of one of Drake's adventurers, straddling his quarter-deck, staring out into space for new worlds to conquer. As I approached I felt his vitality strike out at me. And when he jumped down, although we were almost of a height he seemed to tower over me, adding to my feeling of inadequacy. Compared with him I was the creature underground, crouching in the dark. The pity I had once felt for him seemed almost an insult.

He eyed me up and down as if not certain of what he saw, not giving a damn, arrogant as a prince.

'I've been looking for 'ee,' he said, hard and direct, no greeting, no regret. 'We've not met since that day in Gransters, plenty of water under the bridge since then.'

He eyed me again, as I had used to glower at recalcitrant witnesses. 'There be talk,' he said, abrupt about that too, not mincing words. 'Em Pelruan's been up to tricks. The females here be some cats when they'm provoked, all teeth and claws. Hear you stood up to her and got mauled.'

He didn't smile but for a moment there was a flicker in those deep-set eyes. 'She's had it in for us, you know, for all of us Tregarns; some deep Celtic thing, I suppose. But you be the expert about that.'

Again that quick, penetrating glance. 'Took a shine to my Paw did Em,' he said, deliberately. 'After my Mam died. Proper handsome man, not a grey hair to his head. But he had eyes only for my Mam and when she died, well, he died too, no interest left. Em couldn't accept that. Thought I turned 'un against her. Then, when her mistress and me broke up, didn't she think 'twas the same thing. Took her mistress's part, been atter me ever since, like a bloodhound on the scent, paying me back twice for something that never was my fault.'

He stared above my head, his eyes suddenly blank. 'I make no excuse for what I done,' he said. 'What's been between me and the Tregarans be mine to bear or cast off as I see fit. I bain't a monster tho' as some makes out, eaten up with pride. Nor be I out to hate 'em all, as John Tregaran thinks. But I know what's right.'

'Can't be right,' he cried, 'to have them two to mend what took years to break. They'm not strong enough. And if they fail, 'twill turn 'em hard, make Alice what they say she is, another Evelyn Tregaran. I shan't have my Alice spoiled, shan't have them use her for their whipping boy.'

He leaned forward now, grasping both sides of the stile as if forcing the stones apart. 'But Alice won't give in. Stubborn, see. Can't seem to get young Tregaran out of mind, for all I've argued myself hoarse. Is convinced he won't forget her neither, trusts him blind, even if he makes her wait. Well, I can't speak for him. But what's between me and Alice be mine to make, no call for anyone to interfere.

'They say it isn't fitting for a girl like her to be left alone with the likes of me,' he went on, more quietly now. 'Say it bain't proper. For all I keep her tight, they say she be running wild. Don't care much what they say, Em be only a mouthpiece for her betters. But to pretend Alice be sitting there at home, waiting for her lover, and he off and running, that be a lie that's hard to fight. It got me thinking. Now Tom's gone, there's just the two of us. Suppose this war don't end soon, and they takes us older chaps, that would leave Alice at their mercy. Can't say what put it in Tom's head to go; can't say I blame him. But what I feels about this war is better left unsaid. Only this. Alice be in my charge. And I puts that first.'

He flicked his fast look at me. 'Don't speak of fault nor blame,' he said, 'nor who caused what in the past. But you did us a good turn once, and I don't forget. So that's why I've come to ask 'ee a thing that's been in my mind. They say 'ee be a great up-country chap, with great up-country friends. I wants 'ee to ask them to find a place for Alice. She'd be safe then, out of gossip's reach.'

If he had asked me to fly off to the moon I couldn't have been more startled. It took me a moment to understand that he was asking me a favour; the way he looked at me, and spoke, he might have been granting one. But I did understand that it wasn't only gossip he feared, it was Alice herself. *Stubborn, see?* In her quiet way she still resisted him. I thought, she's got him beaten.

He can't keep her shut up for ever and she won't back down!

He went on talking, suggesting this, suggesting that. I scarcely listened. An idea had leapt into my mind with the precision of a bullet. It sounds pathetic now, I dare say, naïve and clumsy. I had no idea whether it would work or even if it should. But the thought of her going away had struck me like a blow. At all costs I wanted to avoid that.

I framed my reply carefully, more carefully than I had ever prepared a case. One whiff of what I felt and he would be off. So when I spoke, it was so casually that he almost lost my drift and I had to repeat it twice. 'If it's work she wants, let her come to me. We've been looking for a good housekeeper.'

In those days a girl of Alice's age and class would have found nothing demeaning about entering into 'service' as it was called. Apart from the cannery there was little else she could do in Tregaran and the fact that she had remained so long at home had already set her apart from the other girls, might even have caused their dislike. Had there been anywhere else nearby except Tregaran House itself, or houses of Tregaran cronies, she probably would already have gone there, not as housekeeper, of course – that was a position for an older woman – but as a housemaid. However, since I was a stranger, an old semi-recluse bachelor, I could be forgiven a mistake of that sort.

I didn't mention money, I was too clever for that, but I did speak of days off, holidays when she could go home, stressing things that I thought he would like, improvising as I went along, still in the same vague way so that he wouldn't suspect any ulterior motive. I also slipped in the thought that she would 'gain experience', not so much to impress him but her. He could take it in any way he

148

pleased but I meant her to think of it as a preparation for when she married John. For I still pretended that although I was making this offer for myself I was also helping them. And for a long while afterwards I kept up that pretence of being a benefactor to them, although a secret one. For my part, the thought of having Alice under my roof, of having the chance to see her every day, of having her dependent on me, made my heart pound. But I swear in all innocence I never expected more than that, wanted nothing in return, had no desire other than the simple one of being in her company from time to time. And if the cynics of this world raise their eyebrows in disbelief, I make no other plea on my behalf; let the facts speak for themselves as they unfold.

I could see Zack weighing his response. He wouldn't have known on what tenterhooks I hung, overcome with my own temerity, terrified of failure, terrified of success. And perhaps my very offhandedness made him sense some underlying strain, although he couldn't have known the truth. But at this point Em Pelruan's accusations actually helped rather than hindered me. No harm in him, Zack must have thought, just an old faggot. He would never have asked my help in the first place if he had suspected danger. At best he may have considered we were like two watchdogs circling a pet lamb, neither trusting the other completely, each determined to outdo his rival. I never liked Zack Tregarn more than when, like Tom, he showed his loving care for Alice; I never trusted him more than when he held my fate in his hands and I outwitted him.

What convinced him in the end was practicality. 'Don't want for her to be sent away,' he confided, 'in disgrace. Nothing she's done wrong. Why should they win?' By 'they' he meant Em Pelruan and Evelyn Tregaran and their ilk. And when I promised him, still in that same

149

vague way, that I'd keep her presence quiet (meaning I'd not tell John), tacitly promising my house should not become a rendezvous; when he had ascertained the work I had in mind was 'genteel' – arranging the ordering of the house, seeing to the linens, overlooking the other servants, tasks of this kind (which actually Hodges did to perfection); when he had calculated again the merit of having her still close against her being gone completely, I knew I'd won.

'Right then,' he said, bending down to lift up his axe, hefting it easily as if it were a stick. He must have caught my gaze and misinterpreted it. 'In my mother's day,' he said, 'they used to send women and children in the mines. Crawled on all fours they did, along tunnels only a few feet wide. Air so bad a candle scarce would burn, and the water so hot 'twould scald 'ee to death. Mind, I don't mean here, this were always small stuff. And I don't mean the Tregarn women worked like that, not even on the surface picking ore. Our women were better off than that. There's no call for Alice to work at all, 'cept she seem to have set her heart on it. If she agrees, 'tis done.'

There was the snag, what Alice thought. True to my word I said nothing to John fearful of prejudicing the outcome, made easier by the fact that I never saw him since he had left Tregaran. For a week I lived balanced between hope and despair. In the end Zack must have presented her with an ultimatum of his own, an either-or, one of which must have been terrifying.

'Either you work for Mr Cradock,' he must have said. 'Take him as he is, 'tis a fine house and you'll do no better in these parts. Or you go away for good, out of harm.' Better a devil that she knew than one unknown, and Em's insults would have passed over her head, not something young girls knew about. In my person, both

150

she and Zack would have seen little of the devil. As far as she was concerned I was John's friend; she had seen my friendship for her family. My interest may have appeared as the one thing she could count upon. For the rumours that Em circulated, the cruelty of her one-time friends, the change in Tom, all these could be borne as long as John remained constant. But how long would John wait? If she now went away, what hope would there be of ever seeing him again; how could he find her; what future could they have? At least in Cornwall they had a chance.

There was one other reason why she consented. Afterwards, remembering her attempts to change her speech, her way of imitating John, I think she may have seen coming into my house as a means to 'better' herself, not knowing that for me at least she was perfection as she was. Poor soul, she may even have thought that if she came to live beneath my roof she could turn herself into a 'lady'. In short, she consented to live with me for her lover's sake. And that, too, I accepted.

'It's some kind of 'ee, sur,' she told me the day she arrived. She was wearing a pale blue dress I had selected with care, remembering in detail her colouring, shape and size. Her trim feet were encased in neat boots, made for walking. She carried her belongings in a wicker box, and her hair was neatly tidied under a hat. I stifled the urge to pull off hat and shoes, let her run bareheaded, barefoot, as she ought. I had already inspected the room she was to use, seen all was fresh and neat, had been prowling up and down, waiting for her arrival. Now, seeing her, I was struck dumb, speechless in her presence.

'I admit 'twere a godsend,' she was saying in her forthright way. 'I didn't want to leave home. This way I still be close, to ut and Zack. And John.'

She brought the name out deliberately. 'I know what's

correct,' she hastened on. 'I'm not after favours. John thinks the world of you. He'll be that pleased you've taken me on, but we'll not use that to our advantaging.' She smiled at the thought. 'I'll be happy to work my share. And when John comes, for he will when he's time, when the harvest's done, why then I'll give notice, regular like, nothing underhand.'

She picked up her basket. 'I do hope 'twill be soon,' she said, with a sigh. 'I want 'ee to know that. He spoke once of Christmas but like the war I suspicion it'll drag on after that.'

She sighed again, and said no more. Whatever worries she had, she kept them to herself. But I think even then she guessed something of my position. Something about her choice of words had been deliberate, suggesting constraint. It would not have been like her before to distinguish between 'underhand' or not. But that may have been the effect of her other experiences and nothing to do with me. In any case, I suspect I had already given myself away. Men of my rank and age did not often inspect their maid's rooms, nor choose their clothes, nor hover around them. But determined on her part to make things work, she may have tried to overlook all that.

On the other hand, she may have heard fresh gossip. Evelyn must be enjoying the newest twist and would not be loath to share her pleasure. I pictured her in her great drawing room, surrounded by her sycophants. 'My dears,' she'd cry, her eyes bright with delight, 'you'll never guess. Do you know what the old fool's done, besotted with her himself?' She would whisper in their ears, hands busy patting their arms, as if to draw them close, making them part of her delight. 'First a master's son; now a master himself, even if a decrepit one. Hodges must be beside himself.' And she would laugh, stretching out her glass to be refilled. 'Hodges must be in a fret, his old queer with a servant girl! Save my son all manner of complications, won't it, if he wants to be saved, that is. Otherwise, pistols at dawn, I suppose, duel to the death, and may the best man win.'

Except by then, perhaps, it wasn't her younger son she was worried about, if she ever had been.

Despite these doubts, despite Hodges' real and deserved reproach, despite the war in France and this local war of wills, I can honestly say the next few weeks were the happiest of my life. To have the object of one's affections close, to know she slept at night in the attic over my head, that she watched the same slide of moon along the walls, listened to the same sough of sea, was joy unadulterated. In my infatuation I saw her presence everywhere. The masculine severity with which Hodges had maintained the house softened. The vases of flowers, the bunches of asters and wild autumn leaves, the rearranged papers and books, the plumped-up pillows, the neatly laid fires seemed to reveal her influence. No need for Hodges to sulk, or the rest of the household to complain. She wore her position lightly, careful to offend no one. For the first time my house, with its sterile works of art, with its wealth and influence, became a home. The scent of lavender blended with beeswax, the smell of the sea came in with the sun. It was as though windows which before were always shut had been thrown wide open to let in the light.

Scrupulous to a fault, I did not get in touch with John. I could, should have, written him. That was what a true friend would have done, making light of the situation, jokingly suggesting I was taking over from him 'for a while'. I often framed the first sentence in my head. 'Dear John,' I'd write, 'as a way of compromise I've borrowed your Alice.'

I never finished more than that first line. I no longer

wanted to 'borrow' her, nor 'for a while'. Borrowing was not enough; I wanted to keep her for myself.

But, whatever the reason, his absence left the way open for another rival.

Since I had lived in Tregaran I had only met Nigel twice, and on both occasions had been singularly unimpressed. Now, in a gesture of goodwill, he came to pay his respects. Like many vain men he was sensitive to nuance and probably sensed my original dislike, so he made a special effort to be charming. He was in uniform, belt and buckles gleaming, captain's pips prominent, young Lochinvar off to war and wanting to be admired. He told me he had put his father's estate to rights – propped up his father's debts, he meant; the skirmish with the villagers was mercifully patched up, he'd never meant to let it get out of hand; he regretted being hard on them – sentiments he thought I would like. While he was away, off to the front, he wanted to ensure that all things were 'neat and tidy' (his expression).

He may have meant what he said. He certainly wanted to eradicate the unfortunate impression he had given of himself. And he certainly wanted to instil his military enthusiasm, which even then to my ears rang a false note.

'Just an informal visit, sir,' he said cheerily, poking his head in the study window, impulsively boyish. His fair hair was impeccably groomed, his teeth white, his smile Evelyn's, with all its promise of intimacy. As I looked up he saluted me with his swagger stick. 'Off myself in a few days, champing at the bit, just waiting for things to hot up in France.'

He must have been referring to the Allied attack on the Marne which was just beginning and his grey eyes gleamed at the thought. He looked what he wanted to be, the best of England's youth, worthy of what we were fighting for. I thought dourly, he's talking too much. If he's that eager, why isn't he already there? It seemed to me that he would make a competent leader, efficient, unsentimental. His men would follow him. But he would never have that charisma which his father had believed he had. And men wouldn't die for him, as they might his brother.

He continued to chat, casual chat about the weather, the crops, country matters that he thought would amuse, nothing about hunting or shooting which he had heard I didn't like. Suddenly a look came into his eyes although he never stopped talking, a faraway, contemplative look as if his attention had been diverted.

From where I sat I couldn't see beyond him, for he blocked the view, but I knew instinctively what had caught his attention. With a clarity that shocked me, I even knew what he was thinking, as if I was looking into his mind. He wouldn't have seen Alice in years, I suppose, not since they were children. He would have heard of her, though. Over the years mother, father, brother, all at different times in differing ways they must have talked of her, defended, attacked her, depending who they were. But he wasn't prepared for what he saw.

He knew her at once, that much I vouch for. And when, without haste, he had finished his little prepared speech (to which I scarcely bothered to reply, overcome with some dread I can't explain) he saluted me once more, just touching the brim of his cap which he wore pushed back at a slant, and strolled off down the garden path towards the gate.

I sat frozen. All I could think of was something an old judge had often said. 'Never trust a man who wears his hat askew.' The words 'never trust' beat in my head like a drum. So I sat and thought about that judge and my days in court as if it didn't matter that I never witnessed that first interview. I had no need to. I could reconstruct it without any help. I already knew exactly what he would say and do.

Alice had gone into the garden to pick some herbs from the front flower-bed. She made them into country brews that steeped for hours and scented the house. Thinking she was alone she would have been singing to herself, an old nonsense rhyme or some Cornish song whose original meaning was forgotten. I haven't mentioned her voice before, light, wistful, floating slightly off-key like thistledown. Sitting there on the grass in front of the herb border, her blue skirts spread, she would have seemed what perhaps in one sense she was, a daughter of the house, protected and cherished, her beauty the perfect foil to his, her innocence as alluring as she was.

She'd know him, too. His clothes, voice, face would give him away. 'You'm John's brother,' she would say, astonished into speech before he had time to introduce himself, and when he stopped in surprise, not liking to play second fiddle to anyone, 'Nigel Tregaran. John said we'd meet one day, when the time was right.'

She meant when they were married or when the quarrel had been patched up; she would have liked to tell him that she grieved because John was estranged from his family; she had never wanted to be the cause of a quarrel. He took her remark in another sense.

'What better place or time,' he said. 'What better setting.' He smiled a boyish smile and spread his arms to take in the fringe of sea, the stretch of lawn, the country charm. 'Raphael's Madonna in the Meadows!'

She might not have known who Raphael was but she would recognize the admiring tone. She bent her head, went on with her picking without a word, her fingers nimble among the stems, an occupation she was used to, as natural as breathing, hoping he would leave.

He stood watching, tapping his boots with his stick. 'You're not what I expected,' he said suddenly, 'not a bit.'

When she didn't look up again he continued standing, as if trying to get his balance, looking suddenly stupid, not liking to confess what it was he had expected, not willing to leave until she asked.

'What are you doing here? How long will you stay?' The trite questions must have come out against his will. Her stillness, her preoccupation, would have been new to him. He would have been used to girls whose concentration was on him.

She still paid him no attention. What she thought, and felt, and did, were none of his business, and again her lack of response would have irked him. He tried another tack.

'I hear you're waiting for John to name the day,' he said. 'I'm sorry about the delay. But our father's affairs were complicated and the estate still isn't settled properly. John will have to be patient about the Sawer place, as will I, before we get our due.'

He was hedging now, trying to remember exactly what she would have been told. After all, she might well be thinking that if John had had his father's gift as promised, there would be no waiting at all. 'Matters of this kind, legal matters, always drag on. I know John thinks I'm to blame. He's impatient, of course, and I can see why.'

He let his voice trail off. 'Having seen you I can,' was what he implied. He meant it as a compliment, a rather heavy-handed one, intended to flatter. And again would have been irked that she let it pass by. Country girls, unsophisticated country girls, usually weren't so hard to please.

He continued to speak of John, guessing that was the way to break her reserve; his admiration for John, his respect. He knew his brother was doing what he wanted, more power to him. He disliked their estrangement, after all there were only the two of them left. His wish was to 'make up', as children say, before the war swallowed him; he'd feel better in France knowing that his brother and he had come to terms; at this time of crisis there was no room for petty quarrels – mouthing platitudes as if he believed them, trying them out for the effect on her.

Although she did not look up or stop her picking she was listening intently. She would know that what he said was at variance with what John had told her. Doubts would still linger. He was too suave, too facile-tongued; words rolled off too readily. If he felt these things so strongly, why didn't he tell John himself; he must know where John was; hadn't he driven him from the house?

John was in no mood for reason, the reply would come easily. John was in a pout. Couldn't she act as emissary and bring them both to a meeting point?

When she said, 'Like my brother, Tom, John feels lonely away from home,' he knew he had her caught.

'I remember Tom,' he said. He was leaning on the gate now, flicking at the dead flower-heads, watching her long white hands.'Tom Tregarn, the one we all admired. Never thought he'd have to take the fault for my brother. Which regiment's he in, what rank, has he been shipped abroad?'

Officer-brisk now, he would ply her with questions, rapping them out as reluctantly she began to reply.

When he said, 'I'll keep an eye open for him then, perhaps he can be transferred,' her expression brightened for the first time.

'That'll be some kind,' she would say eagerly, echoing what she'd said to me. 'He's miserable so far from home.' But when he began to elaborate, she would turn away again, confused. She must have remembered suddenly to whom she spoke. Tom'd be the last one to take help from him.

He must have sensed the thought. 'I'll keep my name out of it,' he told her, a condescension on his part. 'We can't lose good men because of stupid quarrels. That's something else I meant to say. The older people' (he meant his mother presumably) 'harp on about the past. We young 'uns don't have to.'

It was what John had said. Again a trace of a smile would have brightened her face. For the first time she may have thought that this man wasn't the Nigel of John's description; had war really changed him that much? To keep the smile there he would wax eloquent, reminiscing about that past, dragging up old stories he must have heard, admitting he'd often wondered about the three of them, always the three. All of this would be meant to please, was not exactly a lie. Like his mother he had that easy facility of making lies sound like the truth. And for a moment there, in that peaceful garden, he almost might have believed himself.

I repeat, I didn't have to be there to know exactly what he said, when he smiled, when he advanced, when he retreated, like a cunning player in a cunning old game. Against such skill she had no defence. Innocence is its own reward perhaps, but it's also its own curse. And I knew how she would look, at moments puzzled then equally quickly relieved. I knew it all; I had seen it happen before when my own brother stole my girl in similar fashion.

I don't know how often they met after that. I came to dread the afternoons she had off. He didn't come to the house again, too shrewd for that, but several times I spotted him riding through the fields. It could not have been coincidence that each time Alice was paying her weekly visit to Zack.

159

Nigel made a fine figure on horseback, stiff-shouldered, upright. I remember thinking sardonically that it was too bad there'd be little use for cavalry in this war, already bogging down in trench mud. He'd have done well in a battle charge, the Charge of the Light Brigade, for example, blown to bits in the Crimea. Of course I didn't really want him dead, but since the death of my brother I had never hated anyone so much.

I would wait for Alice's return, pacing up and down in my study, occasionally venturing out to the gate to see if she were coming. I imagined her breasting the hill from the village, panting a little with effort, for she always brought something from Tregarn, cuttings of flowers, home-made jams, pastries she had baked, a regular Little Miss Riding Hood. He in turn would be sitting smoking under the hedge, or come sauntering down towards her as if by chance. Or, equally by chance, he'd come cantering along some path, pulling to a halt in a splatter of leaves as she approached. How English he would look, how much a gentleman, leaning down to take her basket perhaps, smiling with pleasure.

'Good evening, Miss Tregarn,' he'd say, polite as a courtier, courteous as if in a drawing room. 'You're back early, late,' whatever time it was. 'What have you been up to today?' All the little things I'd like to ask and didn't have the courage to, all the things she'd tell him that I longed to know.

It was during this time that my feelings towards her too began to change. 'You're a fool!' I wanted to shout at her, 'you're playing with fire.' Common sense told me to say nothing. For all I knew, he pursued in vain. She might well have passed him by without a word, ignoring him. But if he asked again about Tom, offering her impossibilities; if he promised to be reconciled with John, knowing all the keys to unlock that shyness, I knew her silence would soon crumble. I never trailed him or her, I had lost the desire.

Even when she came in through the garden gate and I caught the sound of its familiar click I never found an excuse to come into the hall as I once had done. I sulked alone. There was no reason for suspicion of her except my jealousy. But jealousy now had full hold of me, destroying happiness.

CHAPTER EIGHT

The reason for Nigel's prolonged leave continued to puzzle me although in the early days of the war military matters were still haphazard, 'gentlemanly unorganized'. He must have persuaded someone he was needed badly at Tregaran, he may have told the truth, that he was waiting for orders, 'chafing at the bit' as he had put it. I became suspicious. In any case, whether he was bored or not, pursuit of Alice must have appeared as a nice distraction, something to keep him amused.

I never figured out exactly what his 'game' was. At first I thought it was to injure John; why should John have all the luck? It would pay John out to steal his girl away. Then I became convinced he meant to play with Alice out of spite, to get even with all the Tregarns. Sometimes I even suspected his mother's work 'Go on,' she might have urged him in that coarse way she sometimes had. 'Have some fun; show our John what she's really like.' She would laugh, her braying laugh. 'Prove I'm right,' she'd say.

One thing I was certain of. Like all handsome men Nigel believed girls were automatically attracted to him. I was sure that he felt her disdain, if she did disdain him, that is, was only pretence, to lure him on. And if she really did spurn him he would be even more intrigued, failure a new experience for him.

I should have warned John. But I didn't, not out of fear of interference, but out of chagrin. No one likes to see an idol turned to clay, no one wants illusion spoiled. And what was I to warn John of, that his brother was buzzing round Alice like a bee, that Alice was the honey pot? I told myself it wasn't my affair; let him find out for himself. Let him fight his own battles. It wasn't John I was worried for, it was myself.

As for warning Alice, I didn't dare. All the disadvantages of my position now revealed themselves. The disparity of age, position, background, rank, stretched in an enormous gulf which I couldn't bridge. I had foolishly thought I knew her well, now I was faced with the truth that I didn't know her at all. We had never talked, I mean alone; we had never shared emotions, thoughts. She had never confided in me nor I in her. I had no idea what her real feelings were. All I felt about her was locked in my own mind; in one way I'd invented her. The only bond between us was our mutual regard for John, and under the circumstance that would keep us apart rather than draw us close.

I had no right, again that word, no right to question her. I certainly had no hold on her, no reason to complain about what she did or did not do. And that, too, was hard to accept.

Unable to cope I withdrew, pretending nothing was amiss. My only hope was that she might confide in me. I pictured her full of remorse, penitent. 'What's to be done?' she'd say. But I knew this was unlikely, was a fantasy in a world where fantasy no longer had a place.

So the days passed; they seemed like years. Nigel lingered on, profiting by his brother's absence to ingratiate himself with Alice, using his interest in Tom and John to keep her own interest, perhaps using his imminent departure for the the war as a way to win sympathy. I veered

163

from indifference to rage. Like Shakespeare's Mercutio I could have cursed both families. What were they to me or I to them, a stranger, on the periphery of their lives? But sometimes I almost wept for all those wasted years, for all that had been lost and now was about to be lost again.

The night Alice received the note, the air was taut like a cord. As yet there were no clouds, the moon was huge, a harvest moon, and the wind was a whisper, rising out of the west, harbinger of storm. I had fallen into so deep a sleep I never heard her leave the house. It was some other sense of alarm, some familiar dread that made me start up, my heart thudding.

I heaved myself out of bed and went to the window. Against the moon the sky seemed black, without stars, and the garden below was lined with shadow where darkness had settled in layers. Only the treetops stirred, etched sharp as glass. I remember how a last leaf spun round and round. I remember the autumn smell of damp and mould.

Suddenly a different flutter caught my eye, white, moth-like, something long and ruffled about the hem. I remembered John's description of her dress. I leaned on the sill, listening. Far off, but distinct, I heard a click, the rusty hasp on the garden gate.

A blackness took hold of me. True, there were others in my house more apt to creep out at night, the Doreen who'd admired Tom, for one. And there could have been a dozen innocent reasons why she went, emergency, sickness, things like that. I knew it was Alice who stole like a thief to meet a man I despised, to cheat the man I thought of as a son. For the first time I felt what Zack had felt, I shared his pain.

I threw on my clothes and went after her. I can't say now what my purpose was or what I would have said or done if I had caught up with her. Or even if I meant to catch her. But I had to go. It never occurred to me that she went to find John. By now I had so forgotten John that I supposed she had as well.

I had no difficulty in following her. Even inside the house she'd left a trail of unlocked doors and windows, as if she didn't care who saw her, as if she had no shame. My anger grew. How dare she make a fool of me, I thought, how dare she betray my trust? For the second time in my life I knew what murder meant. Had I seen Nigel then, like Zack I could have killed.

She had taken the cliff path and I went after her. I made good time, faster than I would have dared in daylight. I ignored the constriction of my heart, the giddiness that comes from lack of breath. Like a man possessed I found new strength and energy. And when I came to the cliff edge I plunged over it as she had done, as if launching myself into space. I was determined now to follow to the end, to be present at this intended perfidy. It was my own betrayal I was witnessing as much as John's.

By sheer chance I stumbled on the little track she must have known by heart, otherwise I would have fallen from those cliffs. Better perhaps I had. It snaked about, a faint line in the bracken fronds, and I edged along it step by step, clinging to the roots and stems, sometimes fumbling on hands and knees. I couldn't see clearly which was just as well, the drop would have sent me into panic. And when I emerged at last on to open rock, I found myself some twenty feet above her, with half as far again to the beach.

I was in shadow where the cliff-face curved, but she stood in moonlight, her white dress shimmering. At the time I was sure she couldn't have heard me, the sound of the sea, the noise of her own descent would have hidden any I made. And she didn't turn round, just peered into the void, shading her eyes with both hands. The main stretch of beach was dark but further out the sea was bright and the rocks where she had sat to talk with John were rippled in silver around the base. If I had wanted I could have climbed down to her; I could have shouted out, warned her of my presence. Even then I could have stopped what happened before it began. I didn't do anything. For from my higher vantage point I could see the little speck of light, the red end of a cigar.

She must have seen it too. She gave a start, her foot slipped, the familiar shower of stones rattled down the slope. A darker shape detached itself from the rocks, a man strolled towards her, a lazy assured walk, as if he never had had a moment's doubt, as if he had been sure she would come.

It was Nigel, of course. I knew the walk by heart. And she recognized him when I did. He must have come earlier, and been lounging there, confident, content to wait. I closed my eyes. I saw her as she had been once, sitting on that rock, throwing shells. Wild as a gazelle, impudent, mocking, in that instant she had won my heart.

''Ee forgot the tide,' she'd say, picking limpets off to throw at John. 'Can't come no further out than this.'

Her voice was unchanged from the one which had spoken to John those years ago, but the words she used should have alerted me.

'Didn't expect you so soon,' was all she said. She continued to stare along the beach as if still looking for something. When at last she asked, 'Where's John?' my only thought was, why mention him? Why speak of one brother to the other when you're about to play the first one false? But wasn't that your nature even as a child, weren't you always a flirt?

'He's late,' Nigel's voice rang hollowly. He might have shrugged. 'What do I care?' that shrug said. 'To hell with him.'

166

She moved again; there was another slip of stone. I thought, if she doesn't watch out she'll fall. I almost wanted her to. In a moment I would reveal myself, tell her what I thought of her, order her to quit my house. Out of sight, out of mind, out of my life.

'He'm never late like this.' She sounded worried now. She hesitated. I imagined the frown between those tranquil eyes. I saw her bite her lip. 'Well done,' I thought. I wanted to applaud. 'You almost have me fooled.'

She was rummaging in her pocket now, had drawn a slip of paper out. ''Tis his writing, look,' she said. 'Something must have happened. He . . .'

Nigel had been moving steadily up the beach, had climbed the rocks at the base of the cliff, and now with one bound he scaled the last so that his head was almost level with her feet. He smiled up at her, with that smile so like his mother's. 'Don't fret,' he said, supremely confident. 'It'll be all right. I'm here.'

She caught the nuance at once. Suddenly her voice sharpened with suspicion. 'When did he give you this?' She held out the paper again. 'I don't understand,' she said. ''Tain't like him to send a messenger. Are 'ee sure 'twas meant for me?'

For answer he grabbed her legs.

There was a smothered cry, a great rattling of stones; they fell together in a tangle of skirts, she uppermost, he taking her weight. I heard them sliding down the cliff. Then silence.

When I dared look he was on his feet, kneeling beside her, trying to make her speak to him. And she was lying on her back, pushing his hand away, her arms thin and white like peeled twigs. He could have snapped them apart.

'Didn't mean to frighten you,' he was saying. 'Lie still and get your breath. But I couldn't leave without seeing you again.'

He suddenly leaned back, said almost petulantly, 'All right, I lied when I said that he'd be here, that the letter was meant for you. What's so bad about that? I'd do damn all to get you on your own.'

When she didn't say anything, more coldly now, 'Look, it was your idea first that he and I should make up. I only wrote him because you wanted me to. His note was in reply to mine, it was easy to alter. All I had to add was time and place. I knew you'd never come otherwise.'

'But I'm here instead,' he said, confidence back in his voice. 'I'm here to look after you. He's no good for you. I am. Come on, Alice Tregarn, enjoy yourself, there's a war on.'

His voice became solemn at that word, lugubrious. 'War's no picnic,' he was saying. 'I may be wounded. I may be dead or dying. Show some pity, it's not much to ask.'

I remembered what John had said. *Sometimes I think the way to her heart is to be in trouble.* Nigel would use that, too, for all its worth.

She said something then, I couldn't hear what, but it made him start up and scan the cliffs. 'There's no one there,' I heard him say as I shrank back. 'But if there were, what would I care?'

He took another step forward, cupped his hands and shouted until the rocks rang, 'Do you hear up there? Alice Tregarn's mine.'

Was he still playing a part? The moon suddenly caught his laughing full-fleshed face, bathing it in light. His grin could have been full of malicious glee, his laughter full of triumph. Or it could have been genuine pleasure. He could have been deceiving her, or himself. I think, for a moment there, he almost meant what he said.

While his back was turned she scrambled beneath him, like a crab, gathered up her skirts, raced across the sand as she used to do. She had lost her shoes; her bare feet kicked up the grit as she ran towards the sea as if she meant to plunge right in. And for an instant he stood rooted to the spot, staring after her, as his brother had done.

Then he was bounding behind her, over the rocks like a hunting dog sure of its prey, catching up with her at the water's edge. He splashed after her to pull her back; the surf broke around them, her skirt billowed like weed.

'No escape that way.' He was panting, dragging at her arm. He shook himself, as if suddenly aware how wet he was. 'Damn it,' he said, 'you've ruined my clothes.'

He held her close, tilted her chin. 'And damn your eyes for looking like that. What have I done? Tonight's my last night here. Don't I deserve some fun?'

The wind funnelled the words up, that treacherous wind. I thought, I think he means that too, I think he's scared.

She was straining away from him, trying to pull her arms loose. She shook her head. 'No,' she was saying. 'Let me go.'

'Damn it,' he cried again. There was anger, passion, in his voice. And fear perhaps, fear for himself. 'I'm tired of it. You've been fighting me since we met. There've been enough other women in my life, why should I waste this last night chasing you? If I'm to die I intend to have something to remember you by. I deserve that much.'

Suddenly he stooped, swept her up, carried her back towards the shelter of the cliff, although she struggled against him, using arms and feet. When he dropped her, 'There,' he panted, 'it's not so bad, is it, just a bit of harmless fun. Who's to know if you did, who's to find out if you don't tell?'

His voice sank to a whisper. 'He won't come, you know,' he said. 'No use to shout. He's changed his mind, he doesn't care.'

'It's over for him,' he went on, brutally harsh, brutally cunning, his last trick. 'That's what he said, over with, done with, finished. That's the message I was to give you.'

She gave a shudder, as if her heart was being torn. 'Stop,' I wanted to shout at him, and to her, 'He's lying.' I couldn't say a thing.

'But I care,' he went on. He reached out to touch her but she jerked away. 'Listen, Alice. John's a fool. If you were mine I'd keep you under lock and key, I'd never let you go.' And that was the last thing that he may have half-meant.

Her cry was wild then, haunting as a bird's. She flailed at him. 'It bain't so,' she cried, 'I can't believe you.' But her whole body, her whole self, said the opposite as if what she had always feared had come true.

He held her tight now, looking down at her, and now there was triumph complete as he bent his mouth on hers. 'But you believe in fate, don't you,' he said through pursed lips. 'Well I'm yours. We were meant, you and I. So why resist?'

Those words reverberated around the cliffs, they reverberated in her ears and mine, like the echo of the centuries, like the sound of doom.

I still could have helped her. I could have gone crashing down that last incline to the rescue, wasn't that what she would have wanted? Lacking John, wouldn't she have turned to me at last? And when I failed her, didn't she fight against Nigel until her strength was gone, until she succumbed to him in the sweetness of that night? Didn't she scream until he again stopped her mouth with his?

I wasn't there to hear or see. I couldn't stay to watch what a brother did, to cuckold me a second time. Why should I stay? Wasn't he only doing what I wanted to; wasn't it my place he was taking there in the dark? I only know I crawled away, vomit hot as bile, tears of impotence.

Next morning at dawn the fishermen found her wandering along the beach, her dress in shreds, her body bruised and cut. She was alone, they could get no sense from her and her seducer had disappeared.

They thought at first she must have fallen, in the darkness missing the path; the cliffs were deadly treacherous near the edge. A miracle, they said, to have avoided worse injury and to have escaped the tide. They carried her back to Zack Tregarn ('Take me home,' she'd said) and he received her tender as a woman. But when they laid her down and withdrew, then the whispering began. What was she doing out so late at night? Her arms, did you see her arms, those bruises never came from falling; the rips on her dress were not from thorns. Had John Tregaran shown his true self at last and left her there to drown? And if not John Tregaran, then someone else, she never was there alone . . .

Not a word she answered them, proud as a peacock. 'Tis naught,' was all she would say. ''Twill pass.' But it wouldn't pass, although Zack shut out the world, like a hermit guarding a treasure.

'Why didn't she tell me?' John was to say much later, as if her silence lay on him like a weight. 'She couldn't have believed that I'd forgotten her, as soon forget myself. I went once to see her, it must have been two weeks after; Zack bolted up the door, threatened to blow my head off if I came any closer. She must have been inside, crouching in her room, listening to him, weeping for us both.'

Years of denial held him taut, a touch would have broken him. 'Like a fool I obeyed. I was afraid to do her harm; just by being there I harmed her. I should have broken down the door, that's what Zack would have done. Instead I played the gentleman and withdrew. Like my father I held back, pretending nothing was wrong.'

He drew a breath, a man confessing to a sin. 'I should have dared Zack to shoot,' he said. 'I should have got her out whatever the consequences. I told you I stayed away because I didn't want to make things worse - as my father did. That was my crime too, you see. God knows we both paid dear for it.'

But that was after the bitter years.

I repeat, a long hard while was to pass before he told me this. Or before I saw him again to make my own confession. And to fill in those gaps which silence and grief had made incomprehensible.

So I never did speak to Alice. All those meetings I had anticipated with such loving concern, those moments of cherished intimacy evaporated without substance. Only in my nightmares did she ever approach me again. I dreamed of her every night, waking up drenched with sweat, my heart racing. I call them nightmares though they were not the sort where one struggles to speak through walls of glass or chases endlessly after disappearing figures lost in mist. She always appeared clearly, sometimes sitting in her May Queen chariot. I had to fight my way through the hawthorn to get at her. The cart sides were too high, the thorns made a barbed fence, the smell of wilting flowers reminded me of death. She stared above my head into a vast distance. And sometimes she came across those cliffs where so much of her story had taken place and stood by the stone stile, her white dress torn, her face wet with spray. Her brother waited behind her, his pickaxe strapped to his back, his tall figure enshrouded in his black coat like some medieval Reaper.

'I heard 'ee that night,' she used to say. She always said

the same thing, it never varied, although I tried in vain to think of new excuses in response. 'No use to deny it; I knew 'twere 'ee. Always were one to traipse behind; they warned me of 'ee.'

No word of reproach or blame, no 'Why?', just stating a fact and leaving it at that. 'Thought 'ee'd hear me shout,' she'd go on. 'Thought sure 'ee'd come forward then. 'Twould have scared 'un off for all his brave talk. Mr Cradock's not one to leave a friend, I thought, he's been so good to us. Or if for some reason 'ee'd already gone, I was sure 'ee'd tell John.'

And when I began to mouth words that wouldn't form, 'Couldn't tell 'un meself,' she'd continue. 'Wouldn't be fair to 'un. Bad enought as 'tis. I'd rather he knew naught than have that knowledge strangle him.'

'Didn't you trust him?' I strained with effort to understand. 'He loved . . . loves you; wasn't love enough to overcome even that?'

She smiled her enigmatic smile. 'There's only so much that loving can patch together,' she said. 'Nigel was right. 'Twas all meant, years ago, afore we was born, doomed afore we began. And as I forfeited love, so love abandoned me.'

She would walk away then, across those fields, away from me, away from Tregaran where she too belonged. And I would wake up to another day of guilt.

There remained one other to be heard from, and that was Tom. He was still up north in an army camp learning to be a soldier. Since news of what had happened to Alice couldn't be hushed up long, I presumed someone would write to him. Not Alice herself, she wouldn't have imposed her troubles on him. Not Zack, he'd be too proud. Tom sent a wire asking me to meet his train, so out of character I knew at once something of the kind must have happened.

He would never have received or sent a telegram in his life. I pictured him in some Yorkshire village struggling with the form while a postmistress he couldn't understand tried to help frame his thoughts. Sixpence for twelve little words, he'd have been horrified at the cost. They say handwriting reveals character. I remembered his from before: the open vowels, the looped 'p's and 'q's, the large consonants, penned like a child. By contrast how curt that wire seemed, how impersonal, the printed letters cold. They were like a hint of the change in him.

He gave date and place but not the time. I was tempted to ignore the request. The station he mentioned was a distant one, not the usual stop for Tregaran and I didn't relish sitting for hours on a draughty platform. Yet something compelled me on.

After what had happened I knew I was an idiot, doubly so, to involve myself again, perhaps be obliged to confess my guilt. But perhaps I had been living here too long and was caught by fate myself.

There weren't many motor cars on the roads in Cornwall in those days and I was sure mine was recognized, although the chauffeur left it round a corner, out of sight, and I sat in the back, trying to while time away, trying to calm my nerves.

The station was small, nestled in banks of rhododendron. The tubs of autumn flowers were done, their colours bleached by rain. More than a month had passed since that last fine night; we were in October now. While in France the autumn weather had bogged down lines of trenches into which soldiers dug like moles, here at Tregaran we were in the lull before the winter storms. Every morning blanketed us in fog; every night hoar frost coated the gardens. My own apprehension that day appeared part of a natural phenomenon.

When I saw Tom clambering off the train, at first I was glad I'd come to help. He moved like an old man, tunic carelessly unbuttoned, cap awry. His feet that once had moved like a cat's through the Tregaran woods clumped hopelessly out of step, the hobnailed boots striking sparks. He had no overcoat and shivered in the easterly wind; he had no luggage, no ticket, no money. He couldn't have eaten all day for the hour was late and he explained that he had climbed on the train just before it left, had hidden when the conductor approached, had ducked out of sight when he'd seen anyone in military uniform. I paid for his ticket myself, mollifying the station master with a tip. When I asked about his leave pass, 'Don't matter any road,' he said, wolfing down the sandwiches I offered him (for I had come prepared for a long wait). 'They'll put me in clink again, sure as sure.'

He gave a sour grin. 'Don't seem to please whatever I do,' he said. 'Don't seem to get forrard to that war, just spit and polish in the coldest, dampest place, damn me, I've ever knowed.'

He was striding up and down the platform now, eating as he went, making me run to keep up with him. I don't think he noticed how fast he went. He had taken off his cap and at every turn stopped to throw back his head as if taking in great draughts of air, as if where he'd been had stifled him. He had begun to seem more like his usual self but his next blunt question should have told me how much he'd changed.

'What's this about Alice then?' He accompanied it with a look that also should have warned. Suspicion was in that look, and contention. And a kind of smouldering rage, all foreign to his character.

'Got me a letter, see,' he persisted when I didn't answer. He pulled the cheap envelope out of his back pocket as if to show it, just as Alice had done, then hesitated for a moment and stuffed it back again. 'Written by a friend, some friend, not to sign her name, poking her old snout where she shouldn't. Told me Alice had fallen from a cliff. Or been pushed. Told me to get home to prevent worse.'

He shot me another look, so like his brother I almost commented on it. But if the good-natured giant who saw no ill in anyone had disappeared, the man who had wanted to protect his sister had not. Protection was still engrained in Tom like a second skin.

'And that's not all,' he went on, grimly censuring. 'Said she'd been attacked and made to look as if she'd slipped. Said it was the man she were with. Said she were wandering all night, out with someone as no maid should.'

He spun round on his heel. 'Said 'twere John Tregaran. Or you.'

Again the look. 'Got to know the rights of it afore I go back home. Don't know what to think meself, none of it makes sense.'

For a moment then he really sounded like his old self. He stood there, ticking his fingers off, trying to arrange the facts. 'Not John. John wouldn't have to fight for what she'd loving give. And not 'ee. 'Ee'd not have it in 'ee for one thing. And then there's what Em said, begging the mention. Not that I hold with filth but that bain't here nor there.'

He brooded for a moment, his habitual courtesy at odds with suspicion. 'All I do know,' he said at last, 'is the whole thing stinks or my name ain't Tom Tregarn.'

He suddenly took hold of my arm. We had reached the end of the platform where it dropped off into the bushes, a sharp steep drop covered with rocks down to the entrance of a tunnel. The rails glimmered thinly in the evening light, steel grey and hard. 'Got to get to the bottom of things,' he said. His grip tightened through the cloth, bruising the bone. 'They say we'm in this war for the women and children, poor Belgian folk done to death by the Boche. But who's to help our own? We'm the little men of this world, not much cop in the greater scale of things. We'm expendable, that's what they calls us, and that's the long and short of ut.'

He spoke as if recognizing a bitter truth. 'But no one does my Alice harm without paying a price. And God help whoever 'twas,' he added softly, 'even if 'twas some-one I held as friend.'

I can't reproduce the menace in that whisper. The dark green leaves, the glittering rails, the lonely arch of stone all seemed to reinforce the threat underlying his words. One false step, one push, and I'd have gone crashing down that slope into oblivion.

By now my cowardice must be well apparent. Certainly my hatred of violence was as inbred as it was intense. Thought of danger, discomfort of any kind, made me sick with apprehension. Yet in this instance I tell the truth when I say that it wasn't fear for myself that made me hesitate. 'She were in your house,' he was continuing, almost to himself. ''Twere up to you to keep her safe. I'm counting on 'ee see, to discover me who 'twas. That's why I asked 'ee to come. Of all the people I do know, you be the best trained; you know the law and its cunning tricks. All I know is it must have been someone she was familiar with, she'd not go off with anyone.'

I said at last, the words dragged out of me, 'It wasn't John, I vouch for that. He's as much in the dark as you. More, since Zack won't let him near the house.'

'He'll let me,' Tom said. 'But this time it bain't Zack that's got me worrit. 'Tis Alice. She'd rather die than talk.'

'Perhaps silence is better.' I tried to think of things to

177

say, all the while edging surreptitiously away from that perilous drop. 'Let things rest. Given time . . .'

'Time,' he scoffed with a smile, the smile sardonic. 'Time, 'ee says. Why, man, 'tis time we haven't got. Not if there's a child.'

And once again his bluntness took me off guard.

He was still watching me, holding me as if afraid to let me out of sight. 'That's summat 'ee didn't think of,' he said softly, 'what old bachelor would? But 'tis natural. That's living for 'ee, mister, not books and fancy talk. Now I do know 'tis spread abroad that 'ee doted on our Alice. The other girls teased her something fierce; Doreen, she what was parlour maid to 'ee, was always on about it even afore I left. I don't say there was wrong in ut, but you was party to things you oughten have been. So do 'ee speak up now, for I believe 'ee knows the truth.'

I said slowly, heavily, the words forced out of me, the confession as painful as the guilt itself, 'It's not how you think. And it's not what you want.'

'I'll be the judge of that,' he said.

So I told him what I'd seen.

Not all of it. Even in that moment of crisis some self-preservation kept a check on my tongue. And some of what happened I couldn't tell anyone, have never told, except here. Nigel's claim to her that night, I couldn't bear to repeat it. Nor could I speak of Alice's response. I certainly didn't reveal my presence; that was something unexplainable. But every word I uttered gave it away, as surely as if I had admitted it. And when I had finished, 'God be damned,' he cried, his face pale. He let go my arm, leaned back against the bushes. His shoulders shook. He might have been weeping. 'God be damned. For if what 'ee says be truth we all be cursed.'

He covered his face with his hands and stood motionless. Then slowly, his voice muffled, he said, 'And if what 'ee says be truth then God pardon 'ee for knowing.'

He straightened up and looked at me. 'God forgive 'ee, Paul Cradock,' he said, 'for what 'ee've seen, and what 'ee've done or not done.'

He shook off my restraining hand; he shook off my mumbled attempts at explanation; he vaulted over the station wall and went scrabbling through the rhododendron bushes, like a hunted animal, scattering a trail of broken twigs and leaves behind him. When I hurried out to the road there was no trace; he had disappeared into the countryside which he knew like his own self. The short autumn twilight was closing fast, darkness covered him. All I could do was go home and wait.

CHAPTER NINE

Tom spent that night sleeping rough. He didn't go straight to Tregaran House as I had half feared, nor did he go to Tregarn. Like the cunning poacher he'd been, he went to earth while he laid his trap. There were plenty of homes in the village where he could have asked for a bed but apparently he had lost faith in the villagers. In his poaching days he had what he would have called 'bolt holes', strategically placed hollows under trees or half-buried ditches where he could hide or take shelter in emergencies. Although now he was a fugitive in a larger sense, running from military law and having in mind a more desperate venture, these secret places were to serve him well. He even discovered an old change of clothes kept somewhere in a canvas bag, into which he stuffed his uniform. I learned all this, and his subsequent movements, long afterwards and how I did so will be told in time. I set things down now in order as they occurred, without comment. I don't say if I approved or, if had I been in his place, I would have done the same. I have less right than anyone to judge. All I do know is that like a steamroller Tom was hard to start, harder to stop. And the Tregarn temper was at last roused in him, flame hot.

And he learned fast. By first light he had walked across country to a neighbouring town where he wouldn't be known. From there he sent a second wire. It was addressed to Nigel Tregaran. Tom himself might be a forgotten private in his northern training camp, so much for the promises Nigel had made on his behalf; everyone knew where Captain Tregaran was and where his regiment was stationed. It was close to home, close enough for Nigel to return easily. By now Tom had seen enough of army efficiency to know there was a good chance his message would arrive before Captain Tregaran was posted abroad. It was terse, this message, short and direct, with a hint of menace. 'Your return is urgent.' He signed it, 'A friend'. He must have smiled his new sardonic smile as he printed those words. Let others learn how friendship threatened, let Nigel sweat.

Tom then turned his attention to his own needs. He bought food: rolls, potted meat, store jam, things he normally would have scorned had not prison and army fare made him less finicky for Alice's home cooking. Along the way he 'scrumped' apples from a well-known orchard, and after dark fished in the cliff pools as he used to do. That night he stayed in his brother's mine, close to the entrance so he could keep a lookout but far enough in to light a fire. Most of the time he sat staring out to sea. Just before dawn he climbed the cliffs and went along the path to where he could look down at his old home. The wind had drifted to the south, bringing rain, and he huddled under a hedge, a scarf thrown around his neck, thinking, remembering. Then, when a faint curl of smoke showed against the darker grey of sky, he retraced his steps back along the railway track.

There was a cutting halfway where he could overlook both the station and the road which, at this juncture, had to pass the railway line. If Nigel were to come at all he would certainly come without delay, and by either of these routes. And when, towards late afternoon, a Staff car jolted across the track in a spray of mud Tom felt excitement surge, similar to when a deer nosed towards him in the woods. After that, sure of his prey, he returned to his lookout point on the cliffs.

It was well after midnight when he approached Tregarn cove. By then he must have been cold and wet for the rain had continued all day long and, except for the apples, his food was gone. But only when he was sure all the windows were dark, not even a glimmer of firelight, had he come down off the cliffs and made towards the house. The wind had freshened into a gale. Although the tide was out great breakers were foaming over the rocks and running hard ashore almost to the edge of the beach. Their surge and retreat drowned all other sounds as he approached the gate and went up the garden path.

He had a special trick for getting in which he had often used in carefree days, around the back where the walls were part buried in the slate of the cliff, up a side creeper thick as his arm, headfirst through the pantry window whose clasp he lifted with his pocket knife. He swung over the sill, let himself down gently so as not to disturb anything.

Hams dangled from the rafters; there was a faint smell of milk mingled with sloe and elderberry, herb wines were fermenting in glass jars. He looked around him. In other times he would have paused to help himself from the plate of fresh-baked buns, would have gone, boots in hand, down the narrow passage with its oak panelling, crossed the uneven flagstones, stirred up the fire with more logs he himself had chopped. Now he didn't hesitate, went past the dresser with its pewter plates, up the crooked staircase, avoiding by instinct the board that creaked.

At the top he paused outside Alice's room. There was a niche in the wall in which she always kept flowers and, even on a night like this, he smelled their faint fragrance, the last of the season's growth, picked in the garden's sheltered spots where the salt wind hadn't torn them to bits. He listened. A few steps away was his own room, and beyond again, Zack's. Both doors were closed, no glimmer of light showed anywhere. He listened again, then lifted the latch and slid into Alice's room under the garret with its sloping roof so low he had to duck his head. He knew it in the dark as well as his own: the window a faint square set thick into the walls; the white blur of the bed; the little pinewood chest he had made for her when she was grown, the familiar scent of lavender. For a moment, then, the whole of what once had been came back to him, as vivid as it was beloved. He closed his eyes, feeling along the wall for support as happiness followed by pain swept over him in bewildering sequence.

Quiet as he was she must have heard him. A movement from the bed made him halt. Alice was sitting up, arms outstretched as he remembered her as a child. She must have been dreaming for she was smiling. 'You'm some late,' she cried, 'where've 'ee been at?'

Then reality returned. Her expression altered, the smile disappeared, she rubbed her eyes. 'I'm some glad you've comed,' she breathed. 'Oh, I did want 'ee to.'

In one stride he crossed the room, finger to his lips. 'Hush,' he said. But there was no sound except the wind in the chimney and the sea.

'Don't fret, my love,' he said. He took care not to come too close to the bed for fear of making it wet, and for a moment he too smiled. 'Nothing to worry 'ee, now I'm back.'

But when taking in, for the first time, the state he was in she began to ask how he'd got there, where was his uniform, why hadn't he let them know he was coming? 'No time for that,' he said. He took her hand between his own and, as he began to chafe it to bring some warmth, asked slowly, 'Is it true what I've been told?'

She didn't let go his hands, too proud to turn aside, but her cheeks were stained with pink where before they'd been white.

'And 'tis who I'm told 'tis, 'tis him?'

He didn't have to mention Nigel's name, she knew who he meant, and reluctantly she nodded. He pushed her hand away, leaned against the bedpost just as he had leaned against the bushes when he'd first heard the truth. Perhaps until he'd seen her he had still dared hope. Perhaps he had had just a glimmer of a thought that what he had planned need never be enacted.

And perhaps she guessed what he had in mind.

Frightened, she sat upright quickly, trying to put her thoughts in order. She'd had plenty of time to think them. Now they came tumbling out, all the pent-up thoughts she'd had to hide, only because she hoped to prevent a worse disaster. 'Listen to me, Tom, please understand. I don't blame 'un. I don't blame no one. It was only when they all said, when he said' (she meant Nigel, she never could bring herself to speak his name) 'when he swore John no longer cared, I felt lost. Half of me knew 'twas false, yet 'twas like the other half didn't. The other half always had known it couldn't work, 'twas too much to hope for. And without 'un I was in one of them moorland bogs, no way out, no way in, sunk deep for ever.

'And when he said' (again she meant Nigel), 'I were his fate I felt as if for the first time he made sense. 'Twas as if John and I were never meant to have what we both desired, as if we was destined always to be on the verge of it, never truly catch it hold. First he had to leave, then you did. The squire's death, the quarrel, even your return were all of the same pattern. That night I felt that all those centuries of hate rose up for one more chance, that I had become part of Zack's great disappointment, that happiness and hope had turned their backs.'

Tom said slowly, 'Then you don't care for him, the other one?'

'No, no, no.' She started up, shaking her head so violently that her thick plait thumped against the pillows. 'That don't change. 'Tis John, always was, always will be. I don't love no one else, nor no one else love me. The other were only playing with me. Love don't enter into ut.'

She took a breath. 'I think he were afraid, Tom,' she said. 'He had to go off fighting. Under that brave talk he were empty, like a pithless reed.'

Tom hadn't expected her to defend him. For a moment he was thrown off kilter.

She sat on the edge of the bed, twisting and turning the lace hem of the sheet between her hands. 'Afterwards, when he left,' she said, 'I stayed on. I didn't care what becomed of me. I'd of drowned meself perhaps if they hadn't found me. But 'twas too late.' She repeated the phrase slowly. ''Twill take another hundred years before 'tis finished with.'

She squared her shoulders. Under the cotton night-gown they were childish thin. 'I've got over that,' she said. 'If it were just myself I'd live it through here. Won't be the worse I've knowed. But there's Zack, and you, and John. 'Twouldn't be fair on all of you. Nor on the child.

'I've said naught about that neither to anyone,' she said. 'I waited until I were sure. But now 'tis so I needs must go away, as soon as possible.'

She turned to her brother then. 'I want 'ee some bad, Tom,' she said. 'Don't fail me. 'Tis hard enough as 'tis. I'm mortal afraid 'ee'll do something foolish.'

She caught his hand again. 'I can't fight Zack on me own,' she said. 'And killing wouldn't be no good; killing would just mean more deaths and 'tis the living that matters.'

There was stillness then in that little room, although outside the wind beat against the window-panes and the waves roared. Tom stood motionless. After a while she roused herself for one last effort. 'Their father said we'd all been interlocked for years,' she said. Her eyes were fierce with unshed tears. 'Years and years of hate, revenge, I don't know what. I felt a part of that, and so perhaps did he. That's what was between us, all them years. Killing won't spare the future that, 'twill only make it worse.'

She came up to him and, almost absently, he held her close as he used to do. He felt her body tight as wire with fear now, for him too. And gradually some sense returned to him. He looked at her, expressionless, his resolution struggling with his real self.

'I meant for to kill 'un,' he told her. 'That's what I'm come for. I had it in mind to shoot 'un down like a mad dog that mauls sheep, without mercy.'

She took a breath.

'But I see you'm right. Killing'll be no help.' He brooded again. 'So here's what we'll do instead.'

It was his turn to talk then, whispering, cajoling, explaining. Some quickness, not usual to him, seemed to have got into him, making him razor sharp. To every argument she had he brought out one of his own; to every denial its counterpart. He had an answer to each of her questions, even when she asked how he planned to arrange it. And what about John, and Zack? How would Zack not know?

'What's Zack supposed not to know?' Zack said.

He stood in the doorway, a candle in his hand. The wax had smouldered and dripped in the draught. He was fully dressed but from the state of his clothes and ruffled hair it was clear he had been lying down, perhaps had fallen asleep. When he set the candle on the chest they could

186

see he had his rifle with him; the barrel gleamed in the guttering light.

'Been waiting for 'ee, boy,' he said to his brother. 'Knew 'ee'd come. Couldn't keep 'ee away for long where Alice is concerned. Knew I'd get no sense from her until 'ee did.'

He took a step towards them, his face suddenly heavy with suspicion. 'Always were for whispering,' he said. 'Always after shutting me out. So what are my brother and sister plotting without my consent? What are they up to that I'm not to know? And what's the truth of all that's happened that she spill it out to you, blithe as a bird, and keep me in the dark?'

They didn't reply. Or rather Tom didn't. Alice got up, in one fluid motion wrapping a shawl about herself for warmth. Her feet were bare. All their lives her brothers were to remember her bare feet; long and slender they were, as were her hands, lady's feet, made for lady's work.

'My dear,' she said. There was a sweetness in her voice that took the hurt away, as if all his anger had become hers to bear. 'Don't pay us no mind. There's no call for 'ee to feel left out. The blame be mine, if blame there be. 'Ee warned me often enough to mind myself. But since my fall' (she meant him to take her literally, but she may have been thinking in metaphorical terms as well) 'since my fall from the cliffs I've had a change of heart. I've bided here with 'ee; no one could have been more kind. But we can't live like this, shut away for ever. I don't speak of John . . .' her voice trembled at the mention of his name but she went on '. . . I don't speak of anyone. But 'ee've let me go before, 'twas 'ee who suggested ut. Now let me leave as 'ee planned, far from here, where I'll be safe. All is blighted for me here, and that's a fact, no way round ut.

187

'I don't want to leave 'ee,' she said. Tears were rolling down her cheeks but she made no move to wipe them away. 'I don't want to leave 'ee here alone. But 'twill be better so, believe me 'twill. I beg fer 'ee to let me go.'

She made a move towards him but he barred the door. 'Not until I know the whole of ut,' he said.

He had set the gun down beside him, now he grasped it once more. 'The three of 'ee always thick as thieves,' he said. 'If you think 'tis John you'm running to, think again. You'll not marry John, there's another fact fer 'ee. Not over my dead body. Or his.'

''Tis not John I'll marry now,' she said. She bit her lip, hesitating, torn between telling him the truth.

Tom came up behind her, lifted Alice out of the way. 'This be between you and me, brother,' he said. 'I warned 'ee long ago she's not your life to live again. So let her pass. I'll see her well cared for when we leave, no charge on 'ee.'

'If you leave!' Zack's face had darkened again. 'If you leave!' He mimicked the word. 'You think leaving will cure all. 'Tis in here, girl, like a brand.'

He suddenly threw up his arm and thumped his chest. 'Branded for ever,' he said. 'No running from. And if you go, you don't come back. I shut the door behind as I've kept it locked afore. I . . .'

'Stop,' Tom said. His own voice had thickened, his eyes flashed. 'Take that back. No need to speak more wrong where wrong's come. She be gone beyond us, Zack. Let go, I beg of 'ee afore 'tis too late.'

'And if I don't?'

'Then,' said Tom softly as before, the second time he had made the threat, 'I make 'ee to.'

He lunged at his brother, aiming for his gun arm. In that small space there wasn't room to struggle, and Zack couldn't raise the gun to shoot. Both men went crashing against the pinewood chest, splintering it to bits. The curtain-rod fell off the wall, the plaster showered over their heads; Tom drove his fist in his brother's face.

They were of a size, equal height and weight; Zack was more than a match for the younger man. But Tom was fighting with a fury born of desperation. Never before had he hit with such intent. He forced his brother against the door, pinning him there in a wrestler's grip while trying to bring him to the floor.

The door was made of solid oak planks but the hinge was rotten. Suddenly it gave way in a splintering of rust and wood. It fell outwards into the passageway and the open stairs. Taken off balance both men went with it, rolling backwards down the steps, smashing the banisters, while, panic-stricken, Alice went scrambling after them. Tom fell heavily, landing on one arm, knocking his head on the bottom post so that for a moment he was dazed. But he fell on top. Pinned underneath him, on his back, Zack lay still. A trickle of blood began to creep from beneath his hair, his eyes closed, his colour gone.

Desperately Alice tried to reach him; Tom's heavy form impeded her, and she couldn't get him to move, no sense in him either as he nursed his arm, shaking his head so that the splatters from his own cut went swinging from side to side. Then his sister's screams seemed to rouse him. He rolled over heavily, feeling for Zack. For a moment there was silence, then, 'He'll be all right,' Tom said. 'Knocked 'un silly that be all. Stupid bugger, coming on like that.'

He picked himself up gingerly, limped to the sink and began to splash water on his face, while Alice remained on her knees trying to make Zack speak. 'Leave 'un be,' Tom said, not turning round. Deliberately he took up a towel and held it to his gash, then flexed his arm and shoulder carefully. 'He'm out cold.' He spoke through

189

the folds of the towel. 'A knock like that'll not hurt 'un. In younger days he were used to ut, best damn wrestler ever I did know from here to St Michael's Mount.'

He came and stood over his brother and sister, looking down at them. 'Saves us a lot of trouble then,' he said without expression. 'Answers the problem like. What he won't know won't harm none, and we'll be gone afore he's come to.'

Alice was still trying to bring Zack round, had dragged a cushion off a chair, was feeling for the cut under that shock of thick black hair. 'You'm mad,' she said. She sat back on her heels, her own hair loose. There were bloodstains on her nightgown, his blood or Zack's, it didn't matter. Her affection was shared equally between them both but the injured man had first claim. 'We can't leave 'un like this,' she cried. ''Twouldn't be human. And look at you, you'm in some state yerself. Just let me see to 'un and . . .'

Tom shrugged. 'Please yerself,' he said dispassionately, 'but to my mind 'tis the best thing that could've happened.'

He bent down and seized her arm. 'Listen, girl,' he said. The old Tom had disappeared, the new Tom spoke in that hard, almost callous, tone that was to become habitual. 'No time to waste, sitting yakking over what might or might not have been. I'll see to 'un; you pack yer things. And when 'tis light we'll leave. No point in lingering. There's work to be done.'

He pulled her up and pushed her towards the stairs. 'Hurry now,' he said. 'Or have you forgot what we'm in this fer?'

She opened her mouth as if to argue, closed it, wrapping her arms about herself protectively. His voice and expression must have given her pain. And yet, she knew he spoke sensibly. Slowly she started up the shattered stair, picking her way over the broken railing, all the while watching him as if he were a stranger as he moved swiftly about the room, finding rope to tie the unconscious man's arms, settling him comfortably before tying him, putting out food and water for themselves. What she must have felt in the wreckage of her room, what she grieved for, wept for, as she put her small possessions in a bag, what she must have thought, one brother lying hurt, the other focused on the completion of his plan to the exclusion of everything else, between them both no comfort to be found. Of all the misfortunes that had come crowding in upon her so unexpectedly, out of nothing, like a summer storm, perhaps this was the hardest, to leave her home and older brother in such a way. And yet Tom spoke the truth. As for John, although she still longed for him, of the three he was now the most lost to her.

When she came down the stairs again, dressed in black as if for a funeral (and so it was, the funeral of her hopes) she found all prepared. Zack had not regained consciousness but his colour had come back and he was breathing easier. Tom had seen to his injury, bandaged him with rough strips of cloth, had spread blankets over him to make him comfortable, done everything except give him liberty. 'When we'm away,' he said, 'I'll send word back. Jeb'll come to tend to 'un, no call to fret.'

But she lingered. 'It seems hard,' she said, 'to leave 'un tied like that as if he were some kind of calf. If we could only wait to speak to 'un.'

She cried out suddenly, 'His last words to me were a curse. I can't bear ut. We be cursed enough as 'tis.'

Tom took her arm. 'Enough of that,' he said roughly. 'We've got to look ahead, no turning back.'

Together they went out of the door, locked it, hid the key under the usual broken flower-pot. Arm in arm they went down the garden path, Tom shut the gate, they followed the familiar cliff path. The storm had blown itself out overnight, the sun was just coming out of the mist, bright red, a ball of fire in the sullen grey of the sky. *Red sun in the morning, sailors' warning.* Behind it lay great banked clouds, beneath it the sea was streaked with purple where the currents drifted; the grey surface heaved.

'Rain again afore night,' Tom said, 'but we'll be well away out of ut.'

They walked on, tension growing between them. All the old ease of comradeship was lost, it too had become a casualty. At the turning where she and John had met on the night of the poaching Tom turned aside to the village while she either sat beside the ditch, using her cloak against the wet, and looked at nothing, or walked up and down by the hedge where she and John had left their childish notes, how long ago it seemed when they had quarrelled about writing! 'I'm afraid we'll forget,' he'd said, 'afraid you won't wait.'

'Who else is there but 'ee?' she'd answered him. 'But 'tis not the waiting that bothers me. 'Tis all that past, all those four hundred years of hate that we've inherited . . .'

Tom returned within the half-hour. 'There, that be taken care of,' he said. In the sunlight he looked tired. The long gash across his forehead was red and raw and one eye would turn black. He seemed, not confident exactly, but as if he were caught up by a wave that rolled him inexorably towards some destined shore. 'Now for the last.'

He took her arm again, drew her on, his hand hard and unyielding. They walked on side by side. No one saw them pass, too early for the schoolchildren, too early for the women going to Truro market, if they still used this route. Sometimes Tom went ahead to hold back the briars; sometimes she had to reach up to unhook them from his coat; the wetness left by the rain showered over them, the

192

ground underfoot was treacherous with puddles they had to jump across. Once she had walked here like this with the man she loved; but she never mentioned it. That too was part of what she had lost.

When they came within sight of Tregaran House she did falter, as if she could not bring herself to look at it, as if the strength had gone from her limbs. But Tom, who all this while had been forcing the pace, refusing to let anything break his stride, Tom didn't stop. He settled her out of the wind beneath a hawthorn facing the sea, then crossed the open parkland and leapt the fence. She crept out to watch him, unable to stay alone, and saw how the fence was laced with raindrops and how the bushes were criss-crossed with spider-webs, thousands of them strung with drops of moisture like miniature lights. The mist was ankle-deep; it swirled around him as he walked, and when he passed two deer broke from the cover of the woods, the deer that he and John had wanted to stalk.

In the morning light the stone façade of the house glowed honey-smooth, and the open shutters and great sprawling terrace gave it a strange continental look which at the time she could not have appreciated. What its width and depth and weight did make her aware of was of all that power and prestige, all that wealth of which her son, had he been born from the man she loved, would have had part as his rightful inheritance but which now she never would claim on his behalf.

She watched Tom mount the steps, two at a time, saw him hammer on the door until it opened and he went inside. Then she drew back and let down her veil. The die was cast; now there could be no turning back.

Tom had hammered at the door until its very timbers shook. When the sleepy servant opened it, fumbling with the bolts in his haste, Tom pushed it wide and went in. He had never been inside the house before, at least not this part of it. His place had been through the service entrance to the kitchen where he had sometimes come with lobster or crab. The sight of that oak panelling, the gilded coat-of-arms, the portraits hanging in dim ranks did not intimidate him. They were as much a part of him as they were of the Tregarans. And when Nigel came halfway down the stairs, disturbed in his dressing by the noise – for the banging on the door, the startled servant's shouts had penetrated to the bedrooms – Tom was ready for him.

He pushed the man aside, pushed aside Em who had materialised from her housekeeper's room and was bearing down on him.

"'Tis 'ee I wants,' he said. He flung out an arm, the uninjured one, and pointed. 'And if 'ee knows what's good for 'ee, 'ee'll listen.'

'Or set the dogs on you.' Nigel held his ground. He was only partly dressed, braces dangling, shirt undone. A white towel was draped round his neck; he might have been in the middle of shaving. He looked pale; perhaps he too had had a sleepless night, but he was ready to bluff things out.

Tom laughed. 'No dog that lives harms me,' he said. 'But I bain't here to boast. What I want is something else, what's yourn to give and mine by rights to have. So turn these other buggers away so we can talk.'

He watched comprehension leap into Nigel's eyes. Then Nigel turned, ran back, to telephone the police perhaps, to put distance between him and Tom, to find some way to hold Tom off. Tom pushed past the servants, took the stairs at a bound. He had Nigel round the neck in a wrestler's hold before Nigel had gone a dozen feet. 'Turn the others away,' he hissed in his ear. 'We'm talking in private.'

Nigel tried to struggle, tried to shout for help, he

couldn't break that Cornish grip. 'And if I won't?' he was choking out.

'You'll regret it,' Tom said. 'I'll make 'ee.'

And that was the third time he used threat.

Only then, seeing that he meant what he said, did Nigel go limp. He let Tom gesture over the banisters. The servants reluctantly drew back out of earshot, whispering furiously among themselves, overcome with curiosity.

Nigel must have known what Tom meant, he must have guessed from the telegram, but he was still able to argue. 'What the devil do you want?' he croaked. He fingered his throat and swallowed painfully. 'I've given up the cliffs, isn't that enough?'

Tom laughed again. 'Bain't be mines or land I be atter,' he said, 'that be my brother's work. 'Tis my sister we be speaking of.'

He pointed once more. 'My sister, Alice, that you attacked, and ruined.'

'What's he talking about?' Behind her son, Evelyn Tregaran had come along the wide corridor. She must have been awakened by the noise for she was wearing a dressing-gown, a long silk creation edged with fur which swept the carpet with a faint rustle. And when Nigel, hearing her, tried to mutter it was nothing, he didn't know what Tom was here for so early in the morning, 'You fool,' Evelyn suddenly whispered, 'what have you been playing at?'

The whisper was proof, if proof were needed, that until now she had been ignorant of Nigel's actions, unless she were a greater actress than she seemed. She turned on her son. 'Fool,' she repeated, her anguish rising as if a knife were being twisted in a wound, 'you've never betrayed us with that sister of his.'

But she didn't lose her sense of urgency. She fumbled behind her for a door, opened one at random. 'In here,' she said. 'No need for all the world to hear what's got to be said.'

The room was small and dark, an unused bedroom whose windows had been closed too long so that the air seemed trapped inside. She stood close to the bed and looked at the two men in front of her. 'I'm willing to talk,' she said, taking charge. She spoke calmly again, in control, ignoring her son. 'If it's money you want I see no problem.'

She turned to Nigel then. 'Of course it's money,' she said. 'Don't stand there bleating, just offer him anything, pay him off.' And when Nigel tried to speak, 'The quickest way is best. Just ask how much.'

She looked defiantly at Tom. 'One hundred, two, three?' In those days that was a small fortune.

'I don't want Tregaran money, missus,' Tom said. He blocked the door with his wide shoulders. 'No money 'ee've got could buy my Alice.'

Gone was his simple air, his simple smile and speech. He matched her cunning with cunning. 'All I want is to be paid in kind. A marriage today, now, at once. Vicar Trevenn's expecting it. I arranged it with him. All 'ee've got to do is to confirm the time and place. And then separation until the baby comes.'

'Baby, whose baby?' Evelyn started to stutter. She turned once more on her son. 'What's he talking of?' she cried again. 'What's John done?'

'Not John,' said Tom, 'him.' And again he pointed at Nigel.

Nigel had begun to perspire, sweat running down his cheeks where the lather was scarcely dry. For a moment he resembled his father when he had been at his most truculent and he opened his mouth as if to deny the charge. But, at the withering look his mother gave him, he shut it fast. When finally he tried to speak, mouthing ignorance, excuses, blame, it was the faltering into silence at the end that condemned him. And when she said, 'So that's what you've been up to while you've been here, you stupid fool,' he flinched as if her insult pained him. Tom's accusations hit him hard but he was equally afraid of his mother's condemnation.

Her eyes narrowed. 'And if we challenge?' she asked, 'who's to prove the child is what it is? Whose word will be believed, a jailbird's, that wretched girl's? Or ours?'

'Don't challenge,' Nigel burst out then. His colour had changed, that fresh look he always had suddenly seemed peaked and white. He wiped the sweat out of his eyes with the towel and pushed back his hair nervously. 'Don't do anything. Think of the scandal . . .'

'Scandal!' She pounced on the word. 'You might have thought of that before you ruined us, scandal every way we look. But two can play the same game. They won't get away with it; we'll call their blackmail.'

'Call what you like,' said Tom. 'To my way of thinking it can't be blackmail, if there's a letter of proof. You'd not want your other son to swear in court he sent it to his brother here to arrange a meeting with him. You'd not want it known that your son altered and used it to trick Alice.'

I've said he had learned fast. Now he showed it.

'And you'd not want witnesses to prove what was done that night.'

He spoke more softly now. 'For there was a witness. So afore you think to besmirch that family name you'm so proud of, do 'ee consider the facts. An officer and gentleman'd find them hard to live with.'

Nigel was already pleading with his mother, catching hold of her arm, his handsome face caved in. He might have forgotten Tom was there to listen, he was so absorbed in his own fears. 'I'll be cashiered,' he said, 'they'll drum me out of the regiment.' He was almost blubbering. 'They'll send me overseas. I'll lose that HQ job. If this leaks out I'm done for, even Archie can't buy me off.'

Tom looked disgusted. 'As for 'ee, live with this thought,' he said. 'Bad enough to take yer brother's girl, but to lie and cheat to do ut, why, if I were 'ee I'd be ordering my pet vicar now to go forwards with that service quick, afore I takes the matter into me own hands. A simple service like, over and done within the hour, that's the best for all of us. And then we'll be off, out of yer lives as 'ee've always wanted.'

Evelyn sank down upon the bed. In that moment her face too crumpled, all her vivacity turned to stone. It was as if she had aged by years, gathering the folds of her gown across her breast as though picking at the shreds of ambition. She never said another word, sat with her black eyes unwinking, as if she were gone into some private hell where they could never follow.

Nigel straightened his back. 'Very well,' he said, his voice low. 'I have no choice. I accept. As long as we keep things quiet I'll do anything you say.' He gulped, wiped away the sweat once more. 'But you're wrong about one thing.'

He looked from his mother to Tom, almost defiantly. 'It wasn't all the way it sounds,' he said solemnly, 'it wasn't all for nothing. I did feel something for her, you know, and so did she for me.'

'Then 'ee'll be happy with this last point.' Tom ignored what Nigel said, the disdain in his voice more shaming than any actual words. 'No one is to know, ever. Least of all Zack. And John. You'll swear to that then, or I won't answer for the consequence.'

'I swear.' Nigel was still shaking. 'And I'm not to see Alice again? Or talk with her, nor tell my part?'

'No,' said Tom. 'That was her side of the bargain. So you see, missus,' he turned back to Evelyn, "'tain't no use to carry on, we'm all in this together, no one to win or lose, losers all. You have your son ready within the hour, and we'll be on the train right afterwards. And there'll be an end to ut.'

He opened the door and strode down the stairs under the haughty stares of those family portraits. So perhaps they had looked when the first Tregaran had stolen a Tregarn daughter. At the front door he paused. Evelyn remained collapsed on the bed but Nigel had followed him to the head of the stairs.

'And be damned to 'ee,' Tom said, 'to all of 'ee. Greed was what first fuelled your fire, and greed will kill 'ee. But 'tis the child I be thinking of. He'll have as fair a start in life as I can give 'un. Nothing from you or yours, mister, only that disgrace don't shadow 'un.'

What followed was done fast in strangely orderly succession. Evelyn must have been persuaded by her son to agree, while Nigel himself waited in a frenzy of anxiety, seeing ruin whichever way he looked. What arguments Nigel used, repetitious ones, disgrace, dishonourable discharge, scandal, eventually he must have convinced her to tell the vicar to proceed. And Vicar Trevenn in turn, sweating himself in impatience to hear from her, perplexed with wonderment since Tom's early morning visit had alerted him, the vicar obliged, even though the banns hadn't been read and the haste was unseemly.

Nigel met Alice and Tom within the time agreed, not wearing uniform now, soberly dressed, to match her black. The service was gabbled through, a truncated affair a few moments' long, the bridegroom muttering the words as if they stung him, the bride veiled like a widow. There was no ring, no exchange of congratulation, no one else present except Tom whose rounded letters followed

Alice's name in the registry book. But as Tom led her away Alice stopped and raised her veil, breaking her own one condition – that she not speak to the man who was now her formal husband.

'If it be so that we don't meet again,' she said, her voice had not lost its lilt but had a crystal ring to it like glass, 'I want fer 'ee to know I'll never speak good or bad of 'ee to our son, let 'ee be as dead to un. But since you said you wanted something to be remembered by, then think that of him. I'll let 'ee know when 'tis over with. Then 'ee be free to do as 'ee please; I have no further claim on 'ee. But whatever there be fer 'ee in years to come, know that we both have reaped what were sown without our wish.'

She readjusted her veil, walked on with Tom. They went towards the railway station speaking to no one else, boarded the train without a word, turning their backs on all the inquisitive looks, crossed the bridge that divides Cornwall from the rest of England, into exile.

Nigel left the same day, driving back as he had come, a broken man. What passed between him and his mother after the wedding defies imagination. I presume she must have forgiven him, her favourite son, but his treachery would have cut the deeper for that. And if, on leaving, he burst out, 'I could have loved her, I would have. I'll not have that damned brother of hers making more trouble, but you were wrong about her, Mother. I'll make peace with her one day,' that must have been a wound from which Evelyn never recovered.

Zack Tregarn regained consciousness to find his neighbours hanging over him. As he had promised, Tom had alerted them. The blow to his head would have killed a lesser man, it was a blow to his pride that changed Zack. But when he started up, remembering what had happened, Jeb Miller held him back as no other dared.

'Tis too late,' Jeb told him. 'So lie still and mend. They be gone, no coming back.'

For that is all the village ever knew, whatever whispers made their round, that Tom had come to take his sister out of gossip's reach, let Zack rage all he could.

Nor did John know. 'I confronted Zack at last,' he said in those days long after when distance and horror should have mitigated the pain, when time should have healed it, and hadn't. 'I demanded news of her but it was too late. He told me he didn't know where she was and from his look I believed him.'

He brooded, dragging up those memories which he had spent years trying to forget. 'They made no pretence where they went,' he said after a while. 'I followed them as far as I could. I forgot that laying false trails was one of Tom's tricks; he was good at it. At Paddington station I found the cabbie who had taken them to some small London street, then a blank. They vanished into the city's vastness as if they were at the bottom of the sea. I never went back to Tregaran House, certain of my mother's complicity, certain of her malice, unable to bear what I was sure was her pleasure at my loss. For the same reason I never sought out my brother, safe in his Staff Office job. By some roundabout way I heard Tom had gone back to serve his prison term in a military jail, was let out, was sent to France. It's easy to sink from sight in those damned trenches. And I went off to war myself – what else was left for me?

'I could have borne it all,' he said, unwittingly echoing her, 'if they had only shared it with me. I would have taken her, child and all, and been proud. What would that have mattered? It wasn't my pride this time that stopped me. I have never known a day's happiness, never a night free of nightmare, until I found her again.'

And that too was after the months and years of bitterness.

CHAPTER TEN

So that was how the break was made that both families had wanted. Those lives through which I myself had found life, into whose secrets I had crept, were blighted. And of those who remained behind the greatest change was seen in Zack, who overnight became an old man.

He made no attempt to follow Tom; he never mentioned Alice's name; he cut her off as he said he would. He let his mine go to wrack and ruin, although in fact it never was much more; he dragged Tom's boat high off the beach and left it to rot against the garden wall until wind and rain weathered the sleekness I had once admired. Its planks staved in, its deck covered with moss, it lay on its side like a skeleton, and children who used to roam freely through the cove came to fear and avoid it. They avoided Zack too, spoke of him as some ogre who watched them suspiciously, gun in hand, ready to chase them if they came too close.

Thus he lived for several years, eking out an existence, gypsy style, taking Tom's place as poacher. He never joined up, was fined for loitering in Tregaran woods which he made his playground. Twice he was arrested for theft – his disregard of both fine and arrest showed his scorn of the ruling class upon whom he laid blame for his family's disgrace (still without knowledge of the true facts).

Evelyn Tregaran didn't tell him the truth. Nor did she

tell John, fearful of his reaction, torn between wanting him to suffer and not wanting him to profit. While both her sons were abroad, John in the trenches, Nigel behind the lines, she was left to bear this thought alone: that if the marriage itself was anathema, worse was the reason for it.

Divorce or annulment would not change it, even if either had been possible. Both would mean acknowledging a wedding had taken place; both would mean publicity, talk. And after Nigel's parting message she must have doubted in any case if he would agree. For supposing if, through some miracle, the marriage could be dissolved, and Nigel could be saved, and supposing she could find some sure way to lay the blame on Tom and his sister, the reason still remained – the child.

Reason and consequence, they merged as one and drove her mad. She could not accept that Alice's child was her son's heir, that a Tregarn bastard (so she thought of it) could inherit all of Tregaran; whatever disgrace she feared, this surely was the most hard. So until the child was born – and died (illegitimate babies often died at birth, perhaps for once Alice would oblige) – she too withdrew into her shell, living alone with Em, using only one wing of the house, seldom venturing out and never meeting anyone. Gradually the other servants left, driven away by her temper fits caused by her drinking. Her hold on local affairs waned, the little court over which she'd queened so long sank into oblivion – Evelyn Tregaran too changed; grew older, embittered, as she saw her life's ambitions come crashing into ruin.

Mathew Trevenn, her religious accomplice (as he guiltily thought of himself), also kept quiet. He blamed the war, finding precedence in the many hasty marriages of the time. But these other marriages, although made in haste, were still acceptable, were not underhand or furtive, or *wrong*, as he felt this one to be.

How often the poor man must have sat fingering the ill-omened marriage lines which, out of some cautious foresight, he had had the sense to register on a blank page. How often he must have longed to confide in his superiors to lessen the burden of responsibility. The reason for his complicity was common sense. In those days church advancement still depended upon local patronage, and he had no desire to offend his benefactress. So he salved his conscience with fasting and prayer, hoping that everything was 'proper', wishing, if truth be told, he'd never set eyes on Tregarans or Tregarns to be enmeshed in their quarrels.

As for the village disinterest, it was largely due to the war. By then the casualty lists had had their numbing effect, those lists which like a medieval plague were to decimate whole communities. Names like the Marne and Ypres had begun to creep into the news, had begun to dominate people's thoughts. As now the great armies of the world fought each other to a standstill, what did village gossip matter? Alice and Tom sank from sight like stones thrown into a pond, and were forgotten.

How I came to know all these things will later be made clear. As I have said, I merely record them in order as they occurred. At the time I sought consolation elsewhere, returning more and more often to city life where I too could sink into oblivion. I rented a flat close to my former home (which acquaintances delighted in telling me I should never have left). I shut up the house in Cornwall, seldom went back, spent my days in 'war work' such as was possible for a man of my age.

Perhaps that was the one good result of my Cornish experience. Too old to fight, hating violence more than ever, with a free conscience now I felt I could offer legal advice to conscientious objectors. I got myself elected to various committees where my professional expertise was useful in anti-war work. And until the public veered round to my point of view I turned my attention to more practical things, such as supplying soldiers in the trenches with comforts they lacked and helping the wounded and shell-shocked who daily began to arrive in ever more horrifying numbers. The man I once had been would have been incapable of that.

I mention all this because it was in this way I first heard news of John. Or rather, Hodges did. Hodges had stuck with me through thick and thin although his devotion had been sorely tried in these last months, especially when he felt Alice had been 'put in charge' (although as I have explained, she had undertaken the task with such tact and grace that he scarcely had room for quarrel). My return to London, 'where I belonged', was a saving grace for Hodges. No one could have been happier than him to see the last of Tregaran, where he felt I had made a fool of myself. Now, despite his original scepticism, or perhaps because of mine, Hodges had become an ardent patriot who daily scanned the papers for news and kept maps in his room of the Army's advance and retreat.

He came into my bedroom one spring day (we are speaking now of April 1915, the start of the second battle of Ypres), overbrimming with excitement, too elated to observe formalities.

A Tregaran, Private John, had been mentioned in dispatches. 'Conspicuous bravery under fire,' he read, 'cool judgement and disregard of personal safety, rescue of men trapped by gas' (one of the first formal acknowledgements that poisonous gases had been used).

He continued to read aloud with obvious relish, not waiting for my permission: how John Tregaran had crossed the wire into no-man's-land, in full daylight, and risking death had dragged back wounded men from the shell-holes where they had been trapped.

'Must be our Master John,' he said at the end. He folded the paper back into its original crease and laid it on the breakfast tray. 'With that name can't be anyone else. Pity about the rank though. And the company. He should be with his brother in his father's regiment.' A piece of social prejudice I also ignored, proof that no matter what else had changed, Hodges' social values remained intact.

When he had left the room I seized the paper and read the report for myself. Beneath the impersonal official tone I heard John's laugh. *Over the top, through the wire and at 'em.* I thought, God bless you, boy, but this is no laughing matter, this is life and death, and next time you may not be so fortunate.

The second mention followed in the autumn, a decoration this, one of the new Military Crosses, while that dreadful year ground to a halt, both sides inching back and forth over the same small stretch of land. A Lieutenant John Tregaran (he must have been promoted in the field) had personally stormed an enemy redoubt and silenced a machine gun, again without injury to himself, as if he lived a charmed life. And again I couldn't reconcile the John I knew with these daredevil heroics. The John I knew hated violence, had turned his back on the Army, had sworn never to be a soldier. I remembered that in an attack a man's life expectancy was measured in minutes, and it seemed to me he was tempting fate, as if he were trying to prove something.

The third time he was not so lucky.

By the following summer he had been promoted again, to captain, not unusual in a war where young officers were expendable, their survival rate counted in days, not weeks. It was Hodges again who heard of him. Following my example, on his days off he had taken to visiting the soldiers in the hospital wards and had been on hand to welcome the first contingents from a new battle front whose name was to become engrained in our memories.

This battle of the Somme was to see an end to war enchantment. A total of 19,000 men killed in one day, 57,000 wounded, those figures were not for general consumption, were kept secret – perhaps just as well, the mind could not take in the magnitude. We at home were hard put to comprehend the little evidence of war that we actually saw in our daily lives.

Among the wounded who arrived that July day was a Captain John Tregaran.

'Gravely injured, sir.' Hodges stood at attention, hat in hand, like an old warhorse himself. 'Twice led out his men. Love him they do, and that's rare, think of him as one of themselves. Call him "Wild Tregaran", wild as a flicking tick. Say he's one of them, no bleeding stuck-up gent.'

He coughed delicately to cover expressions which he would never have dared use before the war. 'Say he once commandeered a horse, rode it up between the lines, port glass in hand, preparing a cavalry charge. The French girls love him, round him like wasps around jam.'

I couldn't reconcile this description, either, with the John I knew but when, after a few discreet inquiries of my own, there seemed no doubt, I went to the hospital to see him for myself.

The hospital was not far from Kensington (where I had set up residence a few streets away from my original house): a large private mansion which had been commandeered for army use. It was a place I used to know well, had often visited on gala occasions. It was strange to see the front steps, up and down which debutantes had floated, lined now with pale-faced men sitting about in dressing-gowns, tattered pieces of uniform draped about their shoulders. The chestnut trees in the garden were in full leaf, the day was warm, nurses in blue and white were bending over wheelchairs, were helping men to hobble about, were escorting the blind, the lame, the maimed across the grass in its summer green. I had come by taxi and for a while, immobilized by what I saw, I just sat there, looking. Then I paid the fare, and went inside.

I didn't recognize the house either. The furniture was gone, of course, as were the paintings for which it had been famed. The curved staircase remained, but the ballroom and reception halls, the great sitting rooms, had been turned into wards, behind whose closed doors came sudden bursts of coughing, moans, an occasional sharp short cry, like the cry of a bittern. It reminded me strangely of those boyish expeditions through the fens when I had first learned to hate hunting.

A sister passed me, eyed me with suspicion, turned back and pointed out that I was in the way. Pulling myself out of the past I asked for Captain John Tregaran. Immediately her expression softened. She indicated one of the doors. 'He never complains,' she said. 'He's getting on very well but he needs cheering up. You're his father, I suppose. You must be proud of him.'

I didn't enlighten her but when she had motioned me inside his room I stood for a moment afraid to move, afraid of what I'd see. And I thought suddenly, passionately, I wish I *were* his father, I wish he had some claim on me.

There was a line of cubicles like a school dormitory, and a line of figures like schoolboys ready for night inspection. Only the garlands of flowers and fruit that still decorated the ceiling suggested that this room had once had another use. In the bed closest to the window John was lying as if asleep. His face had a startling resemblance to Zack's, something I had never noticed

209

before, some distant kinship that suffering had revealed. The dark hair made an even greater contrast against the white of the pillows, his face seemed sharper, thinner than ever. I thought, thank God he'll be all right, and then, but how old he looks.

He must have heard me for he moved restlessly and opened his eyes. I had forgotten how dark they were. Perhaps he had been dreaming and, like Alice, didn't remember what had happened or where he was. 'Ah, there you are,' he said, 'I've been expecting you.'

Then he seemed to come to himself, a shuttered look passed over his face, he shut his eyes again as if even the effort of speaking was too much.

I took a hesitant step backwards thinking I had made a mistake in coming at all, he'd not want to see me, I'd bring back too much of the past, but he said slowly, so softly I had to bend to catch it, 'Don't go. Just sit a while.'

So I sat beside the bed keeping him company as he'd asked, until after a time, when he really was asleep, I went away again.

After that I went to see him every day. Except for that first time he never spoke to me, except to mumble thanks for the gifts I brought, the flowers and fruit that he never looked at or ate. I felt that although he was there in person, he was not there at all. In some strange way he reminded me of Alice the first time I had seen her, at the May Day feast. He only roused himself when one of the men from his company would poke his head in the door 'to chat', and then he didn't say much, let the other do the talking. He had an easy way with him though, I noticed that at once, no stiff and starchy officer-and-men exchange that was the norm for those days, and the talk, what there was of it, always centred on the 'good old times', the 'do you remember behind the front?' sort of thing. Nothing about the attack itself in which so many of their comrades had been mown down, nothing about the dead and missing. Until one day a rosy-faced boy came in.

He had a country accent I couldn't place and a cheeky grin. It struck me with extraordinary force that although I thought of him as a boy, he couldn't be much younger than John. John must have lied about his age when he joined up. Yet, as his superior officer, John now made an effort to talk with this lad, suggesting things he should take back to France to make trench life more bearable, tactfully offering to pay for them himself. 'See you in a few weeks then,' he said. 'Give the Boche my regards. Tell him I'm coming back.'

They both laughed. When the boy had gone, 'There's a good country chap,' John said. 'His father is a Dorset hedger; between them there's nothing they don't know about earth, about digging, planting, reaping. But not mud like we've been in, mud so deep you can't walk in it, mud so thick it drowns you. Mud that comes from rotten earth that buries you alive.'

I held my breath. It was the first time I had heard him speak about the war or his experiences. I thought, perhaps now he's broken his silence he'll speak again. But against that hope came the realization that he was getting well enough to think of returning. A sense of despair settled over me, all that waste that nothing seemed to stop.

Yet there was one thing I could do for him. All through those long summer afternoons when the sun shone dimly through the speckled glass, and outside the London world churned its accustomed round, I kept the thought to myself. But when one day I found him in the garden under the chestnut trees I knew the time was right.

He was sitting on a bench, his injured leg propped up, his head thrown back rather as Tom had done on the station platform, as if after all those disinfectant smells the scent of trees and grass was as heady as wine. For the first time since I had been coming to see him he smiled at me.

'Only a few more days,' he said, 'and I'll be off. I'm grateful to you, Paul. But I'll be glad to be gone from here.'

He stared over my head at the sky, the robin egg blue of an English summer. 'Hard to believe this is real,' he said. 'Harder still to realize it's part of a city. I sometimes wonder what Tregaran's like these days.'

For a moment a melancholy expression passed over his face, an underlying sadness that I remembered from the past. He said, 'I'm going back to a village where the grass is black, where the trees are leafless stumps, where the ground's so pitted it will take twenty years to plough in it.

'When we weren't in the trenches,' he went on, 'I was billeted on a farm. Before the war it must have been a nice little place, just the size I'd have liked, good grazing along the river meadows, good ploughland above. Now the buildings are in ruins. The farmer's dead, there isn't an animal left for miles: no sheep, no cows, no horses, no birds. Only rats. And lice.'

He laughed without mirth. 'We used to sit up of nights,' he said, 'stark naked, inspecting our clothes by candlelight. You could hear the blasted creatures crack when you caught them with your nails.'

He said harshly, 'Thirty seconds, that's all it took to scythe us down, rows of us, like cutting corn. Have you seen men fall like wheat? Don't know how I survived. Some damn Cornish cussedness, I suppose. By rights I should be dead along with the rest, coughing out my lungs in those shell-holes.

'I've lived through things that killed most men,' he said. 'But do you know, it didn't matter. I meant to die, that's why fate kept me alive. What was there to live for?'

212

That's when I told him, 'I know where Alice is.'

I have said I did not speak to Alice again, but I had had news of her. I didn't tell John all I knew that first day, I spread it over several visits. But I did tell him that Tom had written me, after he and Alice left.

The letter came from that army prison where Tom had served time for absence without leave. Someone else had composed the letter, it wasn't his style of handwriting. (In fact as I found out later, a prison chaplain had written it, incidentally using it to help Tom get a pardon on compassionate grounds.) Despite all that had happened, Tom trusted me in this at least. He wanted me to sell his effects, all those things mentioned in his 'will', to ensure that his sister, 'Miss Alice Tregarn', should have benefit of them. I was to act as his legal representative, and, without consulting Zack, was to set up a fund for Alice and her 'unborn child'.

It didn't take long. I sorted out the affairs of each, and since Zack was not to know, separated what belonged to Tom outright from what was shared with his brother. The final sum was small, smaller than Tom had hoped. Without his knowledge I added to it from my own funds, arranging to have a cheque sent once a month to a Post Office address in the north of London.

I knew the address as well as my own. I could have gone there anytime, waited for her, followed her home. That I never had was part of my penance. But I could tell John.

He heard me out in silence. But when I began to fill in the blanks, carefully, not to alarm him, that was when he cried, 'Why didn't she tell me?' as if her silence was a weight, as if what he said now was part of conversations that should have been held all those years ago.

'I should never have left her.' 'I never meant anger to

last.' 'She couldn't have believed that I'd forgotten her, as soon forget myself.'

The explanations, excuses, the misunderstandings poured out. 'I should have broken down the door, that's what Zack would have done. I could have taken on the whole German army; I'd still be a Tregaran weakling.'

He was leaning against the park bench, tears rolling down his cheeks; everyone had turned round to stare at him. A nurse came hurrying. 'I could have borne it all,' he cried, his face thin and shieldless, all the pain that had been bottled up spilling out. 'I would have taken her, child and all. What would that have mattered? But they set us up proper, didn't they? Friend and foe alike. If not their cannon then our own, if not their gas then ours. Turn and turn about as the wind blows – like a coconut shy, see who can knock the dummies off their perch.'

But that was after the bitter years.

That night he ran a fever, was in danger of a relapse. The sister who was in charge looked at me reproachfully as if it were my fault. And perhaps it was. But after that first day he couldn't let me alone. Barely had I stepped inside his room when he would be plying me with questions, trying to get information out of me, all I had learned from Tom's letters, all I had gleaned from that prison chaplain (for in his anxiety Tom had had to confide in someone).

Some pieces of course I still didn't know – Evelyn's feelings, Zack's ignorance, poor Mathew Trevenn's misgivings – these were things to be filled in later still, in another way, which will also be reported in due course. But what had happened to Alice, the marriage, the birth of the child (for by now the child would have been born and lived), that I could and did tell him. And Nigel's part. And mine.

He heard me out, that shuttered look predominant. When I had finished I sat drained. Then slowly I got up to leave. It seemed to me he needed time to be alone, and I wasn't the one to give him comfort. I almost expected him to tell me never to return. Or perhaps he'd not even speak, just turn aside as Tom had done, with loathing. I wouldn't have blamed him. He would only be hating me as once I had hated, as now I hated myself.

'Don't go,' he said. He was sitting in a window seat in a private room, for since his wound had opened up again he had been moved out of the general ward. He was weak, and when he spoke his voice had a distant sound as if he spoke through lint or gauze. 'Don't go. I'm as much to blame. I should never have left her,' he said. 'Nigel was right at that, I was a fool. I knew she needed me and I failed her. As much as you did.'

He said, 'I've always been jealous of Nigel. When we were boys my father used to say I'd never make a soldier like Nigel would. Sometimes I think I didn't resist being sent away that first time as I should have, simply because I half hoped I might prove him wrong. But in my heart I knew Father never said things to hurt, it was my mother and Nigel that I wanted to prove myself to.

'It all came back when I went to France. Perhaps that's what made me do the things I did, just to spite them. And it wasn't only in soldiering. I wanted to outdo Nigel in everything. My father used to say Nigel had the Tregarn charm. I chased women, too, just to show off. For every woman he's had I've matched him.'

He said, 'Nigel's stayed snug and safe behind the lines, there never was competition. So why did he have to spoil the only woman I ever cared for?'

I said, 'John, listen. I don't often offer advice. In fact outside my profession I never have, except perhaps to you. And I've never talked of my own life to anyone. I was a second son, in a family where my mother wanted a girl. Her disappointment was so strong she kept me in dresses and tied my long hair in ringlets. They used to dress boys like that in those days, but not after they were six! She kept photographs where I looked like a china doll, until I tore them up.

'Either because of that, or because I was by nature gentle, if I may use that word, I couldn't stand up to my brother. He was older, stronger; my childhood was a nightmare of miserable failures. The only thing I was good at was studying, and I threw myself into that. It was something he couldn't equal me at, although he could make fun of it.

'While I was an undergraduate at Cambridge I met a girl, and against all probability we fell in love. We were to marry when I had my degree. How calm and placid those days seem, almost half a century ago, long days on the river, Sunday evenings at church, readings by the fire. I thought a lifetime stretched before us, until my brother appeared on the scene.

'I don't think now he set out to seduce her. I used to. I don't think now she went to him easily. Once I condemned her. I saw myself how it happened, I even understood it. He had everything to attract a woman that I didn't have. Her interest in me waned as his in her increased. I saw betrayal in her eyes, her walk, her smile, but I couldn't stop it any more than she could. And my brother never tried. Things came so easily to him, he wasn't used to restraint. The day they were engaged I left England, vowing I'd not return.

'They never married. I don't know what happened. Perhaps she saw through him, perhaps he tired of her, I couldn't bring myself to ask. When I did come back she was dead and he too had gone abroad. I threw myself into my work, making up for lost time; the law became my life. I never looked at another woman, too afraid to risk loving again. Until I saw Alice.

'Then it wasn't only me you liked,' John said. 'I sometimes wondered. And Mother used to say such awful
things ...'

I looked at him squarely. 'A man who is lonely,' I said,
'may try many ways to find affection. In the East it's not
looked on with such horror as it is here. But that was
not my style; I just was not interested. After love died,
nothing had flavour or taste for me. But even work can't
always keep loneliness at bay. In Alice I suppose I saw a
second chance.'

Again I looked at him squarely. 'It came too late for
me,' I said. 'But not for you.'

The windows were open. A bee droned on the dirty
pane. Outside in the garden a man laughed. 'It doesn't
matter,' I said. 'Whatever happened, it doesn't matter
against that greater thing. Don't waste the moment. It
may never come back again.'

CHAPTER ELEVEN

It took him time to assimilate all of this, but the seed had been planted. In the meanwhile we talked, more freely than I ever had in my life. Things I told him aren't important, thank God he had a forgiving nature; hadn't I seen that before? Things he told me I won't repeat, the wildness, the women, that was an aberration he had to get rid of through talk.

There was one girl, a street girl I think, whom he did mention. He had liked her mainly because she had seemed to like him. He wanted her to be taken care of, 'if anything happened to him'. He couldn't yet speak openly of Alice, except in the past. The future overwhelmed him. And the present seemed suspended, all contained in that little hospital room where, perhaps like his father in his study, he dreamed of some mighty effort and yet couldn't wind up his strength or courage to attempt it.

When he was ready I would be ready for him.

After his medical discharge I took him home to my London flat. He kept silent about the war but I knew that in a few weeks he would have to go back to the front, that, unlike his older brother, he would return to all those hell holes underground, those mazes of ditches and trenches which made Zack's mine look like a plaything. But what would be his purpose when he got there, to die or to live? I had undermined his former purpose to 'get killed' as he'd expressed it. What had I given him to live for instead?

They say that it doesn't matter what a man uses to make himself go on living when hope is dead: work, new hope, even death itself. John had reached that point. But the new hope that I had offered him was like a birthing, it was hard in coming forth.

One day, cunning as a weasel, I ordered the car brought round. It was late October, a cool crisp day with the country scent of leaves and bonfires pervading even the heart of the city. The news from France was still grave – if stagnation, the same old tactics, the same round of advance and retreat are news. I had us driven through the London streets in a circuitous route, our destination a little backwater of a place, north of Islington.

It wasn't a region of London I knew at all, with its narrow rows of houses, many of which were slums. We drew up in front of an open place, or crossing, where several major roads seemed to meet. It was a weekday, the streets were busy, the shops were open and doing a thriving business; stalls spilled what fruit and vegetables they had over the pavements, not a great variety, the war at sea had cut down on food supplies and this wasn't a fashionable part of London. This was where ordinary people scraped for a living, this was how most of England existed. Once, to my eyes, the area might have seemed mean and dirty, not any more, and it certainly wouldn't to John. And it was alive. All the vim and grit of the ordinary 'Tommy' was there in those streets.

From the rolled-down car window John watched with little interest. I didn't say anything. We were parked outside a post office where people came and went, the sort of small post office that sells other things besides stamps: food, newspapers, tobacco. He watched, I waited. And then he realized.

219

'This is it, isn't it?' he said. 'This is where she comes to collect that cheque.'

He sat forward, intent, all senses taut. 'And she's living somewhere near here, in this place?' He didn't say anything else, he didn't have to, the contrast with Cornwall couldn't have been more absolute. 'Do you know . . . ?'

The question trailed off. 'Not the exact address,' I said. 'But it can't be far, within walking distance.' I indicated that jumble of streets with their false country names like 'Lime Grove', 'Beech Avenue', 'Oak Lane', names that a few years ago hadn't been false, names which were all that were left of old England, buried beneath the twentieth-century grime. 'It could be found.'

'And when . . . ?'

I understood him. 'Tomorrow,' I said. 'She, or perhaps someone for her, I don't know which. But it's due tomorrow.'

'And then not for another month?'

That was the thought that stayed with him as we drove home. During the night I heard him pacing with his limping stride, up and down, up and down, in the guest room. In my own way my thoughts kept time with his. It was now or never. Next month, next week, he might not be here. But would she want to see him? Did he want to see her? He had said he had wanted to no matter what had happened, and that was probably still the truth. But there were two difficulties he had never addressed, never mentioned since. And one of them was the child.

As for Evelyn, so for him, the child would be the obstacle.

I knew it had been born alive and well, so much for Evelyn's hopes, but not its sex, or anything about it, what it weighed, what it looked like, the sort of things new mothers love to tell. Did it resemble its father? If it did, would that turn John off? Would he be turned off anyhow? And was it fair to the child to have to share its mother with a man who couldn't care for it?

What sketchy information I had, had been gathered from Tom, one of whose letters had once obliquely referred to Alice's new-born child. True to her word, Alice must also have informed Nigel but she told no one else. Zack didn't know, of course; if Evelyn did, Nigel would have been her source.

What do an old bachelor like 'ee know about such things.

I guessed that John had put the problem of Alice's child to one side. It was too hard to deal with. First things first. The first thing was to see Alice again.

The next morning, early, he asked me to drive him back.

Having made up his mind he didn't hesitate, plunged right in. How would we keep watch without frightening her away? Suppose she sent a friend, how would we know if someone other than she came? (He used the word 'we' deliberately, to make me feel involved.) Suppose she didn't come at all but waited for another day? Suppose . . . I quieted his anxiety as we drove along.

The envelope was distinctive, both in colour and shape; perhaps I had chosen it with this thought in mind. It would be easy to pick out if anyone but she collected it – provided there was someone else on hand to watch. My guess was that she came herself. That cheque was her lifeline. I doubted if she would entrust it to another, who would she know to trust? As for not coming, she had only this money to live on, and the cheque was always cashed at once. No, I didn't know if Nigel had offered her money too. If he had, she wouldn't have taken it. And no, Nigel wouldn't know where she lived, John could rest assured on that. Only Tom knew. Tom and I, and now he himself.

The post office wasn't yet open. We got out of the car

and made our plans. We must have been conspicuous, an elderly gentleman conservatively dressed in a style of thirty years before, tall but bent, with a narrow secretive face, and a young officer, his uniform worn and faded, sign of active service, the limp, the pallor, telling a familiar story, as well known here as in the West End.

He couldn't stand long so I left him by the car, in one of the side cul-de-sacs, out of sight of the main road. I had several reasons for doing this. It would be unlikely she would pass that way, and when she came I wanted to shield them both from the first shock. Besides, I was the one who knew the envelope. And although I didn't say so, I was good at keeping watch! If I also wanted to have one moment of recognition for myself, without hindrance or restriction, he and I understood each other too well by now to have to explain. So I went alone into the post office as if intending to make a purchase.

I must have looked suspicious, my pockets stuffed with groceries, dodging between the crates, pretending to be looking for nonexistent items, stopping to read the notices. The shop section was small and cramped but it had its noticeboard, this type of shop always does: of rooms to rent, of second-hand furniture, of job descriptions by carpenters or painters, all those services people around here couldn't afford and yet made their living from. I read the dirty scraps of paper several times over. The morning stretched away endlessly, every minute seemed an hour. In reality it wasn't long, less than half that time before she came.

Even with my back turned I knew the moment she entered the shop. Her step was as light as that day when she had run from her house down the garden path; I felt the same shock of recognition, the same strange light-headedness as when I had followed her blindly across the sand flats. Her voice hadn't changed either. In that cockney world its lilt was like music; I almost felt the flowers, could smell and hear the sea.

I kept out of her line of vision, behind a magazine stand, could only see part of a skirt, a small hat, her outstretched fingers. She didn't wear a wedding ring, her hair was braided up, the skirt was grey, she stood a hand's touch off. When she turned and left again I went after her, drawn like a magnet.

I didn't accost her, didn't take her arm, didn't speak. That was part of the unspoken agreement I had with John. Instead I hurried to where I had left him, and pointed. The apples and sugar spilled from my overcoat pockets, the newspapers were scattered on the ground. Like a greyhound he was after her, his limping stride quickening as he saw her in the crowd.

It must have pained him but I don't think he noticed. Neither did he notice the way he pushed people aside, nor the stares and shouts that followed. 'Alice,' he was crying, 'Alice, wait for me.'

She turned. She did.

And for the second time in my life I was shut out of Paradise.

When a thing is meant, when it happens spontaneously, the world dwindles into that one moment, nothing else counts. Just as it should be. From a discreet distance I watched, this time not able to listen in, not wanting to. I saw the crowds part, grumbling, laughing, not even noticing, intent on their own affairs. I saw her run towards him, stop, sway as if she would fall. I saw his effort to reach her, his hand clutch her arm, as if she were his salvation.

I don't know what they said to each other, perhaps they didn't say anything, perhaps there was no need. Over two years had passed since that summer of 1914 when John had come back to Cornwall to marry her and their lives had been shattered. None of that mattered.

There was one thing that was changed though, that they couldn't ignore. I had spotted him almost as soon as I had Alice, the little fellow she'd carried in her arms in the Post Office. Now she had put him down so he was clinging to her skirts. I would have known him without his mother – he had her eyes; and his face, colouring, even his expression, marked him as a Tregarn. He had taken one look at this tall stranger who was holding his mother, who was making her cry and then laugh, and then cry again, and he hadn't liked what he saw. He was too little for speech I imagine, too little for walking, but he had style. He wrapped his legs around the man and was hanging on for dear life while he batted away with the other hand. I couldn't help smiling. I remembered what the young John had been like. 'Leave Alice be,' John had said all those years ago. Now without words Alice's son said the same.

I watched while Alice tried to pry him loose, while John hobbled off balance, bemused, lifting his feet like a mastiff attacked by a terrier. The child's face was red, mottled with rage and terror, his black hair stood up, his blue eyes blazed. Only his mother's caresses could calm him. And when he had hiccupped into silence he regarded John curiously. And John regarded him.

Perhaps if he had anything of his real father's looks, perhaps if he had resembled his grandfather Michael, John might have felt differently. As it was he stretched out his hand tentatively, as if the child would bite, touched the soft cheeks, the thick black hair, as if afraid they would melt.

'Meet Philip,' Alice said aloud. 'Philip, meet John.'

She folded her arms about them both. 'And now,' she

said, ''tis best we go on home. We've been waiting fer 'ee, John Tregaran. It's been long enough.'

I never went with them to the tiny house, nor saw the rooms she lived in, nor heard the rest of her story except what snatches John saw fit to tell. I never asked to go there, and he never offered to take me. There are some things that can't be forgiven right away, and I knew and accepted that. Sometimes, though, he told me when he would bring them to the park near my flat so I could watch them together if I chose. I don't know if she knew I was there, I suppose she did, but she never acknowledged me. Yet she never stopped my speaking to the little boy – like a miniature Zack, who would favour me with his uncle's same long stare, sizing me up.

And I suppose she must have agreed to my managing John's affairs when he had to leave again. Like Tom, she trusted me with that. Strange, wasn't it, that in the end it was my legal integrity that counted. And that she trusted me to do one last service for her.

It was not the hardest thing in my life. Letting my affianced bride go free was that, second to telling John what I had allowed to happen to Alice. But this was to jeopardize my legal integrity so I suppose it was important. At the time I never thought of it.

I have said that there were two problems that John had to come to terms with. One was Alice's child, the other was Alice's future.

She was married to a man she couldn't love or like, didn't want to love or like, had only married to give her son a name. That was all she and Tom had intended; in her simplicity she had sworn not to lay claim to anything else, and she hadn't, although in legal terms she could. Be that as it may, the marriage stood. And just as Evelyn

Tregaran would have done anything to break it, so now would John.

Tom had solved one difficulty. But he had created more difficulties in its place.

John spoke to me on the eve of his departure for France. The last weeks had seen a change in him, had made him what I had always hoped he would be, the way I hoped he would stay, if life didn't embitter or spoil him. Funny that his father never saw that promise in him. Or perhaps he did. Perhaps in his diffident way Michael Tregaran knew that out of darkness and shame he had sired one son to do him proud. Perhaps he never spoke of his secret knowledge in case it too got lost.

John was fit, fit as a fiddle, he said, when he came for the last time to my flat. Alice had spared him for a few moments; he had to hurry back. He felt confident that he had got the war 'licked'. 'Just a question of sitting tight and not sticking your neck out,' he had grinned. 'No more riding a charger into the thick of things.' Then more seriously, 'I've cheated Old Man Death without really trying, so I ought to manage when I put my attention to it.'

His financial affairs were in order, but he had only his army pay. There was nothing saved; he'd 'blown it' carelessly, wantonly, away these last two years, much to his regret. But it wasn't only financial security he was looking for, he wanted to take care of Alice and Philip properly. 'It's not enough just having her to live with me,' he was saying. 'She deserves more than that. She's not my mistress. She should be my wife. There's no reason for Nigel to stand in our way.'

Nigel was a problem, John had to admit that. Tom had already warned Alice that Nigel couldn't be trusted to act rationally. He wouldn't agree to a divorce, he wouldn't allow an annulment, dog-in-the-manger that he was, he wanted things to remain unchanged until the war was over. John couldn't wait that long.

He had already written to Nigel, the first time in years, certainly the first communication since that disastrous note which, until recently, he had not known how Nigel had misused. Nigel hadn't replied. He may not have got the letter, post was constantly being lost, or he may have chosen not to answer.

Nor did John know what to do about Tom. He knew Tom was in France although their paths had never crossed. Like his brother, he had promised Alice he would see that Tom was transferred. Unlike Nigel, he meant to keep his word. She hoped he and Tom together could talk Nigel round to a divorce but John himself was doubtful.

'We could try,' he said, 'but it's not always easy to move behind the lines. And Nigel's stationed a fair way back, that makes things more difficult. And even if we do track Nigel down,' he hesitated, 'it won't be simple even then. Tom may have his own axe to grind.'

Tom might be a problem too; Tom might not be willing to help. Finally John had revealed his real concern. Suppose, after all their attempts at persuasion, Nigel still refused? John felt he needed some 'leverage' to make Nigel change his mind. And if he wouldn't, how could Alice's and John's relationship be 'legalized'?

'Not much you can do,' I told him. 'Unless you take the law into your own hands.'

I chose that answer deliberately. I should explain that what he was asking did not come as a surprise. Since I had left Cornwall the matter had occupied much of my spare time. Like Evelyn, I had become obsessed with the marriage, so it preyed on my mind. I had been searching for some precedent. But however hard I had scanned the law books I had not come up with one. Nigel's mother feared the scandal of divorce, I the slur on Alice. A divorced woman was cut off from society; Alice deserved better than that.

I had thought of annulment. But annulment was a church matter. And I didn't trust church law. Besides, it might take several years and Alice didn't want to wait. John didn't say so, but I suppose she might be wanting to have more children, yes, she'd want John's sons.

The more I had thought, the more I had come to one conclusion. The matter would be delicate, taking time and finesse. John didn't have the time; Alice lacked the skill. In their place I was willing to act for them. I offered to go to Tregaran House, to face Evelyn Tregaran on their behalf, and put my solution to her.

I didn't tell them what I had in mind, nor explain what 'leverage' I'd use; looking back I'm not sure I knew myself. I merely argued that logically Evelyn must accept. (Again, I stress that at that time no one knew what her position was.) It seemed to me that if she could be persuaded to agree, if Nigel's marriage could be dissolved, if by contrast John's marriage would seem a relief to her, then half the battle would be won.

I don't say I reached this conclusion easily. Or, having reached it, relished the implementation. Earlier skirmishes hadn't left me scot-free. *I hear you stood up to her and got mauled.* Evelyn Tregaran would have a long memory as far as insult was concerned. Although we hadn't actually met for over two years the encounter was not one I looked forward to. I made my offer all the same. That, too, was an act of penance.

All this explains why, when my preparations were complete, a few weeks after John had left I took the train to Cornwall. My brief was simple: to terminate the marriage, restore the status quo so that Alice could remarry – against an opponent who was formidable. No wonder I was nervous.

It was after Christmas when I crossed the river that separated Cornwall from the rest of England. I felt a constriction tighten in my chest like a weight. Through the steamy carriage windows, that little strip of water, that grey stretch of Plymouth Sound formed a barrier, a barricade, between this western county and the outside world.

Suddenly I found myself back in that strange country where everything was mirror-changed, where the language was different, where thought patterns had a rhythm of their own. Any hope of an easy reconciliation seemed foolish; after all that had happened in this doubt-burdened land, why should I imagine that logic was the answer? There was something here stronger than logic, and it might yet cause defeat.

Nothing had changed, I thought, the dirty little villages, the narrow streets, washed by a freezing rain, the restless sea. I rented a room, not wanting to open my own house, and after a sleepless night was driven to Tregaran along those tree-lined lanes that I'd come to know so well. The elms stood like sentinels, their trunks dark and dripping; the wind caught at the branches and sent the rain splattering.

The thought of what I was about to do overcame me. I was no Tom striding headfirst into battle. I was a Daniel going unarmed into a lion's den. But like Tom, I knew what had to be done; no turning back this time.

Nor did Tregaran House seem different, at least not on the outside. The old stones were still their soft gold-grey colour, the park stretched down to the dip in the fields. Inside the neglect was beginning to show, common to all large houses which are understaffed and lack capital, and the rain poured in a steady stream from a broken waterspout over the front door.

Em let me in, an indication of the servant shortage.

She perhaps had mellowed, at least she gave me a frosty smile as she showed me where to go. It occurred to me that perhaps at last she was happy; she had her mistress, as she had always wanted, for her very own. Or was her smile one of anticipation for the struggle ahead?

Evelyn was seated in her favourite place before the window in the old hall. It was cold and damp and dark, almost like twilight in the middle of the day. The dimness was enhanced by the half-drawn curtains, meant to hide the signs of decay: the mould stains on the ceiling, the peeling paper, the faded coverings of chairs and walls. But when I drew closer to the seated figure I saw there was another cause. She didn't get up, just sat there looking at me with those large dark eyes which already seemed sunken into the folds of skin. Once I had thought Evelyn, not beautiful, that wasn't a word I would have used for her, but arresting, and she had known the effect she had. It must have been painful to her to see how people reacted to the change in her, the diminishing of her physical attraction. She had surrounded herself with dimness to hide it, dim light, dim surroundings, dim clothes. Only her necklaces sparkled, spread out across the expanse of bosom like medals on a general's chest.

I remembered what John had said of her – Elizabeth I, addressing her troops at Tilbury – and I set down my briefcase with a thump to give myself courage for this modern encounter.

She attacked first. 'Why, Mr Cradock,' she cooed, 'you're a stranger. We thought you'd left for good, fled away from us in the middle of the night. He's tired of country living, we told ourselves, and all his rustic friends.'

She smiled. The painted mouth, the jet black hair, the pale skin seemed to swim up towards me from the gloom, like a face seen underwater.

'And what can we do for you?'

When I didn't answer, 'Oh come, now, Mr Cradock, let's not pretend. You'd not be here unless there were something you wanted, would you? And you've not forgotten that when I asked for help you refused?'

For a moment I was paralysed. I even took a step or two back in recoil. She was too fierce, too direct, there was no defence from her. I remember thinking, by God, in a courtroom she'd be viper-fast. The man I had once been would have turned tail and fled.

But I was also remembering what I was here for and that steadied me. In a law court all is battle; it's the luck of the draw who starts and how they proceed. Sometimes you take the offensive, sometimes you let the enemy shoot first. Let her waste her ammunition on me, I thought, my chance will come.

She must have sensed that; she was quick and clever. 'So Paul,' she said, more quietly now, 'shall we let bygones be bygones after all?' She smiled, stood up in her too tight dress with its too youthful lines. 'Are you coming back to live then? You've been gone too long.'

I can't describe the effect of that smile, that use of my given name. She had never called me by it before, and the hint of intimacy closed round me as once it had done. I remembered sitting in this room watching while she greeted her other guests, disturbed that she left me to last. I remembered the soothing touch of her hand.

I drew myself up with an effort. 'No,' I told her, 'I'm not coming back. In fact I'm thinking of selling. I'm here for another reason.'

I looked at her defiantly, eye to eye. 'I'm here on business,' I told her, 'on John's behalf.'

She bridled then. Clutching her shawls and scarves together, she seemed to swell. 'Whatever can you mean?' she said. Then quickly, her voice hard, 'He's no claim on

231

Sawer Farm. Michael was mad to talk of giving it. And it's already been sold. Nigel got rid of it two years ago. It was part of his estate.'

'I'm not here about Nigel's estate,' I said. 'Only about Nigel's wife.' I looked at her carefully. 'And a way to undo a marriage that everyone dislikes.'

'Marriage? Wife? What are you talking about? You're as mad as Michael was.' But underneath the protests she was watching me carefully.

I said quietly, 'The marriage that Tom Tregarn arranged, the marriage to which you agreed and had performed in secret.'

She looked shocked. Like her son she could prevaricate. 'I know of no marriage,' she said again, her voice prissy smooth. 'You must be talking of something else.'

'Perhaps,' I said. 'But don't forget, I'm the witness to what happened on the beach that night. And I've already written to Mathew Trevenn; I know what he knows.'

She knew when she was beaten. She gave a bitter little laugh and sank back into her chair, watching me with that bright dark glitter I remembered. 'You're a fool still, Cradock,' she told me, mocking me for the last time. 'Why should you poke your nose in? You'll not win friends that way. You say you want to help my son. Aren't you hoping to help yourself instead?' She gave a little grin. 'She'll never marry you. And there's no way it can be done.'

I waited until she had spelled out all the reasons why it wouldn't work. She did so almost triumphantly, at least in that she imagined she bettered me. 'So you see,' she said when she'd finished, and it was a long list, she was right, she'd thought of everything except the one thing I was about to offer her, 'there's not a chance in hell. And if there were, why should I agree? What do I owe John? He gave me nothing.'

She suddenly turned on me. 'And why should he expect Nigel to make him happy? What does he matter to either of us? He threw in his lot with you, didn't he? He turned away from his own home. If he's sent you here to plead for him, then think twice before asking for my help. She lived with him like a slut before, what's changed so now? She and he can stew together in their own juice, for all I care. When Nigel comes back we'll take care of things in our own way.'

The venom was undiluted, the hatred as fixed as it had been those years ago. I felt almost sad on hearing it, on her behalf more than his. For answer I undid the lock of my case and drew out some papers. I spread them out on a coffee table, dividing them into two very unequal parts, the information I had found out, had systematically amassed before I'd left.

'This represents Tregaran assets,' I told her, indicating the much smaller heap. 'And these,' I stirred the large one with a finger tip, 'are Tregaran debts. If news of Nigel's marriage leaks out, those debts will probably have to be paid, those loans and mortgages settled. Do you have the money to honour them? To say nothing of the claims that Alice could make on her own and her son's behalf. As Nigel's wife she's entitled to that. Who's to say she won't?'

'How do you know all this?' She snatched at the papers, scattering them in drifts. 'Where did you get this stuff?'

'You told me once I had a reputation,' I said. 'And so I have. I'm thorough. I don't leave things to chance. I want Alice's freedom. I'm willing to pay for it.'

'But it won't work,' she screamed. 'We're caught in a trap, all of us, a goddamn trap.'

I gathered the papers up slowly, clipping them together, an old man, knowing all the law's little tricks.

'In a sense you're right,' I told her. 'But there's more

than one way to skin a cat. And I'm here to do it for you.'

I looked at her again. 'You want Nigel free, John wants Alice. Let Alice go, and her son with her; she forgoes any claim to the estate, John forfeits his own. We dissolve the marriage, everyone is happy, no one knows. And I pay off your debts.'

For the first time ever I laughed back at her. 'You made it easy for us, Evelyn, so easy you couldn't see it in front of your own nose.'

She stared at me openmouthed.

'You know what they say,' I told her cheerfully. 'There's no better criminal than a courtroom lawyer. You kept it all so secret you see. Crime loves secrecy. All you have to do is to destroy the records that your pet vicar keeps. I'll send them to you when I've got them, you can destroy them yourself. And there you have it, no record, no marriage, your son's home free.

'Oh, it's illegal you say. Of course it is, but I'll take care of that. And since you'll be part of it you won't say a word. I can't imagine Mathew Trevenn putting up a struggle either. He's probably counting the moments with relief.'

I stuffed the last of the papers into the case, closed it with a snap. 'So if you've no further objection,' I told her, 'I'll go and finish off my business.'

And I did.

She had one last passing shot.

She had regained her composure. I suppose in those last few moments all sorts of ideas, scraps of ideas, went buzzing through her mind, ways to prevent me, ways to improve the offer, ways to get the money without giving anything in exchange; dog-in-the-manger-like, she still couldn't bear to let John have something, even something she and Nigel didn't want. I've said she knew

234

when she was beaten. But she couldn't resist that one last shot.

She'd followed me into the entrance way, was watching me prepare to step out into that rain. 'You think you've won,' she said. The old cold venom was back. 'Don't you know that in Tregaran no one wins? I thought I had, and look at me, where has it left me? Tell her she won't either. That's our legacy from the past.

'We're cursed with it,' she said. 'In the end it'll bring us down.'

But I didn't believe her then. I drove off through the rain as blithe as a boy, as if the sun were shining and a New Year had begun.

CONCLUSION

There's not much left to tell. As I'd imagined, Vicar Trevenn received me with open arms. It was against his nature to keep secrets locked up so he bombarded me with details. The events of that morning were still crystal clear, he just didn't know what to make of them. He had imagined it was John's marriage that was being arranged, what was he to think when Nigel appeared? And earlier in the morning Tom Tregarn like a mad man, fierce and insistent . . .

'I just knew something was wrong,' he babbled, 'no banns, no ceremony, everything rushed. Many's the time I've asked myself was it proper. Thank goodness I kept the record on a separate page.' He thrust the marriage book into my hands as if it burnt.

I've been a good lawyer. I know when a man's protecting himself. And I've lived a long and blameless life, I know what's right. I never had a moment's doubt of the rightness of what I now did. I thanked Mathew Trevenn for his thoughtfulness, carefully cut out the page, put it with the other papers in my briefcase. Then I replaced the book with the others in the belltower, admired the bells, unusual, probably unique, dating back several hundred years, admired the stained glass and medieval carvings, excused myself from his bleatings, and left.

And that was that. Cautious to the end, I gave Evelyn

a copy to destroy, the original I kept myself. I wrote to John with the news and settled back. Oh, I know there were flaws, no crime is perfect. There would be other ways to find out the truth if one dug hard enough, if one wanted to show that Alice had been married, or was still married. The beauty was, who would want to? Not Evelyn, counting over her windfall; surely not Nigel, free to marry again and beget a real heir; not Alice or John, content to let well enough alone. As I said once to Alice, a little crime goes a long way.

The only pang of conscience I had was about the boy, about what he'd miss. And for a while he was unprotected against illegitimacy, the very thing Tom had wanted to avoid. John, of course, would adopt him and his mother didn't mind. 'He'll be free of all that,' she said.

I did see Alice. She allowed me that privilege or rather, I permitted it to myself. The little boy became our bond. In France the war was almost over. Tom and John were together, keeping each other out of trouble. On their next leave another wedding was planned, a joyful one, all that the other had not been, no need to rush.

In the meanwhile, to set things straight, John meant to make peace with Nigel. Nigel had been furious at first. 'I'll not give her up,' he'd said. But perhaps his mother's persuasions worked. Thought of that money must have appealed to him. John and Tom were unable to reach him but they hoped he would come to them; 'time Nigel had a little taste of war first hand.'

Thoughts of that meeting often haunted me. Like John I wondered what they'd say, how they would greet each other. Somehow I felt assured that the younger would outmatch the older at every turn.

And then, that settled, and the war done, Alice and John, and Tom, planned to go home, to make their peace with Zack and return to Cornwall, make a life there of their own.

'I do long for it,' Alice said. 'Surely we've won that right.'

I thought, let exile end, all curses pass. God be merciful, the past is finished, let new life rise.

The sea at Tregaran continues on its daily round, the tide laps across the open flats, the shallows glisten in the uncaring sun. In my old age I see the three of them as they used to be, always arm in arm as they came down through the trees towards the beach. One is older, dependable, the one who binds them; the second younger, with thin long face and thick black hair and sad eager eyes. The third is light upon her feet, swirling her skirts like moonbeams, her body bent into the wind like a figurehead on a ship.

She smiles at us. *Don't you know my dear, my dears, you'll never be alone again.*

And I am strangely comforted.

AUTHOR'S NOTE

I should like to take this opportunity to thank my friends for all their help and kindness while I was writing this book. My special thanks to Vanessa and Nellie Lide for the typing, to James Lide for the editing, and to my agents and editors on both sides of the Atlantic.

Most of all I wish to acknowledge the beauty of Cornwall, whose mysteries are not yet lost and whose secrets still reveal themselves.